Rainbow
Beauty

WITHDRAWN
FOR SALE

Rainbow Beauty

Strawberry Summer

Kelly McKain

USBORNE

First published in 2013 by Usborne Publishing Ltd., Usborne House,
83-85 Saffron Hill, London EC1N 8RT, England.
www.usborne.com

Illustrations copyright © Usborne Publishing Ltd., 2013
Illustrations by Antonia Miller.

The name Usborne and the devices 🏆 🌐 are Trade Marks of Usborne Publishing Ltd.

Text © 1989 Michael Rosen from WE'RE GOING ON A BEAR HUNT by Michael Rosen, illustrated by
Helen Oxenbury, Published by Walker Books Ltd, London SE11 5HJ, www.walker.co.uk

A CIP catalogue record for this book is available from the British Library.

JFM MJJASOND/13   02803/1   ISBN 9781409540557
Printed in Reading, Berkshire, UK.

Chapter One

"Abbie, love, have you got the things we need for Mrs. Smith?" said Mum. "It's a full body massage and facial."

"I know. Just sorting it," I replied.

I hurried over to one of our treatment rooms, a pot of Blueberry Burst Fresh Face Mask in one hand (my very own secret recipe), and a bottle of Uplifting Rose & Geranium Oil in the other. I folded some towels neatly on the couch and arranged the products on top of them. Then I lit the oil burner to fill the air with the scents of jasmine and ylang-ylang and put on some relaxing music, ready for our client, who was due any minute.

Looking around, I could still hardly believe we'd made all this happen. Every single bit of our Rainbow Beauty parlour was absolutely gorgeous. I loved the squishy purple velvet sofas and old gold-painted reception desk, with its vase of pink roses. The marble smoothie bar with its retro stools was so cool, and the chiller counter looked delicious, with little tubs of face mask arranged amongst the fresh blueberries, mangoes, passion fruits, pears, lemons and strawberries. I loved the glass shelves too, with all our natural, handmade products displayed on them like magic potions, waiting for you to pick the perfect one to cheer you up, or calm you down, or make you feel like you could take on the world and make it your own.

We had quite a few bookings. I guessed that, as it was July, lots of people wanted to get themselves looking their best before going on holiday. The bell over the door jangled as Mrs. Smith came in. Mum smoothed down her pink uniform and welcomed her, smiling warmly.

My sisters were on hand too – Grace took Mrs. Smith's jacket while Saff asked if she'd like one of our fresh juices or smoothies. She chose an immune-boosting green one from the menu (it included spinach and stinging nettles, but tasted really yummy

– yes, honestly!). I made it for her, then Mum led her into the gorgeous oasis of the treatment room.

An hour later she emerged, walking on air, and saying how much she'd enjoyed it. She ended up staying for a manicure with Saff and when that was finished, she bought a bag of Lavender Bath Bombs and a pot of Carrot & Calendula Hand Balm to take home. I smiled as I put them into one of our cute recycled bags for her, which we'd decorated ourselves with little rainbow stamps. Grace worked out her bill and she paid by cheque (we weren't set up for card payments as yet) and then Saff helped her into her jacket.

We all said a cheerful goodbye and once she'd gone, we looked at each other and…

"AAAAAAAAAAAAAHHHHH!!!" we shrieked, so loud I'm surprised the glass shelves didn't shatter.

"She loved it, didn't she?" cried Grace.

"She went with the nail colour I suggested and said it looked really good," beamed Saff.

"She bought the last one of my hand balms too," I cried. "Summer's mum was right when she said they'd sell like hot cakes. I'll have to make a new batch."

"OMG, this is amazing!" squealed Saff. "I still can't believe we're really running this place!"

Then we got into a huddle and started leaping up and down, going, *"Whoo-hoo!"*

Mum raised her eyebrows. "We've been open a week now," she said. "Are you going to be like this after every single booking?" She was beaming too though, and she let us pull her into our bouncy, dancy hug.

We were still jumping round reception when the bell above the door jangled and Summer walked in, wearing a yellow checked sundress and flip-flops. I'd missed her over the last few days. We'd only met a couple of months ago when I'd started at school down here, but we were already used to giggling our way through lessons together, and hanging out on the field with Marco and Ben all lunchtime.

"Hi!" she said brightly.

"Hiya," I said, giving her a big hug.

Mum, Grace and Saff all said hi too and Mum asked how her camping trip had been.

"Oh, you know, field, tent, torrential rain, the usual," said Summer cheerily. "You all look really happy. Is business booming then?"

"Not too bad actually, for a Saturday," said Mum. "We had lots of bookings right after our launch at the town fayre, but we do need to get some more in the diary for the next fortnight, especially during the week."

"Mum, seeing as that was your last client, do you think maybe Summer and I could have a treatment?"

"Go on then, you deserve it," said Mum.

"Thanks, Kim," said Summer.

"Not that you need a beauty treatment," I grumbled, as we went over to the chiller counter to pick out a fresh face mask each. Summer had peachy perfect skin, beautiful long eyelashes and thick glossy dark curls. She never bothered with make-up and only ever wore a slick of my orange flavour lip balm on her pouty lips.

"Yeah, right, like you're not the Blonde Bombshell Babe of Year 9!" she cried. "Well, Year 10 when we go back in September. The one who changed Marco from a super-player to Boyfriend Material."

I couldn't help grinning at that. The Marco bit, I mean. From the moment we met on my first day at school here in Totnes, when he pulled me out of the rain, there'd been this spark between us. And last Saturday, after the grand opening of Rainbow Beauty, I'd finally got to kiss him. But as for the rest of what she said...*yeah, right!* At best, I'm okay-looking, if I wear loads of eye make-up. Otherwise, with my pale skin and lashes and almost white-blonde hair, it honestly looks like I don't have a head. I told Summer that and she rolled her eyes. "Oh, Abs, don't start with the headless thing again!" she groaned.

"I'm just saying, I need a bit more help than you in the beauty department," I insisted. "Especially as Marco's back tomorrow… I don't want him to see me and think I look way worse than he remembered. Right…" I scanned the fresh face masks. "Reviving seaweed and honey should do the trick, I think."

Summer went for a moisturizing one with oats and bananas, then we headed into one of the treatment rooms and got all the stuff out for a full-on pampering session. As well as the face masks, we were planning a luxury body treatment. Basically, you cover yourself in layers of hydrating gel, a blend of oils including scrummy rose and geranium, and delicious shea butter, and when you take it off, your skin is as soft as the proverbial baby's bottom.

Summer and I got undressed to our bras and knickers and Saff helped us smooth it all on and get wrapped up in the cling-film stuff you put on top to help it all soak in. Then we put on our fresh face masks, and lay down top to toe on the treatment couch. Saff put some cucumber on our eyes, told us to "Just relax for twenty-five minutes" in her newly-invented calming beautician voice, and left the room.

Obviously we didn't relax for even *one* minute. We spent the first few sitting up and laughing at how silly we both looked, and then at least another five having a play fight about who had the most couch and trying to make each other fall off the edge. Then, as you've probably guessed, we spent the rest talking about Marco.

"So, lover boy is back tomorrow," said Summer, propping herself up on her elbows and lifting off the cucumber so she could wiggle her eyebrows up and down at me in a *Whoo-hoo!* kind of way. I took mine off too, so I could watch her doing it.

"Yeah. Looking tall, dark and handsome...and probably tanned and more gorgeous than ever." Just talking about him made me feel all yummy and romantic. I'd been expecting to see him last Sunday, the day after THE KISS, but his mum had sprung a surprise holiday on him – a last-minute deal to Italy she got on the internet – so I hadn't seen him since.

Summer rolled her eyes. "If you say so," she sighed. She seemed to be the only girl at our school who didn't fancy Marco. I guess they'd been friends for so long that he was more like an annoying brother to her. When I'd met up with her last Sunday and told her about THE KISS, she'd been a bit funny about it at first. I didn't blame her. Marco's record with girls was awful (seven-broken-hearts-in-eighteen-months kind of awful). And there was also the fact that, last thing she knew (after the disastrous cafe date incident), I'd told him there was absolutely definitely no chance that anything was going to happen between us ever again. Like, never.

Still, when I'd told her about how much he'd put himself on the line for me, and mentioned the amazingness of THE KISS, even Summer had softened a tiny bit. But I knew it would take a lot more than that to convince her that Marco wasn't going to let me down again. Still, now he was my actual boyfriend (whoopee!), perhaps she'd come round. I lay back and reapplied my cucumber slices.

"Well, I hope he asks you out now, that's all I can say," she grumbled.

I sat bolt upright so fast my cucumber slices fell off. "Oh, I kind of thought we *were* going out, you know, after THE KISS," I told her. "That's what a kiss means, doesn't it?" *Doesn't it?* Maybe it didn't. I suddenly felt naïve and stupid.

"Hey, chill out!" said Summer. "Maybe it does. And if not, I bet he'll ask you out tomorrow." She grinned cheekily at me. "Or you could ask him."

"Well, perhaps I will!" I said. "But we're probably *already* going out, so what if I don't need to? Oh, but then what if I think, *We are so I don't need to*, but in fact we're not so I *do* need to? And what if—"

Summer giggled. "Abbie! You should have just rung him last week if this is how you've been!"

"I haven't been *able* to ring him!" I wailed. "Mum would never let me call Italy on her pay-as-you-go. Money's still really, really tight and she doesn't let us tie up the line in case people want to leave messages about appointments on the answerphone."

"Alright, point taken!" said Summer.

"Anyway, what would I say?" I asked her. "Oh, hi, Marco, I'm just ringing to check whether we are in fact going out?"

Summer giggled at that. "Yeah, not cool, I get it. Hey, will you do my toes as well?"

"If you do mine," I said. Even though we felt like mummies in the cling-film stuff, we managed to wiggle ourselves upright enough so we could get those toe divider things onto our feet. Then we chose some polish from Saff's colour wheel and started painting each other's nails. "It would be a lot easier if we could just get boys to fill in a form or something," I said, going back to the theme of *Who knows what they're thinking?*

Summer smiled. "What, like, just as they lean in for the kiss you whip out a clipboard and start asking questions?"

"Yeah! Why not?" I cried. "Question one: are we

going out or not? Question two: if you think so, and if I agree that we are, are you going to be keen for two weeks and then go all mumbly and shuffly until eventually I get so annoyed I dump you, which saves you the hassle of dumping *me?*"

Summer giggled. "Yeah. Or question three: are you going to be fine with me on our own but as soon as your mates are there play it so cool it's as if I don't exist, until eventually I get so annoyed I dump you — which *also* saves you the hassle of dumping me?"

I laughed. "All these scenarios seem to end with us getting annoyed and dumping them!"

"Sounds about right!" said Summer. "Not that I'd know. I haven't even had a proper boyfriend. How sad is that?!"

"It's not sad, it's choosy!" I insisted. "Anyway, neither had I, before Marco. If he even *is* my boyf! But hey, I think we should sort it out. Let's get you set up!"

I was only joking, but even Summer's thick layer of face mask couldn't hide how flustered she got. She started going, "Oh, er, but I, I don't know, I mean, I wouldn't know what to say and it would just be really awkward and what if he didn't like me in that way, even if I thought he probably might and…"

I peered at her, my gossip radar on high alert.

"*Who* probably might?" I asked.

"No one," she said quickly, adjusting her cling-film stuff. "I mean, just, you know, *the guy*, if I fancied someone."

I stared at her but she still wouldn't look me in the eye. "Oh, because for a minute there it sounded like there *is* someone…"

"No, no one," Summer insisted. "Well, my skin might be rehydrating but *I'm* dehydrating. Do you reckon we could hobble out and get some smoothies in this stuff?"

SCREEEEECH! She'd changed the subject so fast I'd got whiplash! Very suspicious! But I knew I wasn't going to get any info by pushing her. She was so private, she'd only clam up completely. I'd just have to wait for the right moment to try and find out more about this mystery guy – if what I suspected was right, and there actually *was* one.

"Yeah, come on, then," I said. "There aren't any more clients booked in today, so no one's going to see us."

We swung off the couch and hobbled out of the room, with the toe divider thingies still on our feet and our arms stretched out in front of us. We caught sight of ourselves in the big mirror and giggled. We looked like mummified zombies – especially me, with my gooey green face mask. With the bananas, oats and honey mask on, Summer looked more like she'd fallen face first into her breakfast. I could hear Saff banging around in the kitchenette, and it looked like Mum and Grace had gone upstairs.

We shuffled across the reception area and stood in front of the chiller counter, choosing what to have. I loved the vivid colours of the different fresh fruits. It all looked delicious. "I'm going for a red vitality one with pear and strawberries," I told Summer. "That'll give my skin a boost from the inside too. I want to look my absolute best for when I see Marco tomorrow."

No reply.

"Summer?" I asked. "Which one do you want?"

Still no reply.

I looked up and saw her staring in horror out through the front window.

Ben and MARCO were heading for the door.

OMG – with bells on.

"WHAT?! I thought he wasn't back until tomorrow!" I hissed.

"Get down!" she squealed.

We tried to dive into the space behind the chiller counter but, to our horror, there wasn't enough room for both of us. The bell jangled above the door as the boys walked in. It was too late to make a run for it – I mean, a *hobble* for it.

"Summer, please let *me* hide!" I begged. "Marco can't see me like this!"

"They're not seeing me like this either!" she squealed, trying to squash behind the counter with me.

"But you don't care what you look like in front of them, do you?" I hissed. "They're like brothers to you."

"Yeah, but I've still got *some* standards!" Summer shrieked.

Too late. We both shot bolt upright as two faces peered over the counter. Just looking at Marco made my stomach flip over. Looking at me was probably doing the same to his, but more in a *throwing up* kind of way.

"Erm, what are you doing?" asked Ben.

"Oh, we were arguing about who was going to… get the apple that rolled back here," Summer said lamely.

Marco grinned gorgeously at me and said, "Nice look." I blushed bright red under my green face mask. What a CRINGE! Still, at least the cling-filmy stuff was white and not actually see-through like the normal kind. I tried to be grateful for that, but it didn't really help.

"Did you have a good time away?" I asked, trying to sound casual. *Meet any nice Italian girls?* I wanted to add. *You know, stylish ones who don't walk around looking like an advert for Mad Mummies Inc.*

"We thought you weren't coming back until tomorrow," Summer stammered. She was blushing as red as I was.

Marco shrugged. "I wasn't. We were going to stay the night with Mum's friends who live near Heathrow, but they were ill, so we came straight home."

Summer's cling film squeaked as she turned to Ben. "And you," she said accusingly, "you said you were at Dartington Hall tackling birds all day."

"*Tagging* birds," Ben corrected, smirking at her. "Why have you got porridge all over your face?"

Summer tried to whack him one but he easily dodged out of the way of her stiff mummy arms.

"Well, we only stopped by to say hi on our way into town," said Ben. "Marco's got band practice and I'm going to play football with the lads."

"We should go and get this stuff off," Summer said to me.

"Yeah," I replied. I didn't really want to go, though. I wanted to stay with Marco and I wanted a repeat of THE KISS. But there was no chance of that happening, not in my current state.

"We could meet up tonight," he said to me.

I got a shiver all down my cling-film-wrapped spine. "Great," I said.

But then Saff walked out of the kitchenette. "Oh hi, guys," she said. "Abs, we're making a new batch of fresh face masks tonight, remember? You have to be there to supervise."

I sighed, feeling my stomach drop into my shoes. I'd forgotten about that – the ones we had were on their use-by date. "I really do, or this lot will probably explode all over the shop," I told Marco.

"She's free tomorrow though," said Saff.

"No, I'm not. We've got clients booked in and—"

"It's Sunday, we're closed," Saff said, doing a *You idiot* face at me.

"Yes we are!" I yelled, then went bright red as I realized that a) I am the uncoolest girl in the universe, and b) Marco hadn't even *asked* me anywhere for tomorrow.

But luckily he just grinned. "Cool. It's a date then," he said.

I stared at him, my mind whirring. Did he just mean that as in the phrase, or did he actually mean it was a DATE? And if it was a DATE, then did that mean we *weren't* going out – because if you're boyfriend and girlfriend already, do you still go on dates? Or did it mean we *were* — because if we weren't boyfriend and girlfriend already, wouldn't he *ask* me on a date rather than just saying it was going to be one?

Summer nudged my arm and I realized everyone was looking at me. "Oh, yeah, cool, see you tomorrow then," I gabbled. "Erm, should I bring anything?" DUH! Like what? A life jacket? Cupcakes? Another classic from the queen of stupid questions.

He just smiled. "Leave it to me, I've got a plan."

I couldn't help giving him a great big green grin then.

"We'd better go," said Ben.

Marco went to hug me, then drew back and said, "I'll leave the hugging, you know, with the green goo and the...is that cling film?"

"Well, thanks for coming by!" trilled Summer, shooing them out of the door.

We just about managed to wait until they were down the road before we let out a massive girly scream, even Saff. "He must really like you," she squealed.

I gave her a big smile. She could be so nice when she wanted to.

"Yeah, I mean, he still asked you out after seeing you like that," she added. "You look absolutely awful!"

"Erm, thanks. I think," I said, narrowing my eyes at her.

She glanced at the wall clock. "Oh, I've gotta go. I'm meeting Emily in town." Emily was a friend Saff had made at the college open day. They were inseparable now and looked so alike, *they* could have been sisters. "You can finish up here and lock up, can't you?" she added, grabbing her bag and tripping out of the door.

So Summer and I were left to hobble back into the treatment room and unpeel ourselves without any help.

"Oh, I wish I could see Marco tonight," I said, still feeling the disappointment running through me. "I just want to be with him, you know?"

She gave me an intense look. "I understand," she said, then quickly added, "I mean, I can imagine."

"Summer," I said, raising my eyebrows at her. "What's going on?"

"Nothing, honestly," she insisted, not meeting my gaze. "*Nada. Rien. Nichts.*"

I was sure then. Something was definitely UP, capital U and capital P. You don't say *nothing* in three languages unless there *is* something. Summer had a crush on someone, and I was going to find out who. Or should that be *whom*?

Either way, her secret wasn't going to stay secret for long.

Well, the next day I woke up feeling A-Mazing and bounced out of my bed (well, the bed Mum and I had to share), and then I remembered why.

It was DATE day!

I used my Zesty Zing Shower Gel and my Lime & Ginger Sea Salt Body Scrub in the shower. My skin felt so smooth after that, and from the body mask the day before (my burning embarrassment really must have helped the oils to soak in!), so I only needed the tiniest dab of Avocado Body Butter before I could get on with choosing an outfit. Oh, and my usual ton of silver and grey eye make-up, of course (and a slick of Peppermint Kiss Lip Balm, for perfectly kissable lips. Ahem and double ahem).

The sun was already burning a hole in the sky at ten so, after spending ages staring at all my clothes, I put on my yellow tunic dress (with leggings underneath – I never get my blindingly white legs out, even in July!) and my silver ballet pumps. I was happy with my outfit, but when I went into the kitchen Saff announced that, with the yellow dress and black leggings, I looked like some kind of giant bee. Well, usually I'd have told her to get lost, but I felt so nervous already – what with it being my first proper date with Marco since we'd kissed – that she totally freaked me out. I was going to remember this day for ALL TIME, so I wanted everything to be perfect. I went and changed into about ten other outfits until I finally settled on my red T-shirt and cropped jeans, which they all agreed was really nice – phew!

Saff did my hair, to make up for the bee comment, and it looked really cool, in a kind of fifties half-up-half-down thing with little clips everywhere. Then, just as I was heading out of the door, having double- and triple-checked that I didn't have anything on my face or clothes, (like, as if that would even matter after yesterday!) Mum gave me £10.

Of course, I gave it straight back. "We can't afford this," I told her.

"We can...just about. You deserve it, Abbie. I want you to go and have a nice day. We all do, don't we?"

I thought Saff and Grace would say it was unfair, but amazingly they agreed. "Yeah, you shouldn't have to walk past those gorgeous little shops in town and not buy even one tiny thing," said Saff.

Grace scowled at her. "I think the point is to buy

food and stuff. Abbie shouldn't have a boy paying for her, it's anti-feminist."

Saff tutted. "No, it isn't. It's gentlemanly," she said.

Then they started having a mature discussion about it (well, okay, shrieking and running round the kitchen table, trying to whip each other with tea towels). "Just take it. Go. Have a good time," Mum said to me, over the chaos.

I grinned at her and put the money in my little bag. "Okay, I will. Thanks. See you later."

Walking into town to meet Marco, I almost had to stop and hold onto lamp posts and things, my legs were shaking so much. And my heart started pounding when I saw him waiting where we'd agreed, leaning on the archy building thing that goes over the road at the top of Fore Street, in skinny black jeans and a grey T-shirt. Obviously it goes without saying that he looked amazing (but I *want* to say it, so… he looked amazing!). My stomach did about twelve backflips and finished off with a triple somersault.

I was torn for a while between walking up the road to actually meet him and just staying rooted to the spot, staring at him. I made myself start walking and tried to ignore the heart-pounding and leg-trembling and act normal.

"Hi."

"Hi."

"You look amazing," we both said at once. Pause. CRINGE.

"So do you," we both said, at the same time again. Bigger pause. Bigger CRINGE!

Marco wouldn't tell me where we were going as we headed down South Street and onto The Grove. It just felt so cool being with him and, shallow I know, being *seen* with him too. I felt like a film star or something. Even better, he linked arms with me when we stepped into the road to let a buggy go by, and he didn't let go again.

It turned out we were going to the Rocket Arts Centre, which Marco had mentioned before but I'd never been to. The band playing the lunchtime session was setting up and the place was filling with people. It had a cool, retro, fifties feel, with a long Formica countertop, chrome and red leather stools, and candy-coloured Formica tables and chairs. I tried to stop staring at everything with goggly eyes and act like I went to cool places like this to eat out, with a *boy*, on a *date*, just us *two*, all the time. We grabbed a couple of stools at the counter and, as one of the staff walked past us with two massive burgers, I realized how hungry I was.

We ordered burgers too (Marco insisted on paying – what would Grace say?), and they came on wooden boards, with a little bowl of fries on the side. Soon the band started up and they were pretty good, mixing songs from the last couple of years with classics like "Sittin' on the Dock of the Bay" and "Great Balls of Fire". Marco couldn't help singing along with loads of them. He started an air guitar routine in the middle of "Wild Thing" and when he finally looked up I did a mickey-taking impression of him.

He raised his eyebrows and said, "Right," and grabbed my wrists, and we had a wrestly play fight that involved a lot of squealing (me) and evil laughing (him) and nearly toppling the stools completely over (both of us). Unfortunately the song ended just when I was letting out an ear-piercing shriek and everyone turned round to look at us. I went totally bright red and we had to be sensible for a bit then.

But a couple of songs later Marco started singing along again and I couldn't resist throwing a chip at him. I squealed as he threw one back at me. "Hey, that had ketchup on!" I cried. "Lucky for you I'm wearing a red top!" I poked him in the stomach, and either he's really ticklish or I'm stronger than I thought, because he *did* tip completely backwards off his stool then and everyone was staring at us again.

Including the manager. Whoops.

I know I'm really sensible normally but the way Marco sprang up from the floor and kind of looked around him, like he didn't know what on earth had happened…well, I just could *not* stop laughing.

He leaned right in close to me, and I thought he was going to whisper something into my ear, but then he jogged my stool really suddenly so I almost toppled off too. I gripped the counter, but I was still laughing so much my arms were going weak.

Loads of people were looking at us by then. And the manager was coming over…

"Time to go, I think," said Marco cheerily, pulling me off my stool and leading me to the door. I tried to catch the manager's eye and smile *Sorry*, but he was too busy glaring at the mess we'd left.

We staggered out into the bright sunshine, and stumbled down the street, still killing ourselves laughing and blaming each other for nearly getting chucked out. Then, suddenly, we stopped.

And he pulled me close.

And we kissed.

I was so grateful that this time I wasn't a) wearing bright yellow washing-up gloves, or b) covered in green face pack, that I forgot to think about which way to lean and we ended up crashing noses. But we got it sorted pretty quickly, and the kiss was out of this world, so I forgot about feeling embarrassed in the end. For a few minutes, anyway.

Until I said, "So, are we actually going out now?"

I know, I know. But it just came out of my mouth before I could stop it. "It's just, well, I wasn't sure because we hadn't actually said, last Saturday, I mean," I gabbled, "and it's not like there's a form to fill in just before you kiss, is there? You know, tick here if you think this means we're going out..."

Marco was looking alarmed.

And yet, for some stupid reason, I kept on talking. "Because that would be crazy, having a form, I mean. Only some kind of insane person would think of having a form..." I trailed off lamely, wishing I could just dissolve into a little puddle on the ground and trickle into the nearest drain, never to be seen or heard of again.

Marco smiled. "Are you saying you want to be my girlfriend?"

Play it cool, Abs, I told myself. I was going to shrug and say, "Sure, whatever, if you want." But when I opened my mouth, unfortunately what came out was "YES PLEASE!" (at about eight million decibels).

Even after that, and despite me having clearly revealed my utter looniness, he still said, "Well, I want to be your boyfriend, so I guess we *are* going out."

So then we grinned at each other and sealed it with another kiss. I couldn't believe it. For the first time ever, I had a proper boyfriend. My *dream* boy. Marco.

Chapter Two

On Monday morning I was walking on air after my first proper date with Marco, my definite BOYFRIEND. When I'd got in on Sunday, and told my lot that me and Marco were officially GOING OUT, the way Mum and Saff reacted, you'd have thought I'd got *engaged* or something. Even Grace managed to crack a smile.

I went down to Rainbow Beauty, and Mum was already in with a client, so I got straight on with restocking and rearranging our treasure trove of delicious, natural lotions and potions on the sales shelves in reception. Now it was the summer holidays, I could spend lots of time in Rainbow

Beauty. We had everything to pamper the good people of Totnes from top to toe, from our rich Seaweed & Honey Fresh Face Mask, to our Rose & Geranium Bath Bombs, Lime & Ginger Sea Salt Body Scrub, Avocado Body Butter and Revitalizing Olive Grain Foot Scrub. Not forgetting a cool little Peppermint Kiss Lip Balm, of course.

For perfectly kissable lips.

And then I was lost in thoughts of Marco again. And Saff and Grace noticed that I was staring into space, and guessed why, and especially stopped what they were doing just so they could tease me about it.

A moment later, Mum's client came out – a young woman called Jayne, who'd come in for a facial with a neck and shoulder massage. We all immediately turned sensible and, as Mum made up her bill, Grace called back a lady who'd left a message, Saff rearranged the chiller counter display to fill the gaps and I tidied the pile of magazines.

Jayne told us what a lovely treatment she'd had and bought some Olive Body Butter and a bag of my little star soaps with orange peel in to take home. Then, "Would you like to book again for next week?" Mum asked her.

"I'd love to," she said, "but I'd better make it next month. We're having to cut back at the moment."

"Of course," said Mum, smiling. "So, shall I put you in for early September? Would a Monday suit you again?"

So Jayne rebooked for September and we all beamed and said goodbye, but as the door closed behind her we didn't do the dancy-huggy thing as usual.

"She did enjoy her treatment," said Mum.

"Not enough to rebook for next week though," Grace mumbled, frowning.

"It's not about how much she liked it," Saff insisted. "So often over the last week, people have really loved their treatments but then when I've tried to rebook them…"

"…they've said they'll call back to make another appointment when they can next afford to treat themselves, or they've rebooked for a long way in the future. Same with me," Grace finished.

"I really thought that if we just made it brilliant here, people would be back every week or two," I said.

We looked at each other. I knew we were all thinking the same thing. For all the fun and joy and yumminess of Rainbow Beauty, making it work was going to be much tougher than we'd realized.

If Rainbow Beauty didn't succeed, we'd lose

everything again – including the flat which was now our home – and be out on the street, or housed in some awful B&B somewhere. That's what we'd faced when we'd first got down here a couple of months back. Mum and Dad had just split up because he'd had an affair. Mum had found out about that, and later about his business failing, meaning we'd lost our house and anything that couldn't be hastily shoved into our suitcases. So, that fear of having nothing – no home, no money, no future – was always in the back of our minds.

"Maybe we were being a bit naïve," said Mum. "With the recession and everything, we should have realized that coming here would be more of an occasional treat for people than a regular thing. We've only got four bookings for next Saturday at the moment. It should be our busiest day – we ought to be fully booked."

"Well, we'll just have to get more clients," I said firmly. "Then it won't matter if they come less often."

"It's not that simple," Mum muttered.

Grace blinked at me. "Actually, maybe it *is* that simple," she said. "But the question is, how?"

I thought back to the arts and crafts fayre, where we'd had a stall and picked up lots of bookings.

"Maybe we need another marketing push," I suggested, "something like the fayre, to bring another load of people in."

"We can check, but I don't think there are any more events coming up—" Mum began.

"It wouldn't have to be an event," I said. "It could be anything, so long as it raises our profile." Then I remembered. I'd just seen it when I'd tidied up the magazines on the coffee table. I riffled through the pile and pulled out the latest edition of *Totnes in Focus*, the town mag. "Look, we could promote ourselves in here. It comes free through the door every..." I squinted at the cover. "...two weeks".

"Brilliant idea!" Saff cried. "We could try and get an article in about Rainbow Beauty, with lots of gorgeous photos—"

"Summer could take those," I said, getting a lift from Saff's enthusiasm.

"And let's include a really enticing reader offer to get people in the door," added Mum. "Good thinking, Abbie!"

"Right, so we need to create an amazing package with lots of free extras thrown in," said Saff eagerly.

"But we can't give too much away," Grace warned. "We don't want to end up even *more* broke!"

"True," said Mum. "We'll have to be careful. Oh, and we should have a theme to make it stand out. Something summery."

"Hmm, what's summery?" Saff mused. "Sunshine?"

I immediately thought of something I'd been messing about with in my ideas notebook. "There's a face mask you can make with fresh strawberries and cream," I said. "That's summery."

"Mmm, sounds yummy!" said Grace, grinning at last.

"And we could add strawberry seed oil, it's brilliant for repairing dry and damaged skin," I added. "And maybe even strawberry powder fruit extract to reduce redness and visible pores. That would give us a fantastic formula."

"Great idea," said Mum. "We could put it together with our signature Rose Body Treatment to create a package. Book that and get a complete facial with special Strawberries & Cream Fresh Face Mask, worth £25, for free."

"Brilliant, and we need a name for it," I said. "How about…the Strawberry and Rose Pamper Package?"

"That's gorgeous," Mum cried, and Saff and Grace agreed.

"And let's throw in a free strawberry smoothie, and a gift-size strawberry moisturizer to take home," Saff suggested.

Grace frowned. "Well, hang on…"

"Actually, I think that's a good idea, Saff," said Mum. "That way it's a complete experience. A small size moisturizer won't cost us much to make, will it?"

"I suppose not," said Grace, "but I'll need to check the exact figures."

"We do give everyone a free drink at the moment anyway," I pointed out, "so why not shout about it?"

"And once people are here I could offer them a manicure with some delicious red and pink strawberry and rose nail polish shades too!" Saff added. "And we could order in some nail tattoos of little strawberries and roses!"

"We'll just have to be careful about how many of these packages we book in," Grace warned. "We can't afford to give too much away."

"Okay, we'll put an expiry date on the voucher and make sure we say only one per client," I said. "And we'll make some larger Strawberry Summer Moisturizers too, so that once they've got into the product through the free gift they can come back and buy more. How does that sound?"

Grace looked at me like Alan Sugar looking at

his new apprentice. "You're learning, sis," she said. "Let's cost it all out tonight though. We need to make sure it really is workable before we throw our money into it. Our *last bit* of money."

Time seemed to stand still then, my heart skipped a beat and Mum breathed in sharply. Grace was staring at the wall and Saff looked like she was about to cry. The fear about not making Rainbow Beauty a success had ambushed us again.

"It'll be okay," I insisted. "We'll get more clients. This promotion will work."

"I'll model for the photo shoot, *obviously*," Saff announced. Well, that made us all giggle, at least. "What?" she demanded. "People will pay much more attention to the article if I'm in it than just looking at bottles of stuff."

"Even if you do say so yourself!" I snorted.

But still, none of us argued. We knew she was right.

"Okay, I'll ring up now, and see if we can get into the next issue," said Mum. She flicked through the magazine until she found the contacts page, leaned across the reception desk and picked up the phone. Then she smoothed down her hair and adjusted her uniform, as if the person on the other end was going to somehow be able to *see* her. We all stood there staring at her, but she hissed that we were putting her off and sent us to reset the two small treatment rooms.

A few minutes later she hung up and announced, "We're on! They're going to give us a whole page to promote ourselves!"

Well, we did manage a little bit of a squealy, huggy dance around then.

Then I rang Summer and filled her in on our plans, and she said how great she thought it was and that she was definitely up for taking the photos.

"That will be a massive help," said Mum when I told her. "I'll write the text for our page. Don't let me forget to mention that you can just pop in for a juice or smoothie or to buy products to take home. People might not realize that. And actually... Oh, seeing as I haven't got another client till after lunch, I think I'd better start making notes right now!"

Saff didn't have any more nail clients until later that afternoon either, so she was planning to meet Emily in town.

"Aren't you going out too, love?" Mum asked Grace. "I remember you said something about it."

"Oh, I don't think I will now," Grace mumbled.

Mum frowned. "But you've told Maisy and Aran you're meeting them, haven't you? You can't just not turn up."

Grace sighed. "I only said I *might* go."

"Oh, come on, you can walk into town with me," said Saff. "They're going for lunch at that veggie place, aren't they? I can meet you back there at half three and walk home with you."

"I'm not really hungry," said Grace.

"Oh, come on, love, it's the holidays and you haven't been out with your friends at all," said Mum. "Just go for a couple of hours. I'm sure you'll enjoy yourself."

"But you need me here," Grace insisted.

"We don't," said Mum firmly. "Abbie and I can do the labels and packaging."

"Oh, right, so I'm no use to you, am I?" Grace countered.

Mum sighed. "Oh, come on, you know I didn't mean it like that—" she began.

But Grace muttered, "If you can manage without me, I really do need to get on with my Maths extension work," and then stalked off.

"Gracie, come back!" Mum called.

"I'd leave her to it," said Saff, as we all watched her head for the stairs to the flat. "She's going through a funny phase at the moment. It's like she's got permanent PMS." And with that she grabbed her bag and jacket and swanned out of the door.

"That's the second time she's let those new friends of hers down," Mum said to me, when Saff had gone. "If she's not careful, they'll stop asking her to go out with them."

"You know what Grace is like," I said. "It takes her ages to get close to people."

"You're probably right," Mum said. "She has always been a homebody. We'll just have to keep encouraging her to go out."

"Yeah," I said. But secretly I felt like there was more to it than that. I thought Grace was really, really unhappy. I didn't say that to Mum though – it would have made her feel terrible, even though it wasn't her fault.

"Will you talk to her, love?" Mum was asking me. "She listens to you."

"I don't think she does," I said, frowning. "But I'll try."

Mum looked at me expectantly.

"Not now, though," I told her. "She's already in a bad mood. I'll have to pick my moment."

That evening we made samples of the Strawberries & Cream Face Mask and the Strawberry Summer Moisturizer and they came out really well. Grace (who was out of her mood by then, luckily!) worked out how much they'd cost to make, and she agreed we could do 50ml ones – we were putting them into rose glass bottles and then in cellophane bags (100% biodegradable, of course!) with a scoop of rosebuds in the bottom and tied up with two different shades of pink ribbon so they looked really special.

Mum had been working on the text for the magazine advertorial and while we were all sitting round the kitchen table with our tea and toast, she read us her rough draft. It sounded really good and we all chipped in with suggestions to make it even better. Summer was at a family friend's wedding, so she couldn't do the pictures until the next day, but everything else was pretty much ready. We just had to get the article, pictures and details of our promotion to the magazine by three o'clock the following afternoon and they'd do the design and layout for us. It was a bit of a tight deadline but we thought we could manage it.

When I checked the appointments diary the next morning, I realized I could get out for a couple of hours, so of course I instantly texted Marco and arranged to hang out with him in town. After the usual forty-five minute wardrobe crisis and help from Saff on the hair and make-up front, I was on my way to meet him. This time my legs weren't trembling so much and I had to stop myself from actually *skipping* up the street.

"Hey," he said, as I walked up Fore Street. He pulled me into a hug and I hugged him back so hard I almost crushed a rib, and for so long I had to force myself to let go. I wanted to give him a big kiss there and then, but some old grannies on a bench were watching us, smiling gleefully, so instead I *died* of embarrassment and hurried Marco up the road.

"So, got any ideas where we could go?" I asked.

"Yep, *here*," he said, with a gorgeous lazy grin.

I looked around. "Where's here?" Did he mean the clothes shop opposite us? Were we going shopping? Not the mobile phone store, surely? I mean, I know boys are obsessed with their phones, but even Marco had to realize that wasn't exactly romantic. He couldn't mean the Elizabethan House Museum, could he? I actually really wanted to go there, but it didn't seem very *him*.

"Here," he said again. He grabbed my hand, and pulled me into a narrow passage behind us. Hidden down there was a really cool little cafe with a photography exhibition on the walls. Marco ordered us coffees from the counter, and chatted to the man making them.

He seemed to know most of the people at the other tables too and, when we went to sit down, he kept going off and doing that *Hey, man* hand thing that starts with a high five and then goes into all these other moves. I recognized a couple of guys from our year, but mainly I think they were sixth-formers or college students. I just sat down and smiled at them from our table. No way was I attempting the hand thing — I'd definitely mess it up and look like a total idiot.

"Cool place," I told him when he finally sat down.

Marco looked really pleased, like it was personally his. "Yeah. I come here a lot with Declan, Tay and Chaz. When Tay's writing a new song, he brings stuff here to show us and we all help out with the lyrics."

Marco's band Headrush did some covers, but I liked their own stuff the best, especially some of their lyrics. "I didn't realize you *wrote* any of it," I said.

He smiled. "Tay would probably kill me for saying this, but we do all chip in," he said. It made me look at him differently, somehow. Like I'd just discovered he was even more deep and meaningful and talented than I'd thought.

He told me all about the band and what they were

working on at the moment and how they were keen to get a demo together to send to producers. And he said that Chaz, their drummer, was making them a web page as well as their Facebook one, so people could listen to their songs online. As he leaned forward across the table, I caught his cinnamon, cedar wood and musk smell, and it took me straight back to the first time we'd met, when he'd pulled me into a doorway out of a storm. I smiled to myself. I'd been sure from the moment I first saw him that we were meant to be together. And now, here we were.

"The website sounds like a great idea," I said. "Got any gigs coming up? You can advertise them on there too."

"Maybe another Music Club showcase at Dartington Hall, but we need something bigger really," he said. "Like the chance to support someone well known. That would get us heard by a lot more people and it would be an in to getting our stuff noticed by producers too."

I loved sitting there in the cosy cafe with its bare brick walls and chunky wood tables, listening to Marco talk. I hadn't realized it before then, but how he felt about his band was the same as how I was about beauty stuff. It was his passion, his way of expressing himself, his *thing*.

When he asked how it was going at Rainbow Beauty, I told him about our plans for a promotion, and the Strawberry Summer Moisturizer we'd created the night before. I talked about what was selling best, and what I planned to try making in the future. Never in a million years had I imagined Marco would be interested in all this stuff, but he sat smiling and nodding and asking more and more questions. What I wanted to talk about next was how Dad hadn't called back again since the day of the grand opening. How I'd been expecting him to, to see how things had gone, or to come down even. How he'd sent a good luck card, which my sisters had decided was such a feeble gesture it seemed to have made them even angrier with him. How I constantly worried and wondered about where he was and what he was doing. But I didn't want to spoil our perfect day out, so instead I focused on the good stuff. Marco seemed so interested that in the end I found myself saying, "Come and help out with the photo shoot tomorrow, if you like. Summer's taking the pictures."

"Oh, tomorrow? I've got band practice," he said. "Sorry."

"It doesn't matter," I insisted. "I know it's really important to get your demo together. Ben's coming to help Summer with the lighting or something, so come by if you finish early and we can all go and do something afterwards."

A while later Marco's phone beeped. He peered at it, frowned and said, "Oh, Abs, sorry, I've got to head off. Dec's managed to blag some rehearsal space right now, because the band that'd reserved it haven't showed up."

An awful wave of disappointment flooded through me, and I felt like throwing myself across the table and clinging to him, like some crazy person, but instead I forced myself to say, "No problem." After all, I was usually the one having to rush off.

We walked back down Fore Street together, and when we got to the side road where he was turning off, I pulled him close and gave him a big hug. The old ladies were still sitting on the bench, blatantly staring, but this time he just grinned and kissed me. And I kissed him back, for ages, and I wouldn't have cared if there had been a whole army of grannies watching.

Mum had a client, Loreen, for a massage first thing the next morning, but then there was no one booked in till two so we were free to start the photo shoot.

Summer arrived about ten, with Ben in tow. "Hi, y'all!" he called, as he wrestled two huge silver and gold reflector boards through the door.

After all the hellos, we sat on the squishy purple sofas and talked about the different shots we wanted to get. First we went for a picture of Saff in one of our lovely fluffy dressing gowns, relaxing on one of the treatment couches, with a face mask on and cucumber over her eyes.

I lit the candles and Ben used the gold board to reflect the light back onto her face, so the lovely warmth and cosiness really came across. Poor boy though, he was looking everywhere but at Saff on the couch, and every time he did have to look at her, he made this serious *I am just being professional* face. It wasn't like he especially fancied her or anything, it was just the effect Saff had on *all* boys – they couldn't help staring at her with their mouths hanging open. Anyway, I made sure you could see the lovely vase of roses in the shot, and a nice selection of our products too, on the chest of drawers.

Summer took about twenty shots and then we all looked back on the monitor on her digital camera and there were some great ones to choose from.

"They look amazing!" Mum enthused, and Summer looked really pleased.

"Fine. Good. Now, let's take some with my face actually showing!" said Saff, and Grace rolled her eyes.

Saff really should be a model or film star or something. She looked completely at home sitting at the manicure station, having her make-up done by Mum. Mum looked like a proper make-up artist too, holding loads of brushes at once and mixing eyeshadow and lipstick colours on the back of her hand. Saff looked stunning when Mum had finished (of course) and Ben had to do his serious *I'm definitely not staring at you apart from professionally* face again.

The plan was to show Saff sitting on one of the squishy sofas, reading a magazine, with a delicious, freshly-made juice in front of her.

"If we do a wide shot, we can get the lovely reception desk and smoothie bar in too," said Summer.

"Good idea," said Mum. "We don't want the place to look empty though. I'll stand behind the desk and Grace and Abbie, you can sit up at the counter."

"What? *I'm* not being in it!" Grace cried.

"It's only the side of your head," said Mum.

"And I'm not sitting up there on my own," I told her, and virtually dragged her there.

"Let me put some colour on your cheeks, love, or you're going to look a bit washed out," Mum said then, advancing on Grace with the blusher brush.

Grace backed away. "No way. I don't wear make-up," she snapped. But I reminded her that we were doing all this to help boost the business and eventually she let Mum put some blusher on her, and a bit of mascara too.

Summer was trying to direct Ben to hold up the silver reflector board and he couldn't seem to get it quite right, so she walked over and moved him around, standing behind him and positioning his arms and body like he was a Ken doll or something.

"Any excuse!" he joked. "You just can't keep your hands off me, can you?"

Summer raised an eyebrow and grinned. "You wish!" she said.

We got some good shots, and just as we were finishing up, Ben's phone beeped. "It's a text from Mum," he said, checking the screen. "She wants me to ring her when I'm free. Dad's away at the moment so she's on her own with Gabe."

Gabe was Ben's adorable baby brother.

"No worries, you can call her now," Summer told him.

"But I thought you needed me?" he said.

"Nah, just prop that board there, on the edge of the sofa. That's right. Up a bit. There. It'll work just as well."

Ben tutted. "So I'm basically doing the job of a sofa?" he grumbled.

Summer smirked. "Not really. I mean, a sofa won't make the tea. You couldn't get the kettle on while you ring your mum, could you?"

"Charming!" Ben snorted. But still, he asked if anyone else wanted a drink and then slouched off to the kitchenette.

"Not too much milk in mine!" Summer called after him.

"You're a bit feisty today!" I told her.

"Oh, Ben knows I'm only playing around," she said. She suddenly looked mortified. "At least, I hope he does." She handed me her camera. "I'll just pop and..." She trailed off and hurried across to the kitchenette.

Summer had saved a spare bag of the rose petals they'd been given to throw at the wedding instead of confetti, so while everyone was having a break, I made a little display table showing the whole Strawberry and Rose Pamper Package, with the free gift Strawberry Summer Moisturizer in its beautiful packaging, and the creams and oils we used in the Rose Body Treatment. I made a strawberry smoothie, and set the products up on a tier of fluffy towels, nestling amongst pink and red petals. Finally, I got my tester batch of Strawberries & Cream Face Mask out of the chiller counter, put it into an ice-cream glass and dotted it with fresh strawberries. Then I added the little notecard I'd handwritten which explained the offer.

There was a lot of laughing and shrieking coming from the kitchenette, and eventually Summer emerged carrying the tea tray. After a while Ben came out too, putting his phone back in his pocket.

"Oh, wow, that looks amazing!" Summer cried, noticing the display I'd just made. She took some lovely photos of it, and then some of the outside of Rainbow Beauty. When she came back in, she said, "You know, the shots of Saff on the massage table and you all in reception would look great as big posters in your windows. If people could see how nice the place is as they're driving past, it would really draw them in."

"Great idea!" cried Saff, obviously enthusiastic about massive posters of herself being on display to the public.

"It really is," Mum agreed. "I'll have to see about

printing costs, but I think we can probably stretch to that."

We all looked at the photos again on Summer's laptop, and voted on which shots to use, and then Mum borrowed it to type up her article. With the help of our neighbour (and Mum's new GBFF) Liam's broadband, which he'd given Mum the code for, we got the whole thing off to the magazine a few minutes before our next client, Sumira, was due.

When the bell above the door jangled I thought it would be her, but I looked up and there was Marco. A huge grin broke out all over my face and I rushed over to him before I even had time to *think* about playing it cool. "Hi! I didn't expect to see you today," I said.

Then Saff completely embarrassed me by grabbing a handful of the rose petals off the display table and throwing them over us, while singing "*Duuuuh-duh-duh-duuuh*", like the wedding march. And typically, Summer and Grace joined in. I blushed about a zillion degrees and goggled my eyes out at them in a way that meant *I'm going to kill you lot later*. "Sorry about them," I muttered.

Marco wrinkled his nose up at Saff and brushed the rose petals off his shoulder. "You said to stop by, and we finished early so—"

"Alright, mate," said Ben, coming over and doing the complicated high-five hand thing all boys seem to have to do. "Are you still on for going into town? Summer's up for it too."

"Yeah, sure," Marco told him. "You can come out, can't you, Abs? We might see a film, or go for burgers." He gave me a mischievous smile and added, "Probably not at Rocket, though!"

My stomach flipped over, remembering our first date, and the messing around. Then it did a double flip, remembering the kiss. Luckily then my brain kicked in and I came back to reality. "I'd love to come," I said, "but I've got way too much to do. I need to go through all the stock with Grace to check use-by dates and see what needs to be reduced. We don't want to have to throw anything away because it's out of date. Then I have to get started on a batch of Strawberry Summer Moisturizer for our promotion."

Marco turned to Saff. "Does she have to do all that *now*?" he asked.

Well, that annoyed me. I mean, I *can* speak for myself, and I do know when I'm busy. Luckily, Saff just smiled and swanned off to get the treatment rooms ready.

Marco turned to me. "Well, if you've got stuff to do…"

The way he said it was a bit off-ish, and I found myself saying, "*Important* stuff. We need to minimize waste to keep our costs down. Every penny counts at the moment. And we have to be ready for the promotion. There's no point doing all this if—"

Then I caught his eye, and a look passed between us. And we smiled at each other. We weren't going to fall out over stupid little things. This was *us*, him and me.

"Look, you know I'm desperate to see you," I told him – and blushed bright red, you know, seeing as my entire family were within earshot (well, apart from Dad, of course).

"Yeah, sure, sorry," Marco said. "You're doing an amazing job. I know how much work it is. I just want to be with you, that's all."

Ooooh, shiver! That sent me into a spine-tingling melt.

"Aw! That's nice," called Saff.

"I want to be with you too," I said, trying to act like my sister didn't exist.

"Can you come over for tea tomorrow though?" he asked. "Mum's cooking, and she really wants to meet you."

I found myself thinking that the Strawberries & Cream Fresh Face Masks weren't going to make themselves, but then I thought, *An invite to meet his mum. As his girlfriend. With some delish food thrown in.* And I ended up saying yes.

My friends were all heading off into town then, so I gave Summer and Ben hugs, and then tried to hug Marco as casually as I could without falling to the floor in a jelly-legged heap. There was no kissing though – Mum, Grace and Saff were watching, after all, and I'd had enough teasing for one day. We all said goodbye and waved them off and then Sumira arrived and we went into professional mode again, welcoming her and taking her jacket and offering her a juice or smoothie.

Mum headed into the treatment room with Sumira, and Saff began tidying up, while Grace and I started on the stock check. That was when the phone rang. I was nearest to the reception desk, so I hurried over and picked it up. "Good afternoon, Rainbow Beauty," I said. "How may I help you?"

"Hi there."

It was a man's voice. And just for a moment, I thought it was Dad. Seeing the frozen, shocked look on my face, I knew my sisters thought so too. Then I realized the man was saying, "I'd like to book a treatment as a surprise for my wife, please. It's for her birthday. What do you recommend?"

"Oh, er, yes, of course. Certainly," I stuttered. Then I pulled myself together, went through the options with him, and booked in a full body treatment with facial and pedicure for Friday. When I got off the phone, Grace and Saff were carrying on as if nothing had happened, but the atmosphere between us had completely changed. I decided to bite the bullet and say something. "Look, I know we've all been expecting Dad to call – at least just to see how the grand opening went…"

"I know! It's so out of order he hasn't!" Saff cried. "How am I supposed to tell him I'm still not speaking to him if he doesn't ring us?"

"*I* wasn't expecting him to call," snapped Grace, reaching for a bottle of Spicy Delight Bubble Bath. She accidentally toppled the whole row over and one fell off the shelf and smashed on the floor. We all jumped and she swore loudly. Then she said, "Look, Abs, he doesn't care about us any more. Get over it."

Her words hit me like a punch in the stomach. All the air swooshed out of my lungs and I couldn't even speak for a second. Then, "He does care," I croaked. "There must be a reason why he hasn't called. Aren't either of you *worried* about him?"

"No," said Grace firmly. "He's made his bed, he can lie in it."

I looked at Saff, but she just shrugged and started wiping down the granite countertop.

"We could ring him," I said quietly. "I've got his number."

They both stared at me then. "What?" cried Grace.

"He gave it to me, when he rang last time."

"Don't you *dare!*" said Saff. "He should be the one ringing us."

I was about to call him anyway – I'd tucked his number into the back of our appointments book and now I reached for it – but Grace looked so upset. "Don't, Abbie, please," she said quietly. "I can't deal with all that right now. We've just got to focus on the promotion."

She looked so small and sad and fragile, as if she might smash into pieces at any moment, like the broken bottle at her feet.

So I didn't call Dad, of course.

Instead I went to fold some towels, and worried about Grace.

Chapter Three

"*Ciao, bella!*" cried Sienna, Marco's mum. "I've been so looking forward to meeting you!" She pulled me into her and Marco's flat and did the cheek-kissing thing (I thought it would be two *mwahs* but she did three, so I pulled back and then had to go forward again – NOT a great start on the CRINGE front!).

"Me too," I said. "Thanks for inviting me." She was just as cool and beautiful as when I'd seen her getting off her motorbike at the school gates (when I'd thought she was Marco's *girlfriend*, but we won't go into that!). And *young*. She'd only been sixteen when she had him, and she didn't even look thirty now.

"Alright?" Marco said, as he stumbled out of his bedroom doorway. He was looking extra-specially gorgeous, in skinny black jeans and a black T-shirt with the name of some band on it that was so cool I'd never heard of it. Even better, he gave me a hug, which meant that I could get swirled up in his cinnamon musk smell.

Music was playing from somewhere as we walked down the hallway (again, it was a band far too cool for me to recognize) and delicious smells were coming from the kitchen. "You go and sit down, supper won't be long," Sienna said, ushering me into the sitting room. "Marco, don't just stand there, get Abbie a drink."

Marco rolled his eyes but he followed her to the kitchen anyway. I took in the huge music collection that filled an entire wall and the big flat screen TV (I was very envious of that – I was *so* fed up with peering at our weeny thing! I mean, you could hardly even see what the embarrassing bits *were* on *Embarrassing Bodies*).

There was a cool vintage sideboard, which held loads of records and an old player. A collection of family photos were arranged on top of it. They were mainly of Marco at different ages, and there were some of him and his mum, and what I took to be his massive extended family back in Italy. I spotted one with a man in too, who had the same piercing blue eyes and slouchy shoulders as Marco. His dad, presumably. Marco was about ten in the picture. He was standing proudly, still wet from swimming, with a medal round his neck and the man's arm around him. I picked up the picture to have a closer look.

"I hope this stuff's okay," Marco was saying as he came back in. "It's some kind of weird lemonade we brought back from this market near Nona's house…"

I held up the photo. "Aw, you were so cute in your little trunks!" I cried.

But, seeing the look on his face, I quickly put it down again. I suddenly felt like I was going through his private stuff, even though it was on display for everyone to look at.

"Yes, that is my dad, Luke," Marco said, pre-empting my question. "One of the rare occasions he actually turned up when he said he would."

"Do you still see him?" I asked. "I remember you saying he moved to Liverpool a couple of years ago."

Marco shrugged. "Hardly ever. He used to be around, but he manages the music venue where he works now. He doesn't get a lot of time off. And when he does, well, it always seems like he's got better things to do than come down here." There was an edge to his voice, as bitter as the weird lemonade I was sipping.

He looked exactly like Grace had the day before. Hurt and bewildered and angry, all at once. Was she still going to be like this in two years' time, like Marco was? Was Dad going to just get on with his new life without us, like Luke seemed to have done? Thinking like that made me even more determined to sort things out with Dad, or at least *try* to sort things out, whatever my sisters said.

I ended up telling Marco what had happened with Saff and Grace when I'd suggested ringing Dad. "So now I feel like I can't call him because I know they don't want me to and I don't want to go behind their backs," I explained. "But I'm worried about him and I do want to make sure he's okay."

I thought Marco would understand how difficult it was, but he just shrugged and said, "I'm with your sisters on this one. If he can't be bothered to ring you, then why would you want to ring *him*?"

I had thought that myself. Of course I had. But I didn't say so. "But what if something's wrong?" I said. "He's our dad, we can't just assume he doesn't care…"

Marco looked wearily at me. "I don't know, Abs. Just do what you think is best, I suppose."

"Supper's ready!" called Sienna. And as we headed through to the kitchen, I was quite relieved we didn't have to talk about dads any more.

Supper was cannelloni (delicious, especially because, unlike the one we made at home, it had all the expensive bits in, like the mozzarella and crème fraiche and fresh basil). As we ate, Sienna told me that at the pub where she worked, they had loads of live music and comedy nights and things.

"Maybe you could play there," I said to Marco.

"Yeah, we're really up for it, but the manager isn't keen because of our age," he told me.

"I'm working on him," said Sienna, as she passed me the salad bowl. "And I'm telling all the promoters we deal with about Headrush in case something comes up somewhere else."

Then she asked me how things were going at Rainbow Beauty and I told her all about our promotion. "Yesterday we made a start on the Strawberry Summer free gift moisturizer," I explained, "but our first batch didn't come out as well as the tester one we made so we had to go back and work out where we'd gone wrong. That means we haven't even started on the Strawberries & Cream Fresh Face Masks. But we're getting there. I've left my mum and sisters to it tonight."

"It sounds fantastic," said Sienna. "I'll book in myself, if I can find a time that doesn't clash with my shifts. You're obviously putting in a lot of hard work."

"It is all taking longer than we thought," I said. "The bottles for the gift moisturizers didn't arrive yesterday by courier like they were supposed to, and we've only just got them now, so we still have to get them all filled and handwrite the labels and package them up. The magazine's out tomorrow and I'm sure we'll be rushed off our feet when people see the offer, so we've got to get everything ready now."

Talking about it all was bringing me out in a cold sweat. My mind started racing, thinking how they'd never get everything done in time without me. And Mum had said they'd be fine making the Strawberries & Cream Fresh Face Masks, but would they? I couldn't even remember whether I'd told Grace how much strawberry seed oil and strawberry fruit extract powder to put in.

I looked at Marco. I wanted to stay here with him and Sienna, laughing and chatting, all evening. I tried to push my panic away, but the thoughts wouldn't go.

"Abbie, what's up?" asked Marco, and I came to, realizing that I hadn't said anything for ages. So then I had to tell them my worries.

"Would it be really rude if I slipped off a bit earlier than planned to see how things are going?" I asked Marco. He didn't say anything, and he wouldn't catch my eye.

"Course not," Sienna said, answering for him. "It sounds like you've got a lot on your plate at the moment."

I smiled at her. "Thanks."

Marco didn't talk much after that though, and I got the idea that he was annoyed about it. That was the last thing I'd wanted – him to take it personally when it wasn't. I wanted to be with him just as much as he wanted to be with me. Surely he knew that by now? I had a horrible, nagging feeling that he just wasn't *getting* the situation me, Mum, Saff and Grace were in. I mean, this was make or break for us. If we couldn't bring in more business, we'd be forced to close, and then we'd lose the flat too. We'd come so close to that before starting Rainbow Beauty, and it had frightened me so much, I could hardly even think about it now. This had to work, it just *had* to. And we all had to put everything into it. There wouldn't be any second chances.

I wanted to say all this to Marco but I couldn't really, not with Sienna there. When we'd had our tiramisu, I thanked them both and started to pull on my jacket. I really hoped Marco would offer to walk me home, so we could talk about it then, but he didn't. I said goodbye to Sienna in the kitchen, did the three *mwah*s thing and rushed out – I felt too annoyed with Marco for not understanding to hug him or anything, and really upset that things had been spoiled in the first place by my stupid panicking brain. He came down the hall after me but I just called out "Bye" over my shoulder and left without turning around.

Back at the flat I found Mum, Grace and Saff in their hairnets and aprons, standing at the kitchen table with the Strawberry Summer Moisturizer stuff in front of them, looking really stressed out. I saw that they hadn't even started on the face masks.

"Oh, Abbie, thank goodness you're back, it's a complete catastrophe!" cried Saff, dramatic as usual.

"We're having real trouble getting the moisturizer in the bottles," said Mum, frowning. "I think we were right to go for a thick, creamy texture, but this bottle shape is making it impossible to decant."

We'd chosen long, thin-necked recycled glass bottles because they looked so glamorous, but it hadn't occurred to any of us how hard it would be to actually get the product into them. Even ice-queen Grace looked flustered. "We're *so* behind," she said. "And these bottles *have* to work. We can't afford to order any others."

"Okay, okay, calm down," I told them, hurrying over to the sink to scrub my hands. "I'm sure we can work something out, we just need to think it through." After trying a few different things, we finally came up with a system using a funnel and a spatula. Once we were in the rhythm of filling the bottles, Mum said, "Oh, Abbie! In all the panic, I didn't even ask you if you had a nice time at Marco's."

"Yeah, come on, let's have all the details," Saff demanded. "Did you smooch?" She giggled and made kissing noises.

"No, we didn't!" I cried. "His *mum* was there, in case you've forgotten!" I told them how cool and glamorous Sienna was, and how she was planning to book in for our promotion, and about the lovely supper. Then I told them how panicky I'd got about everything back at the flat, and how I was worried that I'd upset Marco by leaving early.

"Doesn't he realize how busy you are?" said Grace, looking outraged.

"He just wants to spend time with her," Saff countered. "It's romantic."

"Why don't you try and involve him in what we're doing more?" Mum suggested. "Then he might understand how much pressure we're all under at the moment. You could invite him here one evening. I don't think I can stretch to a posh meal, but if you said about seven, we could have tea and biccies…"

I actually thought that was a really good idea. If Marco could see how much we had to do, and maybe even help out a bit, he was bound to realize it was nothing personal when I couldn't spend time with him. I knew he had band practice the next evening so I texted him from Mum's pay-as-you-go phone and asked him over for Saturday night. I got a reply straight back, saying he'd love to come. He didn't sound moody at all and I started wondering whether I'd completely imagined him looking annoyed. I'd probably been worrying over nothing, as usual. As I got on with filling up the bottles, I thought back to our perfect date and felt all warm and fuzzy about him again.

Two hours later the moisturizer was safely in the bottles, and we all had to admit they looked so fabulous it was worth the effort.

* * *

The *Totnes in Focus* magazine came out on Friday and we were too excited to wait for it to drop through the letter box, so Saff and I walked into town to their office to get a few copies when we had a long gap between clients. The article looked amazing and Saff was dancing around the whole day because she was so pleased with how the pictures had come out.

We all ended up in really great moods actually, even Grace, because from about two o'clock – when the magazine was being delivered around town – the phone started ringing and it just didn't stop. We took loads of bookings for Saturday for the Strawberry and Rose offer, and some people even added nail appointments too, so Saff was going to have a lot of manicures and pedicures to do. The offer was on until the following Friday, and we got quite a few people booked in through the week as well.

"This is a fantastic response, better than in my wildest dreams," cried Mum, when she put the phone down after filling the last slot for Saturday. "Doing these kind of promotions is going to give the business a proper boost."

"We could come up with a different special offer every month from now on to keep things fresh," I said.

"And let's start a mailing list so we can tell people when there's a new offer," Grace added.

"In a couple of years, when I've finished college, we can open a second parlour and I can run it!" Saff cried.

And instead of telling her to get a grip, Grace said, "We could have a whole chain! A Rainbow Beauty empire!"

Then we all jumped round the kitchen, singing that Beyoncé song about girls running the world at the tops of our voices.

On Saturday morning, when we all went downstairs in our matching pink uniforms to open up, we were still bubbling over with excitement. My skin felt (and smelled!) gorgeous thanks to my Mandarin Body Butter, and I'd set myself up for a long day on my feet with my Zingy Lemon Zest Foot Scrub.

Just as we were unlocking the door of Rainbow Beauty, the postman came by and dropped off a long cardboard tube.

"The posters!" Saff squealed. "Quick, let's get them up now!"

"We've probably just got time," said Mum.

So she and Saff stood outside, while Grace and I balanced on the stools from the smoothie counter and moved the posters left a bit and right a bit. Then, when Mum gave us the thumbs up through the window, we stuck them up and went out to have a look.

"I look amazing!" Saff declared, making us all laugh. "What?" she cried. "It's a fact."

It was, actually.

"And the products and treatment rooms and reception and smoothie bar all look amazing too," said Mum.

"Even the side of your head looks amazing, Grace!" I said, making her giggle.

Mum grabbed us all round our waists and pulled us close to her. "Summer's done a great job with the photography," she said. "It just looks so professional now. Like a real beauty parlour."

I grinned. "It *is* a real beauty parlour," I said, "and it's ours."

Mum squeezed us tight. "Girls, I can't tell you how proud I am of you all," she said. "And I love you more than words can say…" Her voice cracked and she squeezed us tighter, blinking back tears.

"Steady on!" shrieked Saff, flapping her hands in front of her face. "This mascara's not waterproof!"

Mum giggled and dabbed at her own eyes. "Fair enough. Right, let's rock and roll," she said, and we headed back in, only letting go of each other so we could get through the door.

We all started getting nervous as we double-checked the number of towels in the chests of drawers to make sure there were enough, and arranged the right products and equipment in each of the treatment rooms so Mum and Saff could get hold of everything they needed without any fuss. We all knew how much was riding on this day.

With only about ten minutes until our first client was due, Mum gathered us together in reception for a pep talk. "Now, today is a taster of how we need Rainbow Beauty to run if we're going to make it a success," she said, in a very serious tone. "It needs to be busy and, ideally, fully booked. We need to reset things in the treatment rooms very quickly, as clients will be coming back-to-back. And it's vital to stick to our schedules, no running over time. Everyone needs to leave here having had a wonderful experience, and ready to come back again, and tell their friends about it. So, this is it, girls. Go forth and beautify!"

"Yay!" we all cried, and gave her a big clap.

"Abbie, Trish is arriving now," said Mum, glancing out of the window. "Please could you get her a Strawberries & Cream Fresh Face Mask out of the fridge and put it in the treatment room, then I think we're all ready!"

"Sure," I said. We were leaving the face masks in the chiller counter until the very last minute so they'd be as fresh as possible for our clients. I strode over to it and straight away I could see that something was wrong. As I reached in, there wasn't that cool sensation on my arm, and then I realized it wasn't making its usual faint hum. My heart started pounding. How long had the chiller been out of action? It could have broken yesterday afternoon and been off all night, or (please, please) maybe it had only just stopped working in the last hour. I opened one of the little tubs of face mask and sniffed the pink strawberry swirl inside. Urgh! The cream had gone off and the whole thing smelled like sick. My stomach lurched because, for one thing, smelling sick always made me feel like *being* sick. And for another, I knew there was no way we could use this batch.

Trish had come in by then and Mum, Grace and Saff were doing their usual lovely welcome routine. "Mum, could you come over here for a second?" I called. "It's urgent."

Mum hurried over. Her face fell when I showed her the broken chiller, and she agreed that we definitely couldn't use the Strawberries & Cream Face Masks. The other types were okay, thank goodness, as they didn't contain such sensitive ingredients, and all the fresh fruit for the juices and smoothies was still useable, although some of it was looking a little the worse for wear. "It's going to be boiling hot today too," Mum said, frowning. "We'll just have to try and sell as much as we can of the most perishable things. Talk up the blueberry smoothie and the energizing juice, to use up the grapes, blueberries and bananas."

Grace and Saff had come over by then to find out what was wrong. "Oh, what a nightmare!" cried Saff dramatically, when I explained.

"Calm down, it's not that bad," hissed Grace.

"Will it all have to be thrown away?" Mum asked her anxiously. Grace knows the health and safety rule book backwards.

"We can't sell any of these face masks to take home," said Grace, "because we can't guarantee the use-by dates now. But we can still use them in the treatments. You'll have to offer clients the others for now and then make up another batch of strawberries and cream ones as soon as you can."

Mum went over to Trish and explained what the problem was, and then came back looking even more worried. "She says she doesn't mind waiting for a new batch of the strawberry one to be whipped up," she told me. "I tried to persuade her to try one of the others but she wants the exact package that she came for. She thinks she's being helpful by waiting, but this is going to throw all our timings out."

"Mum, you should have just insisted she had something else," hissed Saff.

Mum threw her hands in the air. "How could I? We have to make our clients happy, and that's what she wants."

"We'll just have to be as quick as we can," I said. "We can use the strawberries we've got here for the drinks – Saff, you start preparing them. Grace, you dash to the shop for some more, and the cream, of course, and I'll run upstairs and get everything else we need. Luckily the blender's still clean so, if you get the kettle on to sterilize it, I can make a batch up right here." They all stayed still, staring at me for a moment. "Go, quick!" I hissed and they all leaped into action. "Oh, and Mum," I added, "please could you call Liam and see if he can fix this blooming thing!"

Liam came down straight away, carrying his toolbox. He was a builder by trade and he'd helped us out loads with Rainbow Beauty – calling in favours and doing the renovation for just the cost of the materials. Without Liam, there wouldn't *be* a Rainbow Beauty. Although we'd only known him a short time, I couldn't imagine not having him around. He spent a long time on the floor with his head under the chiller counter. "I'm afraid there's nothing I can do," he told Mum and me when he reappeared. "The motor's burned out and you'll have to get a specialist engineer in."

Mum looked horrified. "Well, how much will that cost?" she gasped.

Liam grimaced. "It won't be cheap. They'll probably have to order a new motor specially, if you can still *get* the parts for something this old." He pulled Mum into a hug. "I'm sorry, Kim," he said then. "I can't save the chiller counter, but I can take you for a large glass of wine when you close this evening."

"Thanks," Mum mumbled into his shirt. "I might well take you up on that."

So in the end we had to cram the other face masks and all the perishable fruit for the juices and smoothies into our fridge upstairs until we could call someone out on Monday.

The face mask crisis only put us fifteen minutes behind in the end, which probably would have been okay if everything else had gone like clockwork. But it didn't. Instead we just had one disaster after another.

One of our clients, Elaine, wanted a leg wax as well as her facial, but she didn't ask until she arrived, so we hadn't planned for it. Mum said yes because she wanted her to be really happy, but that just put us even more behind time. So by one thirty, when this lady called Geneva arrived for the Rose and Strawberry Pamper Package plus manicure, we were running over half an hour late. She was going to have her nails done first, but Saff wasn't ready, because Mum kept sending *her* clients over late. When we explained about the delay, Geneva didn't say it was okay, like the other ladies had, but instead she seemed really moody about it.

Then someone came in just to look at the products and she chose quite a few to buy. I was running up and down to our fridge to get more supplies for the juices and smoothies, and Grace was trying to welcome people and make up other customers' bills at the same time, so for a start she had to wait ages to pay. Then when I did serve her, I managed to somehow put something into the till wrong and ended up overcharging her. She came back a few minutes later to explain what had happened and I put it right (and apologized a lot!). She said it was fine, but I could tell she was a bit annoyed. Even worse, that Geneva woman was still in reception and she saw the whole thing and had this really snotty disapproving look on her face about it.

She also tutted about the horrible disaster that happened next – as if we didn't all feel bad enough about it. Two ladies had turned up one straight after another and said they had treatments booked. I'd asked their names and invited them to take a seat, but I was confused about why they'd both arrived at once. I wondered if perhaps one was just having her nails done, but I couldn't find her name in Saff's appointments column. Mum came out of the treatment room then and I called her over. "Oh, thank goodness you're finished," I whispered. "We can get back on top of the time now. Your next client's been a bit funny about having to wait," I added, nodding slightly towards Geneva.

Mum grimaced. "I'm nowhere near ready, I'm afraid, love," she said. "Eshana's just having ten minutes to relax with her face mask on, so I've popped out to the loo. Then I'm with her for at least another ten minutes after that."

My stomach started sinking then. How moody would Geneva be in twenty minutes' time?

"Mum, I'm confused about this," I said then. "I've got a lady called Jane who's going in to Saff first and then to you after Geneva, and here she is in the appointments book, but that lady Sue's come in too, for you she said, and I can't find her name."

Mum frowned at the book. "I can't either," she said. Then she turned the page to Monday, and there at 2.30 p.m. was written *Sue Read*, in Saff's handwriting.

"Oh, no, Saff must have booked her in on the wrong day by accident," Mum said under her breath. "Oh, gosh, I'll have to tell her." She looked like she was going to be sick, and I felt like I was too.

So poor Mum had to explain to Sue what had happened and that we didn't have any space free today, while I stood next to her, wishing there was a button I could press on the reception desk to open a trapdoor under my feet and swoosh me down a secret tunnel, never to return.

"But my mother's come over especially from Exeter to look after the children," she cried. "I was really looking forward to this."

"I'm so sorry," said Mum. "I'm afraid we're having a few teething problems today. I could book you in for the same package next Saturday," she offered. "Complimentary, of course."

"We really are very sorry," I said, feeling all sick and trembly and like my legs were about to give way.

Sue looked like she was about to cry. "I won't be able to get away," she said. "Look, don't bother, okay." And with that she stormed out. Jane very tactfully carried on reading her magazine, but Geneva tutted loudly.

"Oh, I feel awful," Mum sighed, rubbing her face with her hands. "I remember that feeling, it's so hard to find time for yourself when you've got young children. Something like this is a real treat, and we've spoiled it for her."

"Mum, it was an honest mistake," I said. "It wasn't your fault." But inside I felt as bad as she did.

"I know, but—" Mum began. Then: "Oh goodness – my client!" she cried suddenly, and rushed back into the treatment room.

Eshana came out a few minutes later looking very happy (well, that was something, anyway) and as she filled out one of our feedback forms, Geneva went in (thank goodness!).

"I'm going to read Eshana's form," said Grace, as soon as she'd gone. "We need some cheering up. *Very relaxing body treatment*," she began. "*Unfortunately the young lady who did my nails paid no attention when I told her which colour I'd like, and pushed a bright pink on me which I'm not very keen on*. Oh," she said, looking crestfallen.

My stomach lurched again. Things were going from bad to worse to shockingly hideous. "I guess we'll have to say something to Saff," I croaked.

"Say what to me?" Saff said brightly, almost skipping out of the other treatment room. "It's going really well, don't you think? Eshana loved her pink nails."

"I don't think she did," said Grace, waving the feedback form at her. So Saff read it, but I wished she hadn't. It sucked all the energy out of her and she looked as miserable as us three. "And you booked—" Grace began, but I did the goggly eyes thing at her to stop her talking. I didn't think poor Saff needed to know about the double-booking she'd made, not right then anyway. As it was, she only just managed to keep smiling and welcome Jane into the treatment room.

Mum followed Geneva out after only forty-five minutes, looking very flustered. "Unfortunately we're running so late that this lady has to go now," she said. "Please could you just charge her half price, Grace."

Grace looked like she was about to argue that we couldn't afford to give ad-hoc discounts, but the look on Mum's face stopped her. She looked small and miserable and defeated, just like when we first got to

Devon and we were going to be thrown out of the flat. "Again, please do accept my apologies, Geneva," she began.

"Miss Grant," Geneva cut in snootily.

"Miss Grant," Mum corrected. "I do hope you'll come back soon, and I assure you we'll have our timing issues sorted out as of Monday. This won't happen again."

Geneva, Miss Grant, whoever she was, pursed her lips and uttered the smallest "Thank you". Then she handed Grace the exact money and stalked out.

"Oh my gosh, please let this day end!" wailed Mum, as we watched the woman march off down the pavement. Grace and I felt the same, but we had to keep smiling through another two clients. When they'd gone, we just about resisted the urge to throw ourselves on the floor and sob our hearts out. Instead we dragged around, sweeping up and wiping down, putting all the products away and gathering up the used towels for the wash. We didn't speak much – I think we were still in shock from how badly wrong things had gone.

It was then that I remembered I'd invited Marco over for tea. I found Mum in the kitchenette, washing up coffee cups. "Is it still okay for Marco to come round tonight?" I asked her.

She gave me a look of utter exhaustion. "Oh, love, I'm so sorry but I don't think I could face entertaining, not after all this."

I was disappointed, but I couldn't bring myself to argue with her.

"No problem," I said. "I'll see if he wants to go out instead."

"Thanks for understanding," said Mum. "Definitely another night though, very soon. I think I'll call round to see Liam when I've finished these, take up that offer of a drink."

"Sure," I said. I picked up Mum's phone to text Marco about going out, but then I realized that I was far too exhausted and miserable. I'd probably just end up crying all over him again, or going on and on about our terrible day – neither of which were exactly *attractive* options. I thought back to that disastrous time when I'd met him in the cafe, just moments after I'd got all upset about Dad. I ended up running off, crying my eyes out. There was no way I was going to let that happen again. I was desperate to see Marco, of course, but I really didn't want him to see *me* in this state, so in the end I cancelled.

A few minutes later I got *Oh. Okay* back. I hoped he wasn't in a mood about it, but I didn't have the energy to worry about it if he was. I'd explained in my text that we'd had an absolutely terrible day. And I'd already arranged to meet up with him, Ben and Summer the next day anyway.

So, after we'd trudged upstairs to change and have some toast, which was all any of us could be bothered to make, Liam and Mum went over to the pub on the corner for a glass of wine. Saff headed into town to meet Emily, and Grace shut herself in her room with her Maths extension work.

I followed behind Mum and Liam on their way out, saying I was going back down to Rainbow Beauty because I'd forgotten to move all the smoothie fruit back upstairs again.

"Do you want us to give you a hand?" Liam asked.

I forced myself to smile. "No, really, I'm happy to do it," I insisted. "And I need to see what products we sold today; I know we're low on some things now. I'll be fine, you go, honestly."

Mum frowned and I could tell she didn't want to leave me on my own, not after the day we'd had. I said again that I'd be fine, and that I'd probably ring Summer for a chat soon, or go back upstairs and persuade Grace to watch TV with me. "Okay, if you're sure," Mum said. "Lock up after yourself, won't you?"

"Of course." I hugged them both and then Liam put his arm round Mum and they crossed the road. I went to the reception desk and picked up the phone, but then I put it down again. I didn't feel like speaking to anyone, not even Summer.

I started checking the stock, but ended up throwing down my notebook in frustration. I curled up on one of the squishy purple velvet sofas, hugged a cushion and stared into space.

How could the day have been such a disaster, when we'd *so* needed it to be a success? And once again Rainbow Beauty had spoiled my evening with Marco.

I told myself there was no point in crying, but that didn't stop the tears from rolling down my cheeks. It just didn't seem fair somehow. We'd worked so hard, and thrown everything into making Rainbow Beauty work. It felt like fate had just marched in with its big boots on, stomped all over our hopes, and torn our dreams to tatters. Things really couldn't get any worse.

Chapter Four

None of us had been able to get to sleep on Saturday night. We kept bumping into each other in the hallway, going to the loo and getting water and bowls of cereal and stuff. So we all slept in really late on Sunday morning and, by the time we woke up, bright sunshine had been streaming through the thin curtains for at least two hours and we were all mudgy and fuzzy-headed (and, let's face it, grumpy!).

I stumbled into the shower and picked out one of my Orange Zest Soaps, with lovely orange peel in, hoping it would wake me up. It worked pretty well, but I still didn't feel like going into town with my friends. Instead I planned to make a new batch of

Rose & Geranium Bath Bombs with little rosebuds in, so after I was dressed and ready I went into the kitchen, got my apron on and started getting the stuff out.

Grace came in then. "I'll give you a hand if you like," she said.

I stared at the moulds, bowls, spoons and bags of ingredients in front of me and didn't feel my usual burst of excitement. "Thanks, but I think my making mojo has deserted me this morning," I told her. I took off my apron, sat down and flopped my head onto my arms.

"Oh, okay. We could go and mark down the stuff that's nearing its sell-by date," Grace suggested.

"Sure," I said. "I was going to do it last night but—"

"Right, I'm putting a stop to this conversation," said Mum, as she walked in. She looked as casual as she ever got, in immaculate blue jeans, a gold belt and a white shirt. "It's a beautiful day, you've been hard at work all week, let's leave thinking about yesterday until tomorrow. We need time to clear our heads. No one is mooching round here today, discounting stock or doing anything else."

"Fine with me," said Saff, wandering in in her dressing gown. "Emily and I are going to the beach, her mum's picking me up in…oh my gosh, forty minutes!" And with that, she sprinted for the bathroom (Saff needs at least an hour to get ready).

"That includes you, Grace," said Mum sternly. "I forbid you to do any studying today."

Grace rolled her eyes. "That's not very parenty of you," she grumbled.

"Do you want to come to the supermarket with me?" Mum asked her.

"Or come out with me, Summer and the boys," I offered. I'd decided to meet them after all. If Mum was chucking me out of the house, I might as well.

"No thanks, I'll go up to the castle and read," said Grace.

"Do you want to walk into town with us?" I asked. "Ben and Marco are meeting me here."

Grace looked horrified about having to chat to my mates. "No, you're alright," she mumbled, then grabbed her book and purse and bolted out of the door.

"I just don't understand what's up with her," I said. "It's not like they bite or anything."

"She's just shy in groups," said Mum, "you know that. Still, it was really nice of you to offer to include her."

I shrugged. "I suppose I'll just have to keep

trying," I said. "She's going to become a recluse at this rate!"

Mum smiled a little, but she looked about as worried as I felt.

At eleven, I double-checked my make-up and hair, added a slick of Peppermint Kiss Lip Balm and went downstairs.

Ben and Marco were already standing outside Rainbow Beauty. And – can you believe it? (of course you can!) – they were just *staring* at the posters of Saff, with their mouths hanging open like gormless idiots. They didn't even notice me walk right up to them. They did when I slapped their heads though.

"Hey! Why do we get smacked?" cried Ben. "We're *saving lives*, thank you very much!"

I peered at him. "Yeah, right! Pervs!"

"Yeah, we're trying to block the posters by standing in front of them," said Marco. "These could cause a crash. It's a health and safety issue."

"Well, maybe I should take them down, if they're that dangerous," I said.

"Oh no, you don't need to do that," Ben said quickly.

"Go ahead. I've only got eyes for you, babes," said Marco, pulling me into a hug.

"Phwoar!" cried Ben. "Can anyone else smell cheese?!"

"Ha ha," I said. "I think that was cute," I told Marco.

"You want to get yourself a girlfriend too, mate," Marco told Ben, and when he said the word "girlfriend" my legs went all bendy and I had to concentrate really hard so I didn't fall over.

Ben *blushed* at that. He's so sweet! Marco's right, he really does deserve to find someone. Maybe I could find someone for him. Not Saff though. She'd eat him for breakfast.

"Summer's running late – she said she'll meet us there," said Marco. He curled his arm around my waist and we started walking up the road. At least being Marco's girlfriend was something good, even if everything else in my life had gone horribly wrong. He didn't seem bothered about me cancelling the night before either – phew.

Summer's dad's Land Rover pulled up beside us, and Jim, one of her older brothers, waved to us from the driver's seat. Summer sprang down and slammed the door shut behind her, then waved him off up the road.

"Hi!" she cried. "So, Abs, how did yesterday go? I've been dying to hear all about it – I thought you'd ring me last night! Was it brilliant? Did everyone love it? What did people say about the new moisturizer?"

That's when I really had to control myself from bursting into tears. I didn't want my mascara to run for a start, and I didn't want to cry in front of Marco either. "It was just awful," I mumbled.

"Oh, I'm so sorry," Summer gasped. She linked arms with me on the other side to Marco and squeezed me tight. "What happened?"

I was just going to skate over it, but in the end I told them all the terrible things that had happened, and how devastated we all were about it.

By the time we were over the bridge and halfway up Fore Street, she looked as upset as I felt. "Oh, hon, I'm *so* sorry," she cried.

"Yeah, that sucks!" said Ben. "Especially that woman being such a cow. It was your first really busy day! She could have cut you some slack."

"Honestly, it was terrible when Mum had to tell that lady she couldn't have her treatment," I told them, shuddering at the memory. "I just wanted to crawl under the reception desk and die, and Mum was really upset about it."

"It was only one day," said Marco. "You're going to have some bad days, everyone does. Don't let it get to you."

I think that was supposed to cheer me up, but instead it made me really annoyed. "It's not just one day though," I snapped. "Those ladies might not come back. And worse, they'll tell their friends we were running so late, and about the other problems, and *they* won't book in either. Word of mouth is everything. This wasn't just a bad day, this was a disaster!"

I realized then that Summer was staring at me, and Ben was looking very interested in the pavement. "Alright, keep your hair on!" Marco said. He was trying to sound jokey, but I could tell he was really hurt.

Okay, so maybe I was overreacting a bit. But then he was under-reacting, by a mile.

None of them said anything else about the disaster day after that – I'd been so touchy about it they probably didn't dare, poor things. Summer and Ben walked ahead after a while and Marco put his arm round me again. "Shall we peel off and do our own thing?" he said. "We missed out on last night, and it feels like we haven't seen each other on our own for ages."

I realized that he was right – in fact, we hadn't hung out together on our own since our amazing date at the cafe, and that was a week ago now. But still, I shook my head. "Let's stick together, if it's alright with you," I told him. "I've hardly seen those two either, and Summer's going away soon."

Marco shrugged. "Okay, if that's what you want. Maybe we could do something tonight though? There are a couple of decent films we could go and see."

"Oh, I can't tonight," I told him. "I'm sleeping over at Summer's."

"But if you're seeing her later, why—" he began.

"*Working* sleepover," I told him. "We're going to pick lots of apples and pull up some carrots for our juices – Annie's offered them to me for free." Annie was Summer's mum and she had this amazing cottage garden full of fruit and veg. "And she's going to give me feedback on my new gardeners' hand cream formula. It's like the balm I made, but much creamier."

"Oooh, that sounds thrilling," said Marco.

I stared at him. "OM and G, are you sulking?" I teased. "You *are*!"

"I just want to see you, that's all," he grumbled.

I nudged him with my elbow and he tried to keep up his serious face, but I kept poking him until he bent double and cried, "Oi!"

"Oh come on, we've got today," I said, "and the rest of the summer."

He peered at me, and smiled at last. "Right, well, next bit of free time you get, book me in, yeah?" he said.

"Of course," I promised. Ben and Summer were ambling along a few metres in front of us, chatting and laughing. I nudged Marco and gestured towards them. "Let's get them," I whispered.

We grinned at each other, then bolted up the pavement and jumped on their backs with a loud war cry.

In the cafe, Summer and I sipped strawberry milkshakes and munched on Danish pastries while the boys tucked into chicken and chips. It was only half eleven but they were always hungry. We were chatting about this beach party that was coming up – apparently it was a tradition that started in Year 6, a leaving-junior-school thing some of the dads put on. They reckoned it was really good fun and that most of the kids in our year went. I completely forgot about my problems – that was, until Ben said, "So, is your dad coming down soon, Abs?"

The question took me by surprise and I had to slurp on my milkshake for a few extra seconds so I could catch my breath. I'd been thinking about Dad so much, but keeping it to myself. "Yeah, maybe, I think… He's, erm, he's a bit busy at the moment, so I guess we'll see."

"Why would you even want to see him, after what he did?" said Marco.

I got really flustered and when I tried to speak it felt like my tongue was tying itself in knots. "Course I want to see him," I said eventually. "He *is* my dad."

Marco shrugged. "Well, he's not acting like one. He hasn't even been in touch to see how your launch went."

I felt really defensive of Dad, even though I'd been thinking the same thing myself. "He's got stuff going on," I said lamely. "It's hard for him too." I didn't even know if I believed that myself though. "I'm just going to the loo," I said then, standing up suddenly. I hurried off before any of them could say anything else about it.

I stood by the mirror, fiddling about with mascara and eyeliner from my bag even though my make-up looked perfectly fine. A couple of minutes later, the door swung open. It was Summer.

"Are you okay?" she asked.

I shrugged. "Yeah. It's just that I never know what to say when people mention Dad. It seems to twist me up in knots."

"Ben didn't mean to upset you," she said then. "He was just being a mate."

I peered at her in the mirror. I'd caught a glimpse of something in her face but I wasn't sure what it was – not totally sure, anyway.

"Yeah, I know. Ben's really, *really* nice, isn't he?" I said experimentally.

"Yeah." And there it was. Unmissable. Summer, blushing and trying to force down a smile.

I whirled around and pointed the mascara at her accusingly. "Is there something you want to tell me?" I asked.

"No," she insisted. (Cue more blushing.) "Well…"

I absolutely screamed my head off then. "Oh My G! You fancy Ben!" I shrieked.

"Abbie, shut up!" she squealed. "He'll hear you! It's not like anything's happened…"

"Yeah, but you'd like it to!" I cried.

Summer put her head in her hands and stamped her feet on the floor. "Argh!" she cried. "Maybe. I don't know."

"You *do*, and you *do*!" I yelled.

"Okay, I *do*!" she squealed.

"Whoo-hoo – I knew it!" I whooped. I started dancing around, waving the mascara and eyeliner like

95

little pompoms. Then I tried to march her through the swing door and back out into the cafe, still leaping about, but she grabbed my arm and wrestled us back into the loos again. "Calm down!" she hissed.

"Alright, I'll try," I said. I stopped dancing and pulled her into a hug instead. Well, okay, maybe it was more of a headlock. I was just so excited. I mean, those two got on *sooo* well. They were perfect for each other.

"Please, Abs, you have to act normal when we go back out," she begged. "He might not even feel the same."

I winked at her. "Well, now's your chance to find out! Come on, let's go and ask him!"

She looked really scared then. "Are you crazy?" she hissed. "What if he doesn't like me? I'm not risking it. I mean, when we had that walk on Vire Island, just us two, I thought maybe—"

Someone came into the loos then so we had to look sensible. "Thank goodness I'm coming to yours tonight!" I told her, as we filed out. "I need details. Times. Places. EXACT words!" As we neared the boys, she did the goggly eyes thing at me.

"My lips are sealed," I promised her.

"Are you sure you're alright?" she asked me then, suddenly serious again.

I made myself smile. "Sure I'm sure." Part of me did want to talk to her about Dad, but I felt like I wouldn't know where to begin.

"I love it!" Annie declared, rubbing my new gardeners' hand cream into her skin. "It's really creamy, but still very light."

"Thanks," I said. "I'm a bit unsure about the smell though. The carrot oil is coming through quite strongly, even with the calendula…"

"Yes, it can pong a bit. I wonder, if you just added some bergamot… Hang on…" Annie swished off in her long skirt, bracelets jangling. We were sitting round the huge pine table in Summer's kitchen, among a collection of empty mugs and a half-sorted-out pile of recycling.

I loved Summer's whole house, but her kitchen was my favourite part. I adored the open shelves full of every spice you could imagine, the rack of dried herbs hanging from the ceiling and the huge red Aga, which was wafting delicious smells our way as the date and banana muffins Annie had whipped up for our sleepover baked inside it. Summer and I had already dug up the carrots and picked the apples and they were stacked in boxes, next to the pile of muddy boots at the back door, ready for me to take back to Rainbow Beauty in the morning.

Summer put some popcorn in the microwave and got the kettle on to boil for hot chocolate, and a few minutes later, Annie reappeared with a large wooden box, which held her collection of essential oils. She found the bergamot, pulled a saucer from the dresser and added a drop to a dollop of the hand cream. She mixed it and then held it up for me to smell. "That's gorgeous," I exclaimed. She was right – the bergamot really balanced out the carrot oil scent and gave the cream a refreshing, feel-good note. "Perfect for tired-out, chapped hands that have been busy in a veg patch all day," I told her.

"Let's have a sniff," said Summer, so I passed the saucer over and she said she loved it too.

"Put me down for four jars when you make your first batch up," Annie said. "My green-fingered friends went wild for the balm, I'm sure they'll love this too. I'll get my purse."

"You're not paying!" I cried. "Not after everything you've done to help us."

"I certainly am!" Annie insisted. "You're a new business, you can't afford to give things away. Now, how much are you planning to charge for these?"

While Annie and I had a debate about whether

she was paying or not (she won in the end – she was right, we needed every penny we could get), Summer gathered up all the stuff for our sleepover. I picked up my bag and, once Annie had filled a box with the hot, fresh muffins and handed it to me, I headed for the stairs.

"Oh, we're not sleeping in my room," Summer announced.

"What?" I said, confused.

She smiled mysteriously. "I've got a surprise for you. Come on!"

And with that she gave Annie a hug as best she could while weighed down with all the stuff, and headed out the back door. Then Annie and I had a let's-not-squish-the-cake-box-type hug too and I went after her.

We stumbled through the veg garden, crossed the lawn and there it was. The yurt. It was glowing with some kind of inner light, like it had just landed from outer space.

Summer giggled. "I hope you like camping!"

"Oh, this isn't camping, this is glamping!" I cried.

The yurt was completely magical inside. The glow turned out to be loads of these gorgeous little candle lanterns hanging from the ceiling, and there were cosy rugs on the floor and two sleeping bags set out on fluffy sheepskins. "It's fantastic!" I gasped.

Summer's massive hairy dogs Biff and Chip had taken a shine to it too and made themselves at home, so we had to step over their long, stretched-out legs. As soon as we'd settled down and got all our yummy food out, I said, "Right, spill, I want all the details on this *thang* with you and Ben."

Summer grinned at me. "Sorry, I can't speak at the moment," she said, grabbing a massive handful of popcorn and shoving it into her mouth.

"Oh, come on!" I begged. "I need details! When did you start to fancy him?"

She grinned at me and shoved in another handful of popcorn.

"You can't keep this up all night!" I told her. "Soon the popcorn will run out and you'll have to tell me *everything*. Very soon, in fact, if I do this..." I grabbed a huge handful myself and shoved it into my mouth. Then another and another until it was crammed full. She snorted with laughter and several bits of popcorn came flying out, and then she had a coughing fit. "Steady on! Don't choke yourself over it!" I said, still chewing.

Biff was eyeing up the popcorn, so I threw a bit for him and he caught it in his mouth.

"Okay, okay," said Summer, when she'd got her breath back. "I've always liked him loads as a mate, but I suppose it was that last day of term when we were all mucking around, spraying foam and stuff. Remember when we ganged up to get Marco? Well, I turned around and Ben was right there, spraying his can at Marco and laughing his head off. He looked the same as ever – well, apart from being covered in pink and green foam – but he looked different as well. You know, *mmmm* different."

I giggled. "Are you sure you haven't just got a thing about spray foam?"

"Don't laugh!" Summer cried. "Oh, but it *is* stupid, isn't it? It's not like he's going to suddenly start liking *me* in that way."

"Well, you suddenly started liking *him*, so why not?" I reasoned. "Maybe he already does like you, and he hasn't been brave enough to make a move either. Or maybe he still needs to see *you* in a different way too, as more than a mate. When are you next meeting up?"

"He's volunteering at Dartington Hall next week," she said, "you know, with the conservation group. They want to make a new wall display to tell people about the work they're doing and I offered to take the pictures."

"Right, well, that's perfect," I said. "Get some time alone with him and say something."

"Of course I will," said Summer.

I peered at her, impressed that she was just going to go for it. But then she grinned and added, "I mean, like, I'll say 'Hi, how are you, nice otters', that kind of thing."

I swatted at her and she rolled out of my way. "You know I don't just mean say *any old thing*, dipstick!" I cried. "I mean, Say Something, with capitals."

"I *can't*," Summer groaned. "Not till I know whether he feels the same or not!" She rolled onto her tummy and hid her head under a bit of sheepskin. "Oh, this is all so embarrassing and hideous," she cried. "Maybe I'll just stay a spinster for the rest of my life!"

Biff was half on my lap by then and trying to stick his head in the popcorn bowl, so Summer chucked him out of the yurt. Chip followed right behind him as usual, snaffling a muffin from the box on her way.

"You must be able to tell if he's interested," I said, when they'd gone. "You have to act like *you* might be interested, and see how he reacts."

Summer looked at me like I was speaking Japanese. "But how do I do that?"

I stared at her in amazement. "Summer, haven't you ever heard of *flirting*?"

"Oh. Duh. Right!" she cried. "I did *try* that, when we were doing the photo shoot. You know, when I ordered Ben to make the tea…"

"That was meant to be *flirting*?" I gasped. "We all just thought you had PMS or something!"

Summer groaned loudly and buried her head even further under the sheepskin. "See? I'm SO rubbish at it!" she squealed.

"Don't worry, you can improve. I'll help you," I said.

"But, Abbie, I—"

I pulled her up. "Let's *workshop* this," I said, doing an impression of Miss Hicks, our Drama teacher. "Okay, stand up…stretch…shake it loose…" I leaped up and bounced from one foot to the other, like we were actors warming up.

"Abbie…" Summer began, looking unconvinced.

"Trust me," I said. "Okay, time for a bit of role play. So, you're doing the wildlife thingie, and you've got your camera, and you could go, 'Hey, Ben, can I get a picture of *you* with that, like, vole or whatever it is? You're so fit we'll get loads of girls volunteering for the conservation group when they see it'."

Summer stared at me, wide-eyed. "No way! I

can't say that!" she screeched.

I grinned. "Maybe that is a tad too mucho. Okay, then, how about, 'I've got a mad crush on you, be my boyf and give me a kiss, *mwah*, *mwah*!'"

Well, as you can guess, we were just crying with laughter after that, rolling about on the rugs. We kept coming up with even crazier stuff to say and I thought my sides were going to actually split (ouch!). When we'd recovered enough to speak, I said, "Seriously though, there is body language stuff you can do, to show someone you're keen. I saw it on TV. Like, you hold their gaze for a bit too long."

"What, like you with Marco before you got together?" she said, and she did an impression of me staring at him with my eyes goggling out like some kind of crazy stalker.

"I did *not* look like that!" I screeched.

"You *so* did!" she cried, and we ended up chucking the rest of the popcorn at each other and then crushing it into the ground by rolling around having a play fight.

We were really hot after that so we put our pillows together in the entrance of the yurt and lay down with our heads sticking out. The sky was endless, and inky blue, and full of stars. For ages, we just looked at it, without saying anything. Then Summer spoke.

"Seriously though, I'd have to be sure he liked me before I did anything about it. I'm way too scared of getting knocked back. That would just be *too* awful! I'd die of embarrassment and never go near him again!"

I was a bit surprised, because she always seemed so confident in general. But she obviously wasn't when it came to boys. "I'll watch you, next time you're together, and see if I can tell how he feels," I offered.

Summer whipped her head round and stared at me in alarm.

"*Subtly*, obviously!" I promised her. "Not, like, with binoculars and a notepad and stuff! I mean, you try a bit of flirting and I'll watch to see how he reacts."

"Okay," said Summer. "But subtle, yeah – promise?"

"*Subtle* is my middle name," I insisted. "And if we think he does like you, I'll set you two up! And if we think he doesn't – yet – we'll make sure he soon does!"

Summer sighed. "Typical! You're so loved up you want everyone else to be too!" I thought she was still looking at the stars, but she must have seen the cloud going over my face, because she said, "Or not?"

I didn't look at her. "Nothing's really wrong, just…"

She sat up suddenly. "If Marco's messing you around, after everything he said—"

I sat up too. "No. It's not that. It's not him. It's me. I think. I don't know."

Summer looked worried. "What's wrong, Abs?" she asked.

I shrugged. "I really don't know," I told her. "Probably nothing. I suppose it just feels like he wants to see me a lot, and of course I want to see him a lot too, a LOT lot, but I honestly haven't got much time, and I don't think he *gets* that."

"Wow!" said Summer. "Well, I never thought I'd see the day when super-cool Marco smothered a girl!"

"He isn't!" I insisted. "It's not like that. I just… Oh, I don't know. We've got so much to think about with Rainbow Beauty, and Grace is struggling, and I can't stop wondering about Dad…"

Summer looked at me as I trailed off. "Do you want to talk about it?" she asked.

"To be honest, I just want to have some fun and forget about it," I told her.

"Well, you know I'm here for you – anytime, any place…"

I smiled. "I know. Thanks. But I'm fine – I guess it's just that sometimes I feel like there's so much going on in my head since we moved down here, my brain's going to explode."

"Ew, messy!" said Summer. "Not all over my yurt, please!"

I smiled again. It was nice of her to try and make me laugh. "Look, let's not talk about boys all night," I said. "It's really sad when girls do that. Let's play The Future Game instead."

Summer's eyes lit up. She invented The Future Game, and she'd shown me how to play it when we were lying on the field at school, at the end of the summer term. What you do is say what you think your life will be like in however many years' time. Summer's ones were always really elaborate, down to the names of her children and stuff (Rainbow, Phoenix and Tyler, in case you were wondering). And we nearly killed ourselves laughing once when we did "in eighty years' time" and had ourselves living in this futuristic nursing home on Bondi Beach, as two mad surfing grannies.

"Okay, so how many years this time?" she asked.

"Erm, ten," I said.

So, according to us, when I'm twenty-four, I'm going to be a beauty consultant going round to amazing houses in Hollywood and advising film stars on the best products to use on their skin. And my

Rainbow Beauty range will be massive, of course, and I'll be a millionaire and probably live in New York or somewhere cool like that.

Summer's going to come and stay with me when she has her photography exhibitions there, but she's mainly going to travel the world, meeting amazing people and telling their stories. As a famous photographer, of course. As she always says, a picture tells a thousand words.

"Oh, and I know I shouldn't say this because we weren't going to talk about boys," I added, after a while, "but I'll still be going out with Marco, and his band will be really famous. And you might be going out with Ben."

Summer sighed. "I hope so. But it will probably take me about ten years to get up the courage to tell him how I feel, and by then he'll be married to some amazing gorgeous French girl who's massively into nature and that, and he'll have forgotten all about me."

"You need a deadline," I told her. "We're going to that beach party Ben mentioned earlier, aren't we?"

"Of course," she said. "Everyone is. Well, I mean, loads of people from our year. Bex and Rachel will be there, and Olivia and Rose from netball and Iola and Amany from Art Club. Jess's dad and his mate always do a barbecue, and Jed and Jim are coming to help too. I think the boys from Marco's band have been invited. There are plans to build a big campfire on the beach. Thank goodness I'll be back from Cornwall in time. This is going to be the event of the summer."

"Right, well, it's nearly two weeks away, isn't it? So that's your deadline," I said. "By the time we go to the beach party, you'll have asked him out."

"Only if you're really *definite* that he likes me," Summer warned.

"I'm sure we can find out by then," I said.

Summer leaned back on her elbows and smiled. The light from the candle lanterns glinted in her eyes and after a moment I could see she was lost in thought – probably imagining being at the beach party with Ben. I couldn't help thinking I'd been like that about Marco once – totally head over heels and hardly daring to hope he could even like me. Now I'd got my dream boy, and we were crazy about each other, but somehow, reality seemed to keep getting in the way.

I lay back too and looked up at the whole universe of stars and tried to tell myself that things would be okay. Not just with Marco, but with Grace and Dad and Rainbow Beauty and everything.

Chapter Five

"Morning!" I called, staggering into Rainbow Beauty with the boxes of carrots and apples stacked in my arms and my sleepover bag slung over my shoulder. Jim, Summer's brother, had dropped me off. He'd offered to bring the boxes in, but I'd promised him I'd be alright. He'd been staring at the posters of Saff in our window, and I didn't want him coming in and chatting to the real thing. Her head was big enough already.

"Hi!" they all chorused. They were sitting on the purple velvet sofas, with steaming mugs of tea on the table in front of them and Mum with a notepad and pen on her lap. We'd planned to have a meeting this morning, to go over what went wrong on Saturday.

"Hi, love. Wow, that's generous of Annie," Mum said, eyeing up the free fruit and veg. "Did you have a good time with Summer?"

"Great, thanks," I said, putting the boxes down on the smoothie bar.

"How's Jim? Still gorgeous?" asked Saff, watching through the window as the Land Rover pulled away. I ignored that.

"Do you want a tea before we start?" Mum asked me, getting to her feet.

"I'm fine, thanks," I told her. "I had one at Summer's. Well, some kind of herbally thing with twigs in anyway. That's the closest thing they have to proper tea over there."

"Well done on getting all that free stuff!" said Grace.

"I've got orders for four of my new gardeners' hand creams from Annie too," I said. I pulled her money out of my pocket and put it on the table. "I know that's not going to save the business, but it's a start."

"It's brilliant, love," said Mum.

And she wasn't the only one who seemed more positive. Saff and Grace looked a lot more cheerful after getting away from it all the day before. And a really good laugh with Summer was definitely what *I'd* needed too.

"Right, well, let's begin," said Mum, glancing at her notepad. "Girls, I know it felt like the end of the world when everything went wrong on Saturday, but it wasn't."

"Well, not *quite*," Saff chipped in.

"Lots of the clients were happy," Mum said, "or at least they were understanding about the problems."

"In the main," Grace grumbled.

"That Geneva woman was horrible!" added Saff.

Mum sighed. "Can I finish?" she asked. "And it's true that they might not end up recommending us to their friends, or maybe even coming back, but there are still plenty of other people in town who'll try us out. I know a lot rested on Saturday, but thanks to our promotion we do still have more than the usual amount of bookings right through the week as well, so let's just be positive and concentrate on creating a really good impression from now on."

"I second that!" said Grace.

"I, erm, third it, if that's possible," I said. *Poor Marco,* I thought. I realized that I'd been a bit hard on him on the way to the cafe. What he'd said was true – Saturday was only one day and no business gets it right all the time. I just hadn't been in the mood to hear it. Hopefully I could make it up to him when we next met up. Maybe with a strawberry milkshake. Hmm. *Or a peppermint kiss.*

When I came out of my little daydream I found that Saff was fourth-ing Mum's words by chanting, "Go Mum! Go Mum!"

"Good, I'm glad we're all on the same page," Mum said. "Right, now we need to get practical and address the problems we had on Saturday."

"You mean like the stinky sick-smelling face masks?" I asked, with a grimace.

"Well, yes, but we couldn't have predicted that the chiller was going to break down," Mum said. "I called the engineer this morning and he's on his way to look at it now."

"That was quick," said Grace.

"Well, I employed a bit of the old Green girls' charm and he said he'd pop in before his next job," Mum explained. "Nice to know I've still got it," she added, with a cheeky smile.

"What really threw us was how it affected the timing," said Grace.

"Yes, exactly," said Mum. "So, what can we do to make sure a little problem doesn't mess up the whole day? We need to allow at least ten minutes in between appointments from now on, for a start. Fifteen if it's a full package."

"And you have to learn to say no to people," Saff told her sternly. "What really put us behind was you agreeing to do extra bits and pieces once people were here."

Mum grimaced. "I know, I know. I just wanted people to have the perfect experience. But I've learned that lesson now, definitely."

"Of course, it's fine if we've got time," said Grace quickly, "and we should try to shift things to *make* time, like, say, sending someone to Saff first instead so that Mum can spend the extra time with another client. We don't want to say no to making more money unless we absolutely have to."

"But if it's just not possible, I'll say so," Mum promised.

"To make it easier, we could ask people if they'd like any other services when they book," I suggested. "Kind of like, 'Did you know we also offer waxing and eyebrow shaping? Would you like to book anything extra?' Then hopefully more people will think about it at that point rather than once they get here."

"Great idea," said Mum. "Okay, so everyone do that from now on. Right, next on the agenda…"

She checked her notepad. "Nails. About Eshana's feedback sheet—" she began.

"She told me she loved them!" Saff huffed. "If people don't say how they really feel, how am I supposed to know? I'm not a mind-reader."

"Honey, if someone felt strongly enough to write that you weren't listening to them, then you probably weren't."

"I did *listen* to her. I listened to her saying she loved them," Saff protested. "And everyone else was happy."

Mum shook her head. "Not necessarily. You've got to think that for every person who actually *makes* a negative comment, there will be others who felt the same way but were too polite to say so."

Saff was about to protest again but Mum held up her hand. "I know, I know. That might not be true in your case. But we can't risk it. We have to take everything on board and really try to improve. *All* of us."

Saff grumbled a bit but she did agree to make sure that the clients were choosing the nail polish colours *they* liked, and not being pushed into trying the ones *she* liked.

"I've got some *feedback*," she said then. "Grace could smile a bit more when she speaks to people on reception. The way she looks, it's like they're coming to the dentist or something."

Actually I agreed with that and I could tell Mum did too, because she said, "Thank you, Saff. Grace, are you able to take that point on board?"

"Hmph," grumped Grace. Then she caught Mum's stern look and said, "Yeah, okay. But don't expect me to act fake cheerful and be all over people like Saff is. I'm not like that."

"Oi, I'm not *fake* cheerful, I'm just a happy person!" cried Saff. "You should try it!"

"No one's asking you to be someone you're not," Mum told Grace. "We're just saying a smile wouldn't go amiss."

"Fine," said Grace, pulling a sarcastic cheesy grin. "Oh, and I've got a comment. *We* should check really carefully when *we* book anyone in so *we* don't accidentally double-book," she said, eyeballing Saff.

Saff pulled a face back at her and mumbled that it wasn't a big deal, but she'd been really upset about it when we'd finally told her on Sunday. We knew she'd never make that mistake again.

Mum checked down her list. "Right, well, that's everything," she said, looking relieved that she'd survived giving negative feedback to Grace and Saff.

Just then, a van pulled up outside. "And here's the fridge man," she said.

When the fridge man, whose name turned out to be Andrew, was safely installed behind the chiller counter with only his legs sticking out and a cup of tea on the granite worktop above him, we went back to the meeting.

"Grace and I have been looking at the figures," said Mum, "and it's not good news, I'm afraid."

Grace shuffled her papers and cleared her throat. Then she reported, "With what we made on Saturday, and based on the volume of clients we've got booked in, we should just about be able to afford the bare minimum ingredients and supplies to stay in business, for a few weeks anyway. Sorry, but no more inventing, Abs."

Saff and I were shocked at that. "A few *weeks*?" Saff repeated.

"How many is a few?" I cried. "Five? *Three?*"

Grace frowned. "I'm not sure, exactly," she said. "It depends how things go. Basically, we need to treble the amount of clients we have per week to keep going, and we need to do it before we run out of money."

Put that way, it seemed pretty simple – and pretty impossible.

"We'll need another business-boosting idea, in that case," I said.

But no one had anything to suggest.

"We'll just have to all think really hard about it," said Grace.

"And work on building up our customer base slowly and steadily by giving people a really good experience," Mum added.

Meanwhile, Andrew the fridge man emerged from behind the chiller counter and gave us a figure for the repair that made Mum leap up off the sofa as if she'd had an electric shock.

"Not such a bargain after all then," I muttered, feeling gutted. I'd been so pleased with that chiller too, when I'd bought it for a few quid from the free ads.

"We just can't afford that, I'm afraid," said Mum. "Is there anything you can do for us, price-wise?"

"I want to help you out, love, seeing as you're a new business," said Andrew. "I tell you what, how about if I do it at cost? Then it would come in at about three fifty."

"Oh, that's great!" cried Saff.

"Three *hundred* and fifty," Grace mouthed at her.

"Oh," said Saff.

Mum looked crestfallen. "That's very generous of

you, but we literally don't have that money," she told him. "I suppose we'll just have to get rid of it."

"I'm sorry there's nothing more I can do for you," said Andrew.

"No, *I'm* sorry," Mum insisted. "I've wasted your time."

As we watched him drive away in his van, Mum said, "I'm sorry, girls, it looks like we're going to have to keep running up and down to the flat for things all the time."

"Don't worry, burning off all those calories just means we can eat more doughnuts," I said, trying to make her laugh. But I didn't even get a smile.

The postman walked past our window then. "I'll grab it," I said, rushing to the door. "Hopefully my blank labels have come."

They hadn't, but our old neighbours from London, Roger and Laura, had forwarded some stuff on. It was weird, imagining letters landing on the Victorian black and white tiles of the hallway of our house in Ealing. Thinking back, that hallway had been absolutely massive. I mean, we used to *scooter* down it when we were younger. We could almost have fitted the entire flat into it. It didn't seem massive at the time though. Just normal.

I wondered who was living in the house now.

Whoever it was must have been passing our post on to Roger and Laura. Was someone sleeping in my room? Had my purple walls with silver stars already been painted over? I pushed it all out of my mind. It was in the past. And like Mum said, we had to look forward, not back. It was difficult though, when our future was so uncertain. And when I didn't know where Dad was, or *how* he was.

I shuffled through the envelopes as I wandered back in. Most of it was smart clothing catalogues and offers from spas for Mum, none of which we could afford now, of course.

But then I saw that something *else* had come back from the past – to haunt Saff.

One of the letters was stamped with the logo of Arts Ed, the performing arts school where she'd signed up to start a singing course in September, before all this happened. It was back in London, and it cost a fortune, and there was no way she was going now. I tried to slip the envelope behind the things for Mum – after all, the last thing Saff needed was to be reminded of what she was missing out on. But too late, she was already leaning over my shoulder asking me what I was looking so interested in.

"It's for me," she cried, spotting her name, so I had to hand it over. Then her face dropped as she saw the logo. "Oh. It's from Arts Ed."

That put Mum and Grace on edge too.

Saff opened the envelope and we all waited. It was their newsletter – full of exciting articles about the courses and details of fun social nights out for the students, no doubt. Saff sighed and began to flick through it, looking as upset as she had after finding out about the double-booking mess-up.

"Oh hon, I'm sorry—" said Mum.

"It's just a shame that—" I began.

"No way…" mumbled Saff, peering at something on one of the pages. Then: "YEEEEEES!" she screeched, making us all jump. "There's an ad in here, look, it's an open audition for a new TV series! *We're looking for a sassy, streetwise 16-18-year-old girl for a lead role!*" she read.

Grace rolled her eyes. "Sorry to point this out, but you have absolutely no acting experience whatsoever."

Mum and I glanced at each other. Grace was right. But Saff had never been one to let a little thing like that stand in her way. And, from the look of it, she wasn't going to start now. "It's perfect for me!" she shrilled. "This could be my passport to fame and fortune as an actress, then we'll never have to worry about money again!"

"Saff, that's not very likely, is it?" Grace snapped.

"Well, what are *you* doing to help things?" Saff snapped right back. She hugged the newsletter to her chest. "This could solve all our problems. It says to call and book yourself in for the auditions. They're on Friday." And with that she swished off behind the reception desk and picked up the phone.

Grace was about to go storming after her but Mum stepped in. "Let her book it, if it makes her happy," she said.

Grace snorted. "Well, luckily we're not *all* coming up with crazy schemes and ignoring the facts, or we'll never save the business. She's in fantasy land, Mum."

They both looked at me, but I just shrugged. I could see where each of them was coming from. Just then, we realized that one of our clients was about to arrive and we all had to rush around, clearing away our tea mugs and preparing the treatment rooms, so no one said anything else about the audition.

Mum and Saff were doing massages and manicures for the rest of the morning, but they both had a break at half twelve, so Grace and I went upstairs ahead of them and got some lunch ready. We decided on tomato soup even though it was about a million degrees outside. We always used to have it when we were little and I still liked it because it reminded me of us three sitting up at the table together, cushions on our chairs so we could reach, making boats out of bread and floating islands from grated cheese. As I stirred the pan, I did try and bring up the subject of Grace's friends with her. I still wanted to find out why she wasn't going out with them, but when I mentioned them she just completely clammed up, so I had to drop it.

Saff got upstairs first, and of course she was chatting on about the audition, but when Mum came up a few minutes later she had some bad news. "I'm so sorry, love," she told her, "I didn't think about this earlier but I've realized that we won't be able to afford your train fare to London, not with the way things are. I gave the station a ring to check and as you'd be travelling at peak times, well, we're talking about over a hundred pounds, and then there's the Tube on top of that."

I thought Saff would look devastated, but, "Oh, I realized that," she said cheerfully. "Don't worry, there's a coach offer for eight quid return. I've seen it advertised on that board thing outside Somerfield. I'm going to book it now. It's about six hours or something awful, but I've been put in the 4 till

5 p.m. audition group so that's okay. I'll have to stay over with Sabina and get the morning coach back, but I don't mind."

"But you've got nail appointments—" Mum began.

"Nothing that you can't cover," Saff said quickly. "I've checked in the book, and there are only two manicures and a pedicure in at the moment over those days. There's only one where we overlapped but I've called the lady and she can come half an hour early, so it's fine, you can do it."

Mum looked taken aback by that. Saff had it all sewn up. So she was stuck really, and she had to agree.

As Saff started talking about what she might wear for the audition, I suddenly realized…this could be my chance to see Dad.

My mind was racing, trying to second-guess how they'd all react when I suggested it. Then I started thinking that I couldn't say anything after all, in case Mum got really upset about it. But then, as Mum would never let me go up to London on my own, this might be my only chance. So when Saff said, "I'll pop back downstairs in a minute and book my seat on the coach," I found myself blurting out, "Book one for me too." I steeled myself and added, "I want to go and see Dad."

Saying *Dad* was like pulling the pin out of a hand grenade. There was total silence for a second, and I felt like diving under the table with my hands over my ears.

Then suddenly the bomb exploded, and they were all talking to me at once – well, more like shouting. Saff and Grace were demanding to know why I even *wanted* to see him, and Mum was saying it was impractical and too soon. "Anyway, this is all irrelevant becau. · don't have his number," she finished, "so unless he calls again, which he hasn't bothered to do so far—"

"I've already got it," I said, in a very small voice. "I took it down when he rang."

Mum raised her eyebrows. "Did you now?" she said. Then she sighed. "I'm not against you going in principle, love," she said gently, "but I really don't think you should go on your own."

"I have a right to see my dad, you can't stop me," I snapped. *Woah, where did that come from?*

"I'm not trying to stop you," Mum insisted. "It's just, I know how much all this has affected you, and I'm sure seeing him will bring up a lot of difficult feelings. I don't want you facing that by yourself without any support. I'd come with you, but we'd have to cancel our clients and close for two days.

I just can't do that, not with the business in such a delicate state." Her eyes bored into mine, willing me to understand. I gave her a small smile to show that I did.

But she hadn't changed my mind.

"Grace——" I began.

"No way," my sister said flatly. "I'm not going with you. I never want to see *that man* again!"

I turned to Saff. "Maybe if I came to the audition with you, then we could both go to——"

"I don't want to see him either!" Saff shrieked. "Like I said, I'm staying over ... on, but instead he

Grace caught Saff's eye and ... vell——"

look. Oh well, at least having a ... like a stomach those two together.

I took a deep breath. "Look, of course I know I'm rocking the boat by wanting to see Dad now," I told them. "And of course I feel just as hurt as you all do that he doesn't seem to be making any effort with us. But the truth is, I really, really miss him. I think about him all the time. I wonder where he's living, and what he does all day, and why he hasn't been in touch again, apart from that card. My head's *full* of him. At least if I go up there I can have it out with him and then maybe all these thoughts and questions will stop whirling round my mind the whole time, making me feel like I'm on a merry-go-round that's going way too fast."

By the time I stopped talking, they were all staring at me. "I didn't realize it was affecting you so badly," said Mum quietly, looking like she was about to cry.

"Well, it is," I muttered. "Mum, let me go, please. I promise I can handle it."

I really thought she'd say no again, but then Saff stepped up. "We'll take a phone each, and if she gets to *his* and she's, like, hysterically upset or something, I'll go straight round ~~d take her to Sabina's with~~ ~~on't be stuck on her own."~~

~~mile of gratitude and Mum~~ ~~ne might possibly be thinking~~ about it. "But you won't be out of your audition till about five will you, hon?" she said to Saff.

"I could meet Em and Zo in Kensington first," I said quickly, before Mum started looking like she'd *stopped* thinking about it. "I could just go to Dad's at teatime, then if I need Saff she'll be there for me."

Mum frowned. "You'll have to check with him," she said.

"Yeah, he might not even be around," sneered Grace. "He's obviously been far too *busy* to phone us."

I ignored that and dashed downstairs to call Dad before Mum changed her mind. I grabbed the bit of paper from the back of the appointments book and dialled the number. It was only when he picked up that my heart started pounding.

"Hi, Dad, it's me. I mean, Abbie," I said.

"Oh! Hi, love," he said, sounding really surprised.

I probably should have said "How are you?" and all that stuff, but I just felt way too awkward and weird to chat normally. So instead I blurted out, "I'm coming up to see you Friday teatime, and I'm staying over till Saturday morning, so I need your address, okay?"

I thought he'd be over the m█████████████ just mumbled, "Oh, right, okay,

A pang of pain shot through m█████████████ cramp and I felt like saying "Forget it, I won't bother." But I didn't. Instead I told myself that I was doing this for me, to clear my own head, not for him. He gave me the address, speaking in a flat monotone voice. Then I felt like he was going to say he had to go, so I quickly got in there first and said *I* had to. Even after I'd hung up, my heart was still banging like I'd run up a mountain or something. It was awful – he just hadn't seemed like *Dad* somehow.

Then I had to try and put my hurt aside and pull myself together to call Em. When I told her I was coming up, the reception I got couldn't have been more different. She went mad, screaming and saying she'd ring Zo immediately, and wanting to start a big chat right there and then. But I had to just arrange to meet them on Kensington High Street and then make an excuse to ring off. I couldn't keep up the happy act any longer.

Mum, Saff and Grace came down then and I told them everything was arranged. Mum took the piece of paper from my hand, looked at Dad's address and made a face like she was sucking a lemon. "You're not walking round *that* area on your own," she muttered. "You can take my mobile, and call your father to meet you at the bus stop."

"What did Dad say?" asked Saff.

"Yeah, he said it was fine," I told her, trying to sound breezy.

Grace snorted. "What, just *fine*? Huh!"

"Well, I don't remember his *exact* words!" I snapped. Ahem, *lie*. The fact was, I was worried that if Mum thought he wasn't keen, she wouldn't let me go. And I had to. For my own sanity, I just *had* to see him.

So Saff booked us seats on the coach there and then. Mum still didn't look very happy about it, but when Saff put the phone down, she said, "Well, it's done now. And no more bickering, alright?"

She eyeballed Grace. "We have to all stick together and focus on saving the business."

"Okay," Grace conceded. Then she sighed heavily and said, "Saff, I'm sure you'll get the part and become a famous actress magically overnight with no training or anything, and Abbie, I'm sure Dad will have some totally reasonable excuse for not keeping in touch and you'll both have a wonderful evening of joy."

Of course, she didn't mean a word of it, but at least she was trying to make us laugh. Saff, being Saff, simply decided to believe that she *did* mean it, though. "Aw, thanks, Grace. I knew you believed in me really!" she cried. "Come on, group hug."

So we all huddled in and squeezed each other tight because, whatever our differences, we knew Mum was right. Rainbow Beauty had survived Saturday, but only just. Now we needed to put all our energy into making it a success.

Chapter Six

Monday went much better, and we really thought we'd survived the storm. We had no idea then that there was a much bigger one on the horizon.

"I just don't understand this," said Mum on Tuesday morning. "We've had three cancellations in the last hour." We were down in Rainbow Beauty, getting ready for our first client, and she was behind the reception desk, listening to the answerphone messages.

It was a bit strange, but we just wrote it off as a coincidence. But then, when two of Mum and Saff's clients for the morning didn't turn up, we knew something was really wrong. We only found out what it was when Siân, a new customer, came in for her Strawberry and Rose Pamper Package at half one. She emerged from the treatment room absolutely glowing and as she was paying at the desk, she said, "I wasn't going to say anything, but I've had such a wonderful time, I just *have* to tell you…"

"Tell us what?" Mum asked. We all had that ominous feeling, like when the sky darkens above you and the thunder rumbles.

"That I think that awful write-up you got in the local paper was completely unfair," Sian said, signing her cheque with a flourish.

What?!

We were all very careful to keep looking normal (even Saff, once Mum had nudged her) but we were completely shocked. "My Terry spotted it this morning," Sian told us. "He was telling me to cancel my appointment but I said no, you have to go and judge for yourself. And I'm so glad I did."

Mum had to nod and smile and say "Absolutely" and "Thank you so much" as if she wasn't upset at all. But as soon as Sian had gone, Saff dashed upstairs and grabbed the local paper, *The Totnes Echo*, which we'd put straight into the recycling pile when it had arrived that morning. We all gathered round as she put it on the coffee table and riffled through. Then we found the article and I thought I was going to throw up all over it.

Beauty Goes Green, read the headline.

And then there was the byline: *by Geneva Grant.*

"Oh my gosh, it's that awful woman who was here on Saturday," Saff gasped.

"Oh, no, no, no," Mum groaned, cradling her head in her hands. "She was a journalist! And she saw all the problems... This can't be happening."

"*With its inviting façade and welcoming shabby-chic interior, I had high hopes for my visit to new beauty parlour Rainbow Beauty,*" Saff read. "*But I'm afraid to say that my experience went rapidly downhill as soon as the surly receptionist took my jacket—*"

"I am not *surly*!" Grace cried.

"*...and informed me that my therapist was running twenty minutes late.*"

Mum groaned again.

"*I selected a complimentary fresh juice and a poor flustered-looking girl had to dash off somewhere and come back through the front door, clutching the ingredients (I later found out that their refrigeration unit had broken). NOT very professional. I ended up waiting no less than thirty-five minutes in reception, and as I dehydrated, the juice became a distant memory—*"

Mum winced. "Yes, I suppose we should have

offered her something else. It *was* very hot in there," she said.

"Don't defend her," snapped Saff, "she could have asked for another drink if she was thirsty. This is all completely out of order!"

"I am not *surly*," Grace said again.

Saff sighed and continued. "*...and I watched a total shambles unfold before my eyes. One lady left in distress after finding out that her appointment had been double-booked, meaning that there was no space for her, and another was overcharged by the poor girl who was running in and out with fruit all the time (perhaps she was suffering from heat exhaustion)...*"

Mum gave me a really anxious look then.

"I was *fine*!" I cried. "I'm just rubbish at maths!"

"*By the time I was taken into the treatment room,*" Saff read, "*I had to ask the therapist to curtail my massage as otherwise I'd have been late for a meeting. So, while I'm sure in the right circumstances my experience would have been heavenly, with beautiful handmade products and an indulgent ambiance, these were* not *the right circumstances, and I left more stressed out than I arrived.*"

"Okay, okay, please, just stop!" cried Mum.

"That's pretty much it," said Saff. "Apart from, you know, avoid the place at all costs, that kind of thing. Silly cow," she added, with venom.

Grace looked silently furious and Mum looked devastated. I don't know what I looked like, but I felt sick and shocked and battered. It was like the roof had just caved in on us and we were standing in a pile of rubble, everything destroyed. "We might as well have never done all this," I said quietly. "No one will come now. This is going to close us down."

I could tell how much that shocked Mum and my sisters. I was usually the positive one, after all. But I just didn't have it in me any more.

"She *did* say your products were beautiful," Saff pointed out. "And that the treatment would have been heavenly if—"

"Face it, it's over," I said flatly.

"I'm afraid you might be right, love," said Mum.

We all felt like going upstairs and curling up in our revolting spiny beds and having a massive cry and then going to sleep for a very long time. But we had our final client of the day arriving in ten minutes so, despite our world crumbling around us, we had to carry on.

What else could we do?

So Grace and I reset the treatment rooms, and when Trish, one of our lovely regulars, arrived, Mum found a smile from somewhere and offered her a juice.

"Thanks, Kim," she said. "But I'll just have water, please. I don't want Abbie running up and down the stairs on my account."

"Oh, but it's no trouble—" Mum began.

"That silly woman has no idea what she's on about," Trish said, waving her hand at the local paper, which was still open on the coffee table. "Such petty complaints. Every new business has teething problems! And if she'd wanted another drink she should have asked for one—"

"That's what *I* said!" cried Saff.

"Don't you worry, love," Trish told Mum. "I've told all my friends that that article was a load of rubbish!"

"Thanks," said Mum, in a small, choked voice. She looked like she was about to cry, so I did the goggly eyes at Saff and for once she got the hint and ushered Trish into one of the treatment rooms for her pedicure. Then, just after Grace went upstairs to study, Liam walked in. Mum took one look at him and burst into tears.

"Well, if *this* is the effect I have on women, it's lucky I *am* gay!" he cried, sweeping her up into a hug. "Kim, what's the matter, sweetheart?"

I brought the article over from the table and handed it to him. As he read it, Mum sobbed and sobbed, and murmured, "I can't believe she just wrote this without warning us, or giving us a chance to put things right."

Liam was furious. "Too right! Trashing a new business, something that benefits the town – that you've been brave enough to set up in a recession too – how can *that* help anyone?"

"We'll have to close down," Mum sniffled. "We were only just going to survive the next few weeks as it was. And now that half our clients have cancelled, well, we just won't be able to meet the running costs for long enough to dig ourselves out of this hole. Reputation is everything in the beauty business and she's completely ruined ours!"

There was a sickening silence, as what she'd said sunk in.

Then, "I've got a few savings," Liam said. "It's not much, about a grand, but you could get the chiller counter fixed and—"

"Oh, Liam, I wasn't asking for anything," Mum said hurriedly.

"I know you weren't," he insisted. "But please, let me lend you some cash to tide you over. You just need to stay afloat for a few weeks while you build up your customer base again and work out a rescue plan."

"I really don't know——" Mum began.

"I could charge you interest, like a proper bank," he suggested.

Mum took a deep breath. "Okay, yes please," she said. Then she dissolved into tears again and hugged him for a very long time.

When she finally let go, I hugged him too. "Thank you so much," I said. And I didn't just mean for the money. I meant for the faith, as well. Liam believed we could pull ourselves out of this mess, enough to put his own money into Rainbow Beauty, and that gave *me* a glimmer of hope too.

"Right, first things first," he said. "Let's get that chiller counter fixed. We can't have poor Abbie getting heatstroke now, can we?" He pulled an over-the-top horrified face, then grinned at me.

Mum did smile then, a bit.

"Honestly, I'm just rubbish at maths!" I cried again, and I found myself smiling a bit too.

I woke up feeling slightly better on Wednesday. Thanks to Liam's loan, Mum had been able to have Andrew the fridge man back in on Tuesday afternoon to do the repair, so we were fully up and running again. The first thing I did after getting showered and ready was go down to Rainbow Beauty, get the chalkboard from behind the smoothie bar, and write *We sell delicious juices and smoothies to go!* on it in huge letters. Then I put it outside on the pavement, where passers-by and drivers would see it on their way to work. When I went back inside, I cut down a box to make a holder, filled it with leaflets and put that out there too. Mum, Saff and Grace all came down a little while later and saw my handiwork.

"Abs, we're not going to get out of this mess by selling a few smoothies," said Grace.

"It's a start though," said Saff, smiling at me.

Mum just gave me this weird, all-choked-up look, then grabbed me and hugged me tight.

We only had a couple of clients in the morning, both for the Strawberry and Rose Pamper Package, so at about twelve-ish I went back up to the flat to get changed. I was meeting Marco at half past, and I couldn't wait. We hadn't seen each other since Sunday, and it felt like ages. We had the whole afternoon to hang out, and he was going to check whether Summer and Ben were around too.

We met by the church on the way into town, and as I reached him, he lifted me up and swung me round.

I giggled as he put me down. "Well, hello to you too. What was that for?"

"Because you're gorgeous," he said.

I looked deep into his startling blue eyes and I just wanted to hug him for ever and never let go (which would be a bit awkward for, like, playing netball and waxing my legs and stuff, but hey, I'd just have to be hairy and unfit!).

I knew I'd been letting everything get in the way of us two, but I was determined that from now on we'd make time for each other. Starting with hanging out on Vire Island in the sunshine for the entire afternoon with our mates.

"So, did you text Ben?" I asked.

"Yeah, he's already there with Summer," he told me. "She wanted to meet him early, to go through this conservation display thing they're doing."

I had to hide my knowing smile. *Go, Summer!* Maybe she wouldn't even *need* until the beach party to get together with Ben. I imagined us all there under the stars. Me snuggled up by the campfire with Marco, her with Ben. I was so looking forward to it already. It could turn out to be the perfect night – for all of us.

"What are you thinking about?" asked Marco.

I pulled him close. "The beach party. You and me by the campfire…"

"I can't wait," he said. "But we've got something even better than that in store," he added, smiling mysteriously.

"Oh, yes?"

He took my hand and we started walking towards the bridge. "I was going to wait until we were all together," he said, "but I just *have* to tell you now. I've got some absolutely brilliant, amazing news." The way he was grinning at me, I honestly thought he was going to say he'd won the lottery. But it was even better than that. "Me and the band are supporting The Breaks," he announced.

"Oh my gosh, even *I've* heard of them!" I shrieked. "Saff plays their album all the time! That's amazing! This is massive!"

Marco looked so gorgeous, beaming like a little boy in a sweet shop. "It's not a big stadium or anything, but they're from Exeter, so they're kicking off their tour there with a warm-up gig for their local fans, and we're on first."

"Fantastic!" I cried. "There'll be journalists there, and bloggers. You could really get noticed!"

"I know," said Marco. "It's the chance we've been hoping for. You know how Mum's been talking to everyone about us? Well, the support act had to drop out at the last minute and a friend of hers who knows the promoters suggested us as a replacement. They weren't sure at first cos we're so young, but when they heard our demo they were impressed, so—"

"When is it?" I asked. "I'll have to start planning what to wear, like, *immediately*." I grinned at him. "What *do* you wear to be the girlfriend of a Rock God?"

"Rock God? I like it!" he said. "It's on Friday."

My stomach lurched and I felt like I was falling down a huge hole, with nothing to grab onto. "This Friday?" I croaked. "As in two days' time?"

"Yeah," he said. He peered at me. "Are you okay? What's up?"

My head was spinning. I didn't know what to say. I thought for a moment that I wouldn't say anything, and just cancel London and go to Marco's gig instead. But I was *desperate* to see Dad. I knew Mum wouldn't let me go on the coach by myself another time so going with Saff really was my only chance. But then the gig mattered so, so much to Marco, and I really wanted to be there for him. All this was going round in my head and I hadn't even decided what to say when I found myself blurting out, "I can't come."

"What?" Marco cried. "Don't tell me you have to work? This is *only* the single most important thing that's ever happened to me. It could be the start of something. I *need* you there."

"I'm not working, I'm going to see my dad," I explained. "It's all arranged."

That just seemed to make things worse. "Why are you bothering with that waster?" he snapped. "He hasn't bothered with you!"

Anger rushed up inside me then and I wrenched my hand away from his. "That's not true! How dare you say that!"

Marco glared at me and folded his arms. "Well, did he ever ring you back?"

"No, but—"

"Or come down to see you?"

I sighed. "He can't, he hasn't got a car and the train's too expensive and it's tricky, because he can't stay over—"

Marco snorted. "Wake up, Abs! It's just a load of excuses! He could get the coach, that's cheap. He could come down early and go back the same day."

I knew he was right, Dad could do that. I'd thought exactly the same thing. But I couldn't admit that to Marco. Somehow it was okay for me to think those things about Dad, but not for anyone else to say them. "Can't you understand how much this matters to me?" I said in a small voice.

"Can't you understand how much this gig matters to *me*?" he countered. Then he gave me a piercing glare and muttered, "I'm always last on your list."

I sighed. "I'm so, so sorry about the gig. And I know it's true that I don't have much free time, but you know how important making the business a success is. There's no Plan B here, it *has* to work or we'll be out on the street. Why can't you understand that?"

He glared at me. "If I'm too much hassle for you, then why are you bothering?"

"Oh, come on, I didn't mean it like that," I insisted. I tried to take his hand but he pulled away.

"Don't do me any favours," he muttered. "I have got my own life, you know." He sighed and ruffled his hair with his hands. "Look, Abs, Declan's going down to the studio now to rehearse. I said I really couldn't but…I think I will after all. Tell the others, yeah?"

"Hey, hang on, I—" I began – but he was already storming off.

I just stood there on the bridge, feeling stunned, wondering how things could have gone so badly, so quickly. On shaky legs, I walked onto the island and went to find Summer and Ben. I spotted them under a willow tree, talking and laughing together, with a notebook and some sketches spread out on the ground around them.

The second she saw me, Summer knew something was up. She sat me down and ordered me to tell her what had happened.

"I had a fight with Marco," I said.

"What's he done?" she said, then tutted loudly. "Argh! Boys are useless!"

At that point, Ben sprang up like he'd just discovered he was sitting on an ants' nest. He muttered something about joining in the kick-about with some lads just across from us and jogged off.

I told Summer what had happened. When I'd finished, she said, "Shocking as this may sound, Abs, I can see his point."

"Me too," I admitted. "I feel really bad now, but I just got so angry when he talked about Dad like that."

"It's only because he cares about you."

I sighed. "I realize that now. But I wish he'd understand that I *need* to go and see Dad. I need to talk to him. I want an explanation of why he hasn't been in touch. I've got so many questions. It's for my own sake, not his. And this is my only chance."

Summer nodded. "I get it. But you have to make *Marco* get it too. He probably took it as a competition between him and your dad for your time and attention. And he lost. Let him know it's not like that."

I shrugged. "I suppose I could try talking to him again. He said he was going to the studio."

"Oh, right, yeah, of course," said Summer. "He virtually lives at that place."

I threw my hands up in the air. "And I don't even know where it is!" I cried. "I really have been way too wrapped up in my own stuff, haven't I?"

"Go up there and see him," said Summer. "It's round the back of the youth centre on Victoria Street."

I hesitated. "But what about you?"

"Just go!" she said. She gestured towards Ben, who was now running about with the other guys, with no shirt on. "Don't worry about me. I'll be fine here, admiring the view."

So I went straight to the studio, but the guy at the youth centre said I'd just missed Marco. He and Declan had gone off somewhere and he wasn't sure whether they'd be back. I tried the little cafe he'd taken me to, and the one at the arts centre, but he wasn't at either, so I mooched around Fore Street and the High Street for a bit, hoping to bump into him. Then after a while I checked the studio again, but they hadn't gone back there. I thought about heading to Vire Island, but I didn't feel like hanging out any more, so I went back to Rainbow Beauty (I still didn't have my own phone) and left Marco a message (okay, maybe a *few* messages!). I said how sorry I was that we'd argued, and asked if we could meet up. But he didn't ring back.

When I checked the phone on Thursday morning, Marco still hadn't left me a message, so I went round to his flat.

I rang the bell and he opened the door in a faded T-shirt and trackie bottoms, looking all sleepy even though it was past ten.

"Hi," I said.

"Hi." He peered at me from under his mop of tousled curls. His mouth said "Come in" but the look in his eyes definitely said "Go away".

"I came looking for you yesterday and I tried ringing, didn't you get my messages?" I asked, as I followed him up the hallway.

"I ran out of charge without realizing," he said.

"Well, they just said I'm sorry about yesterday," I told him. "I shouldn't have reacted so badly when you talked about my dad like that. And I really do know how much the gig means to you."

He managed a bit of a smile then. "That's okay, don't worry about it." He looked so gorgeous I just had to hug him.

"So, are we cool?" I asked.

"We're cool," he said, squeezing me tight.

"Oops, shall I come back later?" came a voice from the doorway. I turned and saw Sienna in a fuchsia dressing gown, smiling at me. I mumbled hello, blushed about a zillion degrees and put her son down.

She padded over to the fridge in her bare feet and poured herself some orange juice. "Are you staying, love?" she asked me. "Would you like a drink?"

"Thanks, but I'd better get back to Rainbow Beauty," I said. "I just came round to tell Marco something."

"Oh, okay," she said. "I'll come up to your place next week. I need a pedicure. I mean, look at the state of these."

She wiggled her scarlet-painted toenails at me. They looked immaculate, but I said, "Great, see you soon then."

"Isn't it amazing about the gig?" she said. She leaned over to Marco and squidged his cheeks. "I'm so proud of my little boy!" she cried, making me giggle.

Marco groaned. "Mum, can you NOT?"

"I'll be there, right down at the front, giving it large," Sienna said then, doing that rapper-ish arm move thing. Marco couldn't hide his horror and she laughed and said, "The look on your face! I'm only joking! I'll be hiding in the shadows at the back with the other parents. I wouldn't want to cramp your style."

I found it hard to imagine Sienna cramping anyone's style. I mean, it was like Marco had Angelina Jolie for a mum or something. "Come over and say hello though, won't you, Abbie?" she said then. "I bet you can't wait!"

"Oh, I'm—" I began, but Marco cut me off.

"It's going to be amazing, now you're coming," he said. "I'm so glad we sorted it out."

I just stared at him, like, *Hang on, what?*

"Well, I'm going back to bed," Sienna announced. "I was on a late shift last night. See you Friday, hon." And with that she picked up her juice glass and swanned out again.

"Marco, I didn't say I was coming," I said, when she'd gone.

He stared at me in confusion. "But you said—"

"No, I just meant I want you to understand why I need to see my dad so much. It's not for his sake, it's for mine, I—"

"I don't believe this!" Marco cried, throwing his hands in the air.

I folded my arms. "I just wanted to make you understand."

"Well, I don't," Marco said flatly. "This gig is our big chance to get noticed. You could go and see *him* whenever."

I sighed. We were just going round in circles again, like we had on the bridge. "But I explained that. It has to be now, there's no other time."

"It seems like there's *never* any time," he grumbled.

I felt like screaming. He just didn't *get* it. I wasn't going through the whole Rainbow Beauty thing again. "Well, maybe I don't have time for a boyfriend," I snapped.

I felt as shocked as he looked. Had I really said that?

Then I realized it was probably true.

"Maybe you just don't want to *make* time," he said.

"Maybe I *can't*."

"What are you saying?" he demanded.

I shrugged. "I don't know."

"Maybe we should leave it for a while," he said.

I don't know if he meant that, or whether he was just pushing me to see if I'd back down. But I wasn't going to. "Maybe," I echoed.

His jaw set then, and he wasn't looking at me any more, but at the wall above my head. "Well then," he said stiffly.

"Well…"

"I guess this is it."

"I guess so," I said. Panic fluttered up to my throat. He'd back down in a minute, surely? But—

"See you around then," he said.

"Yeah, see you around," I mumbled, then strode back down the hall.

The next minute I found myself standing on the pavement, wondering what on earth had just happened. I'd gone round there to put things right and instead we'd split up. How was that even *possible*?

I was in a daze and I just started walking, with tears running down my cheeks. Half an hour later, I ended up at Summer's. Annie was in the veg garden and she pointed me up to the yurt. I found Summer inside, stretched out on the rugs with her eyes closed, daydreaming. Books, sketch pads and pencils were strewn all around her. It looked so idyllic I just wanted to, like, *move* there and never have to face any of my problems again.

"Earth to Summer," I called.

She opened her eyes and smiled at me. "Oh, hiya.

I thought you might ring me last night. How did the making-up go?"

I sighed and collapsed onto the rugs next to her. "It didn't. It kind of turned into…breaking up."

Summer shot upright, looking shocked. "What happened?"

"I'm not really sure," I said. I told her about the misunderstanding over the gig. "Then it sort of spiralled after I said I didn't have time for a boyfriend," I finished.

She gasped and clapped her hand over her mouth. "You said that? Oooh, serious ego damage!"

"I know. It was awful. But the thing is, as soon as I'd said it, I realized it was probably true."

"Oh, hon, I'm so sorry," said Summer. "I wish I wasn't going away tomorrow. You need your mates at the moment."

"Thanks, but I'll be okay," I promised her. "Anyway, I'm going to London. It'll do me good to get away and clear my head, and have a chance to sort things out with Dad." I sat up and stretched. "Right, enough about me and my depressing non-love-life. Let's talk about you. How was yesterday?"

Summer couldn't help smiling, even though she was trying not to, out of respect for my tragic situation. "It was great, hanging out with Ben. And now I do think if he did know that, you know, I liked him, he wouldn't actually be *sick* or anything. In fact, I think, maybe, he likes me back…"

(Pause for lots of girly squealing.)

"Are you going to Say Something before you go away?" I asked her, when we'd calmed down enough to carry on the conversation.

"No, but I've got a plan to tell him how I feel at the beach party," she said. "At least then it'll be dark, so if he's not interested, I won't have to see the look of horror on his face. And hey, keep watch for me – make sure no other girl whisks him off into the sunset while I'm away, won't you?"

"LOL!" I said. "Don't worry, I'm sure he's into *you*."

Summer grinned. "I hope…I think…you're right."

After loads of hugging and a discussion about which one of us was going to miss the other more, and Summer making me swear I'd ring her if I wanted to talk about Marco, or anything else, I headed home.

I had to tell Mum, Grace and Saff what had happened with Marco, of course. Saff hugged me and Mum wanted us to all sit round and have a big chat about it. But I promised her that I was okay (ish, anyway) and that I thought it was probably for the best (ish, anyway). I also said that after speaking to Summer I didn't want to go through it all again (definitely true).

But when they went back down to Rainbow Beauty to welcome the only afternoon client we had booked in, I didn't go with them. Instead I made a cup of tea and went into my little chill-out room. It used to be the Hoover cupboard but Mum, Saff, Grace and Liam had done it up for me with stuff left over from creating the beauty parlour. I turned on the fairy lights – not much daylight came in through the small, high window anyway, and the sky had turned a menacing grey as I'd been walking home.

The little pools of golden light glowed against the burned-orange paint and made the tiny room feel really cosy. I sat on one of the floor cushions and listened to the crackle of lightning and the rumble of thunder outside. And then, with a frenzied drumming on the open windowpane, the storm broke.

The smell of fresh rain filled the air around me and I couldn't help pulling my sleeves down over my hands and cuddling them up to my face. I still had Marco's signature scent on my clothes from hugging him. That and the rain smell mixed together took me right back to when I'd first met him, when he'd pulled me out of the storm and I'd got all swirled up in his cedar wood and cinnamon smell. It had been so exciting – the electricity jumping between us, the pounding rain – and later, the slow dance in the empty beauty parlour, and kissing him.

How could it have come to this?

We started in a storm – and now I guess we'd ended in one too.

I wondered whether we'd still be friends, and how it would affect our group, and what Ben would say, but then I pushed all that out of my mind. I couldn't think about any of it right now. Not yet.

First I had to deal with Dad.

Chapter Seven

On Friday afternoon I stood outside H&M on Kensington High Street and scanned the pavement for Em and Zo. The coach from Totnes had taken six bum-aching hours (about five-and-a-half of which I'd spent staring out of the window, going over and over what had happened with Marco) and I felt like I never wanted to sit down again. Mum had given me her phone (I'd called her to say we'd arrived safely, of course), and Saff had borrowed Emily's old one so we could all keep in touch with each other. She'd gone off to her audition all excited, looking every inch the A-list star.

Despite everything on my mind, excitement kept

bubbling up in me about seeing my friends and I had to stop myself from jumping up and down on the spot like a loony. We hadn't spoken properly since I'd left London, and we just had *so* much to catch up on. I was keen to talk to them about what had happened with me and Marco too, and get their take on it. We always used to chat about boys and try to work out what was going on in their heads (if anything, LOL!).

In any case, I wasn't completely sure what *had* happened with me and Marco, and I was hoping they could help me work it out. I spotted them coming towards me, arms linked, high-heeled boots marching in unison. Em had had her chestnut hair cut into a bob and highlighted at the front. Her denim cut-offs looked fab – unlike me, she had amazing legs. Zo's glossy black hair was poker straight as usual, but now with purple flashes. I bet *that* hadn't gone down well with Miss Banks at school.

My excitement went off the scale as I dashed towards them and I nearly knocked them down with a huge hug. We jumped around in a squealy huddle in the middle of the pavement for ages, and I only pulled them to the side when I realized that a lady in a wheelchair couldn't get past us.

When we'd calmed down a bit (a little bit,

anyway) Zo cried, "Oh my gosh, Abs, we went into school that day as usual and you weren't there and Danuta Blackstone said she'd seen a big van at your house, and some blokes moving your stuff."

"And everyone was asking us where you'd gone and we didn't know what to say," said Em. "How could you not tell us what was going on?"

"Yeah, we were so worried about you," added Zo.

"Well, it was all a bit of a shock," I said lamely.

"You could have called us," said Em.

"Yeah, we rang your mobile, like, a million times, but you had no signal." They both looked a bit put out then. Well, I suppose I hadn't told them anything at all. I *still* hadn't, in fact.

I did think about making excuses, but in the end I realized there was no point. The only way they'd understand why I'd been so out of touch was if I told them the truth.

I sighed. "It wasn't my signal, my phone was cut off."

They both looked absolutely horrified. "But that's *awful!*" shrieked Em.

"How did you, like, *survive?*" cried Zo.

"It was no big deal," I said.

They just looked at me blankly, unable to imagine how having no phone could ever be *no big deal*.

"It was my phone, not my *leg*!" I added, with a grin.

Still they just stared at me. I'd wanted to make them laugh, but it hadn't worked.

"But you could have Facebooked us," said Em, "or got us on MSN or email. We could have had one of our three-way Skype chats."

"Broadband costs too," I said.

Now they were looking at me as if I was from an alien planet. Maybe they thought broadband was just in the air, like pollen.

"But it must have been terrible," gasped Zo.

"How can you not *care*?" cried Em. "I'd, like, *die* if that happened to me."

I shrugged. "I suppose I was more worried about us having no home and no money."

Well, I didn't think they could look any more shocked, but Zo's eyebrows shot right up and Em clapped her hand to her mouth.

"But surely, your dad..." Zo began.

I thought about glossing over the Dad stuff or even making something up. It was the bit I found hardest to talk about. But I'd started with the truth thing now, and I had to see it through. *The truth, the whole truth and nothing but the truth* and all that. "He went bankrupt, and now he's living in a tiny bedsit," I told them. "He's got nothing."

They actually *screamed* then.

"Oh my god, Abs. You should have come to live with us!" screeched Zo.

"Or us!" cried Em. "You could have still come to school and everything. You wouldn't have missed Finley's party either."

"Thanks, but…we all had to stick together," I said. "We're getting back on track now, anyway—" I was about to tell them about Rainbow Beauty and break the news that I wasn't coming back, but suddenly Em linked arms with us both and dragged us into H&M, declaring, "Babes, you need some serious retail therapy after all that trauma!"

A few minutes later we were in a whirlwind of clothes, holding things up against ourselves, picking out stuff for each other, swapping and matching things to make outfits. It was like I'd never been away.

"You don't think this colour's too strong for me, do you?" I asked them, holding up the gorgeous blue sparkly top Zo had just handed me.

"No, it makes you look really striking," said Em. "I'd kill for your hair and pale skin."

I grimaced. "You wouldn't! Unless I wear—"

"Loads of mascara and eyeliner—" Zo cut in.

"It looks like I don't have a head," finished Em.

I giggled and swatted them with the top.

"How many times have we heard that?" cried Em. "You haven't changed *that* much then!"

"I haven't changed at all!" I protested. And right then, at least, I thought that was true.

"Right," said Zo. "Shall we try these on?"

As we headed for the changing rooms, I said, "You do realize I'm not actually *buying* any of this stuff, don't you?"

"Oh, nor am I," said Zo. "I got a load of stuff last weekend on the King's Road."

"Me neither," Em insisted. "Mum took me to Selfridges on Tuesday and I got some Replay jeans and a Juicy Couture top for Edina's party next week, and I haven't even worn my new Golddigga hoodie yet."

At the changing rooms, the assistant gave us a big smile and said hello really cheerfully. When she counted our things, Zo turned out to have too many, so she asked her to leave one outside.

"But I want to mix and match them as outfits," Zo said stroppily. "Can't you just let me take it in? I'm here *all* the time."

I was shocked by how snotty she was being. I tried to catch Em's eye, but she was glaring at the assistant too.

"I'm sorry, but our policy is a maximum of twelve items, no exceptions," said the girl. I tried to catch her eye and smile, but she didn't look in my direction.

"Oh, come on, that's crazy—" Zo began.

"Give it here, I've only got ten, I'll bring something in for you," I said quickly, and grabbed a top from her.

"Thanks, Abs," she muttered.

We all got our number things and I said thank you to the girl very cheerfully, to make up for the fact that Em and Zo had stalked off grumbling.

As we walked down the row of changing rooms, Zo said, "Silly cow."

"OMG, shut up!" I went, bundling them into the communal bit at the end.

"Oh, come on, Abs," said Zo, "who cares what she thinks?"

I stared at her. I had never realized how spoiled Em and Zo could be. Did I used to be like that? Had I ever sounded like they just had?

"So, has your mum had to get, like, a summer job down there or something?" asked Em.

"Course not," said Zo. "My dad says single parents get loads of benefits. And they give you a free flat, don't they?"

"Do they?" said Em. "Cool."

"No they *don't*!" I cried. "Mum *has* got a job – we all have, actually. We've set up our own business, Rainbow Beauty."

I told them all about it, and, "Wow, Abs, that's amazing!" cried Zo.

"We should come down and visit," said Em. "We could hang out and get loads of free treatments and stuff!"

"Yeah," I said. "Well, probably not free. And only if I wasn't working."

"What, do you have to work a lot then?" asked Zo.

"Yep, all the time in the holidays and on weekends, and after school during term time," I told them. "And it's not all fun stuff. I have to clean the loos and prepare all the fruit and veg for the juices, and when Mum's finished a treatment I have to chuck out the leg wax strips, and *worse*."

"Ew!" they squealed.

I smiled. I don't know why, but I kind of *wanted* to gross them out.

Em pulled on a yellow top and frowned at herself in the mirror. "Yuck. Vile," she declared. "But, Abs, when do you have time to go shopping?"

I didn't say that I wouldn't have the money to go anyway, even if I had the time. I didn't say that

Rainbow Beauty was hanging by a thread or that in a few weeks it might just be a memory. I didn't say that soon we could be out on the street, or in a hideous B&B, or squished into Liam's flat, or Summer's yurt.

I know, I know – I'd decided to tell them everything. But that was before they'd been so snotty. I felt distant from them now, and I didn't want to advertise our problems. I didn't think they'd understand. So instead I said, "The nearest big shops are in Torquay and the buses don't run all that often so I haven't really been shopping yet."

Zo zipped up a green dress and craned her neck round to inspect her bum in the mirror.

"That's nice," I said.

"Urgh, no!" she groaned. "If Damon sees me in this he'll be instantly sick!"

Em gave me a worried look. "Abs, do they even *have* H&M down there?" she asked.

I giggled. "It's Devon, not Outer Mongolia. Course they do! You'd have to go to Exeter, but it's only an hour on the bus."

"Oh, thank goodness for that," cried Em, seeing the joke and hamming it up now. "I couldn't bear to think of you stuck out in the sticks without the latest fashion!"

"So I guess your life's down there now," said Zo, suddenly serious. "You're not coming back, are you?"

"Don't be stupid, course she is," said Em.

I took a deep breath. "No," I told them. "I'm not coming back."

Em looked really shocked, and Zo just looked gutted.

I made myself smile. "You can come and visit though," I told them. "There's a great beach near us, and the town is lovely…"

I'd thought it would be mascara-wreckingly heartbreaking to tell them I wouldn't be back. We'd been so close, for so long. But in the end, it was pretty easy. I talked about how much fun we'd have, and how I'd try to get up again on the coach to see them soon, and after a while we were trying stuff on and chatting again, almost like nothing had happened.

I pulled on a star-patterned top then and they went crazy over it, saying it looked great and amazing and that I should definitely buy it.

"I'm not buying anything, remember?" I said.

"What, actually *nothing* nothing?" said Em.

I'd forgotten that when we used to say *nothing*, we usually came out with two or three things each. And that's what they did this time (Zo said she may as well get the green dress, because it might look okay with a cardi over it).

The starry top looked so amazing, and they went on about it so much, I did buy it in the end. But as I handed over the fifteen quid at the till, my stomach lurched and I felt like I was going to be sick. We needed every penny we could get at home, and here I was buying a top I could do without. The queasy feeling wouldn't go away and as we wandered out onto the street I decided to take it back as soon as Em and Zo had gone home. I felt much better then.

On our way to our favourite cafe, Em said, "Hey, Abs, let's pop in here. It's new. You'll love it."

The shop was a small, posh skincare place called Lily Loves. Em was right, I did love it. They stocked lots of gorgeous little brands, some that I'd heard of and others that were new to me. I tried loads of the testers, and they were divine, but I had to keep my eyebrows from shooting up on top of my head when I saw the prices. I could make most of the stuff for a fraction of the cost, and with completely natural ingredients too. I picked up every leaflet and brochure I could, in case any of it gave me ideas for Rainbow Beauty. I hadn't forgotten that we were all on the lookout for a new plan to save the business.

Meanwhile, Em and Zo were loading up with delicious lotions and potions, and buying two of things just because they were on offer. Zo even picked up a complete six-product mandarin pedicure kit, just because it came in a free gift bag.

"Wow, you two are really going for it, aren't you?" I said.

"Well, we have to *buy* everything now that you're not around to make stuff for us," said Em.

"Yeah, your products are easily as good as this," said Zo. Once again I felt like shushing her, because the assistant was quite close by, but at the same time, I was really chuffed.

"I've nearly run out of those Rose & Geranium Bath Bombs you gave me for my birthday," said Em. "I don't know what I'm going to do when they've gone completely. Hint hint." She beamed at me, batting her eyelashes.

"Okay, okay, when I have time I'll package some up for you and send them in the post."

"Oh, would you?" she cried. "That's fab! Thanks, Abs!"

Zo made me promise to send her some of her favourite Lemon Zest Foot Scrub too, and then they paid for their mountains of stuff and we headed for the cafe.

As we walked down the street, arms linked, shopping bags swishing, all chatting and laughing, I got another glimpse of how it used to be. For a moment I felt like myself, my old self, from before. And I felt really close to them again. I promised myself that I *would* come up and see them soon, and get them to come down. I couldn't exactly see them fitting in with Summer, Ben and Marco. But then, maybe they would – I hadn't even given them the chance yet.

In the cafe, we managed to nab our fave spot – a big comfy sofa at the back – and got stuck into our massively oversized (and overpriced, I now realized!) pineapple smoothies.

I started telling them about Summer, and I mentioned the cool sleepover we'd had in the yurt. I was trying to get across how completely amazing and magical it was, but they just didn't seem to get it. They kept going on about it being cold and muddy (which it wasn't) and giggling about me going to the loo behind a bush (which I didn't). I even told them about the beach party next Friday, thinking they'd definitely be interested in that, but they just still seemed obsessed with it being cold and the where-to-go-to-the-loo thing, so in the end I gave up and changed the subject, asking them what was going on with Harry and Ryan, these boys from The Royal School they used to fancy.

As I listened to a *very* detailed account of what happened at Finley's party, I found myself wishing that Summer was there with me instead, sipping her favourite strawberry and vanilla herb tea and talking about the Ben situation.

Then Em's phone beeped with a text. She showed it to Zo and they both burst out laughing. That bought me out of my daydream. "What's up?" I asked.

"Oh, it's just this stupid thing," said Em. She wasn't going to explain any more but when she saw I was still looking at her, she added, "We had to go on this geeky science day and The Royal School boys went too, and we had to do this fruit fly thing with Ryan and Harry—"

"Urgh, it was disgusting!" said Zo, with a shudder.

"…And then Harry sent Zo this hideous picture, and we sent one back, and the whole thing carried on at the cinema last week, and then he nearly kissed her and—"

"Hang on, *you* used to fancy Harry, didn't you?" I asked her.

"That was ages ago," said Em. "I like Ryan now."

"Why would she have told you she danced with

Ryan all night at Finley's party if she still liked Harry?" said Zo. "Keep up, Abs!"

Seeing the blank look on my face, Em just shrugged and said, "Have you met any fit guys down where you are?"

I shook my head. "Nah, not really." I'd been desperate for us three to get into a cosy corner and talk about Marco, but now I realized I didn't want to share it with them.

"I hope you're not saving yourself for Jake," said Em. Jake was one of the boys we used to hang out with in the park at weekends. I suppose we used to flirt a bit, but I hadn't even thought about him since I'd been in Totnes.

"You know Amelia Fenton-Clarke in 10B?" Zo was saying. "She's always fancied him and then, when you went, she got her claws stuck in."

"But now she's moved on to Jack, you know, Cayden's brother?" added Em.

"You know he asked Jenna out to the cinema and then didn't turn up, don't you?" Zo said to Em.

"No way!" Em gasped. "You didn't tell me that!"

And then they were off, in their own world. I knew who they were talking about, of course — well, mostly — but I just couldn't seem to *care* about any of it any more.

"Abbie, are you okay?" Zo asked.

I'd drifted off into my own thoughts, staring out the window. It must have been for quite a while, because they'd finished their smoothies and I'd hardly touched mine.

"What's wrong?" asked Em.

What could I say? *It's not you, it's me. No, actually, it is you!*

No. That wasn't fair. It wasn't their fault I'd changed so much. But I was shocked to realize how much I *had* changed. I felt a really heavy sadness inside as I realized that whatever we'd had between us just wasn't there any more. I mean, there's a kind of special magic in friendships, and with us three I'd really thought it would be there for ever, wherever life took us. But a couple of months apart and – *poof!* – it was gone.

After another drink for the other two and a lot more nodding and smiling by me while they chatted away, I was almost relieved when it was time to go. When we hugged goodbye I held them really tight for ages and ages, thinking it was probably the last time I'd see them – saying goodbye to the past.

Then I walked down towards Kensington Church Street to get the bus I needed to take me to Dad's. Mum had called the transport helpline to check for me, and written down the bus number and where to get on and off, and also how to get to Dad's flat in case there was some kind of dire emergency and he couldn't come and meet me. I was going back past H&M on my way to the bus stop, and I was still planning to take the top back.

As I passed the lovely little skincare shop we'd been in, I found myself stopping completely still on the pavement and just staring at it. Suddenly everything started whirling round in my head – seeing that they stocked small, exclusive brands, telling my friends I'd package some stuff up for them and send it, realizing how much people up here were prepared to pay for good quality products.

Suddenly, standing on the pavement, I had it.

The Big Idea.

I didn't even know if it could work, and I'd need to talk to Mum and my sisters about it, of course. But I thought I might have just found a way to help save the business.

After a moment I carried on walking, with a new spring in my step, heading for H&M.

Chapter Eight

I got off the bus at the stop for Dad's house, and it was like a different world to Kensington. I hadn't asked him to meet me in the end because I'd wanted a walk and some fresh air before facing him. But as I strode along the litter-strewn pavement, I wished I had done. A car passed, with its stereo up so loud that the *boom-boom-boom* of the bass went right through me, and then a group of teenage boys gave me the shock of my life by suddenly leaping up on the railings and making these kind of monkey noises as I passed them.

I felt like running, but I made myself keep walking normally. There was no point ringing Dad by then.

I wanted to keep moving, rather than stand somewhere, waiting for him. I saw two trendy mums with buggies a little way ahead, so I walked fast to catch them up, then stayed a few paces behind them. I felt a bit safer then, and they were in front of me all the way to the turning for Dad's road, luckily.

The white stucco terrace looked like it had once been quite grand, but now the paint was a grimy grey, with graffiti sprayed here and there on the old front walls. As I walked down the road I passed a bike chained to some railings. Well, what *used* to be a bike. Most of the bits were missing now.

When I reached number 15, I double-checked the address on my bit of paper before walking up the crumbling stone steps to the front door. There were loads of bells, with grubby bits of paper sellotaped next to them. By the bell for Flat 2 there was the newest-looking bit of paper. It just said *Green* in Dad's scribbly handwriting.

I reached up and pressed the bell, my heart pounding. Deep breath. This was it.

Dad buzzed me in and I walked up the threadbare hallway and found Flat 2. When he opened the door I felt such a rush of different emotions that I didn't know whether to hug him or slap him one.

But I didn't do either in the end, because I'd

walked in and seen the state of the flat (well, bedsit). And quite honestly, I think I was in shock.

I mean, I knew it wasn't going to be a palace, but I couldn't take in how awful it was. Our house had been immaculate, and not just because of Mum – Dad had liked things just so, too. But here the window was covered with filthy nets and heavy, half-drawn curtains, making the whole place gloomy and brooding. The floorboards were thick with dust and grime. There were dirty clothes and old newspapers and coffee cups everywhere, and a half-eaten portion of stale fish and chips sat on the coffee table, still in its white paper. The whole place smelled of dirt and grease.

"I see you cleaned up for me," I said.

"Oh, yeah, sorry," mumbled Dad. "Time just got away from me, somehow. Would you like a drink?"

"Maybe some water, thanks."

Dad started to shamble towards the kitchenette, but I said I'd get it. I was shaking by then. The sink was piled with dirty washing-up and there were ready-meal trays stacked on the counter. A container of milk sat on the side next to the fridge, going off. I hadn't imagined things would be this bad. It was really, really awful.

I took a glass from the shelf and tried to move some of the dirty dishes so I could get to the tap to fill it. Then I noticed it still had congealed Coke or something in the bottom, so I looked for a sponge to wash it. The sponge was so disgusting that it would have made the glass dirtier, so I used my hand instead. I took ages, not wanting to go back into that room with Dad.

I had no idea what to say to him.

But when I turned back round, he was standing in the doorway. It was lighter in the kitchenette and I took in the dark circles under his eyes, and the fact that he hadn't shaved. He *always* shaved, even when he had the flu. He was wearing a crumpled shirt with something spilled down the front and his hair was a greasy mess. He looked the same, but also like a completely different person. A big wave of sadness broke inside me. "Oh, Dad," I said.

We did hug then. For ages and ages.

When we finally broke apart, I said, "I can't believe you didn't call us back, or come down and see us. It's like you don't care." I couldn't help it, it just came tumbling out of my mouth.

"What?" he gasped, looking really shocked. "Of course I care! After I called you, and Grace and Saff wouldn't speak to me, well, I thought I should give you girls a bit more time. That's why I just sent the card."

"It was them who needed time, not me," I said flatly. "I needed *you*."

He sighed deeply, and his shoulders crumpled even more. "I'm sorry," he said. "I wasn't thinking straight." He looked around the disgusting kitchen and grimaced. "I'm in a bit of a mess."

"Understatement of the century," I said. "Look, I'm sorry you're struggling, but it's been difficult for us too, you know. We got a disgusting flat and then we were *that* close to being thrown out of it again, and we would have had to live in a B&B and probably be split up and I was so scared. We all were. It was awful. You left us in such a mess." I glared at him.

I might as well have slapped him.

"I know, love," he croaked, his voice choking up, his face full of pain.

I'd wanted to hurt him, but now I felt awful. "Look, why don't you do this place up a bit? That's what we did with ours," I suggested.

He shrugged. "There's no point, I probably won't be here for long."

We went back into the main room. "Well, at least open the curtains properly," I snapped, tugging at them until they were pulled as far back as they would go. I gathered the heavy nets together, balanced on the window sill and knotted them up as high as I could. The window was filthy, but at least a little more light could get in.

"I'm assuming you haven't got a job," I said, gathering up the stale old fish and chips into their wrapper.

"I'm going to the jobcentre every week," Dad mumbled. "But no luck so far. I did get one interview but then they rang and cancelled. I think they found out I'd been made bankrupt."

I sighed. "What about a course? You could train up for something."

"There's no funding," he said flatly. "And anyway, there's nothing I want to learn."

He was really annoying me by then. "What about moving out of here?" I suggested. "Go back to Ealing and get a place in a house-share so you've got some company. This area's horrible."

"It's not that bad once you get used to it," Dad said. "At least people keep themselves to themselves, which is how I like it. And I'd rather live on my own than with strangers."

He was just seeing the negative in all my ideas, without even thinking about them. I felt so frustrated with him I wanted to scream. Instead I squeezed the chip wrapper too hard and ended up with old fish, grease and congealed ketchup on my hands, which just made me more annoyed. "We've had it tough too, you know," I snapped. "But we pulled ourselves out of it and started the business. We had nothing, the same as you."

"You didn't have nothing," he said flatly. "You had each other."

He looked so lost and broken that all my anger rushed away, like water down a drain. "Oh," I croaked. "Sorry, I didn't think... I'm just so angry with you, after everything that's happened... Hang on, I'll wash my hands, then we'll talk, yeah?"

I was just wiping my wet hands on my skirt in the kitchenette when my phone rang. I went and pulled it out of my bag, thinking it might be Mum. I'd promised to ring her when I got to Dad's.

But it was Saff.

I could hardly make out what she was saying, she was crying so much. Something had gone wrong at the audition, by the sounds of it. I asked Dad which Tube stop was nearest and told her to come straight over. I said we'd meet her at the station.

Dad and I didn't talk much on the way to the Tube. I was too worried about Saff to think of anything else. When we got there, we only had to wait a few minutes before she came through the ticket barrier, her sunglasses still on to hide her eyes.

They didn't hide the black mascara smudges on her cheeks though.

"Saff!" cried Dad, holding out his arms.

But she walked right past him, threw herself onto me and burst into tears again. "Oh, Abs, it was awful!" she wailed. "We were all in the theatre waiting for our names to be called, about thirty of us, and *everyone* saw what happened. There are going to be bits in the show when the main character, Jazmin, talks to the camera, and we had to do that bit, but to the panel of TV people…"

We were in the way, so I steered her out of the station and we started walking down the road. Dad followed behind us, listening in.

"The first few girls were really good," Saff said. "They seemed to have been able to learn the whole piece in about ten minutes. I guess it was their stage school training. With everyone who went up, I got more and more nervous and when it was my turn I just fell apart. It was awful!"

"Oh, Saff, I'm sure it wasn't," I said soothingly.

"It was!" she insisted. "I couldn't get a single line out without looking at the script and I kept losing my place. I'd been standing in one spot and then halfway through I remembered the other girls had all moved round the stage while they were speaking, so

I started walking about, but then I lost my place again and did a bit I'd already done. And then when I was finished they said…they said…"

I squeezed her tight. "Go on," I told her.

"Well, this one man really lost it and shouted at me that it was the worst audition he'd ever seen and I shouldn't have wasted their time and then he told me to get out. Everyone was whispering, and some of the other girls were sniggering. I felt so stupid, and completely humiliated, so I just ran." She burst into fresh sobs then.

"That's terrible!" I cried. "He should never have behaved like that!"

Dad had been hovering beside us and he said, "Too right! That's completely unprofessional. I'll go up there now and have a word with—"

Saff turned and gave him a withering look. "Well, it's good to know you still care," she spat.

"Of course I do!" he cried.

"Don't go up there, please," Saff said then. "I just want to forget about the whole thing."

Dad frowned. "If you're sure…"

Saff shuddered. "Definitely."

"Look, just come back to the flat for a while, yeah?" he said then. "I'll make some tea."

"Well, I do need to redo my make-up," Saff

muttered. "Don't think this means I forgive you though," she warned.

"Fair enough," he said.

Saff linked arms with me all the way back and didn't talk to Dad at all. He did try to walk next to us for a while, but the pavement wasn't wide enough, so he had to step back again and walk behind.

I badly needed the loo by the time we got back to the flat. Judging by the state of the rest of the place it was going to be hideous, and I wasn't going in there unarmed. So I left Saff in the main room, staring in horror at the vileness around her, and went to look for some bleach under the kitchen sink. In the bathroom, I found the ancient loo brush too. I cleaned the loo before I went and then I put a big glob of the bleach down the sink as well.

By the time I came out, Saff and Dad were in the kitchenette, *together*, searching for clean mugs. Well, that was something, anyway. Dad handed over some mugs and I found a not-completely-disgusting cloth and started wiping the counter before putting them down on it.

"OMG, are you turning into MUM?" cried Saff, pointing at the cloth.

"Ha ha!" I said. Still, it reminded me to give Mum a ring before she closed up at Rainbow Beauty. Dad vanished into the main room as I got my phone out. I promised Mum that everything was fine, and let her know that Saff was here as well, then put her on the phone. I thought Saff would tell Mum the whole story, but she didn't (luckily for my phone credit!) – instead she just said that the audition hadn't gone very well so she'd come to see me to talk about it.

Then I went and gave Dad the not-completely-disgusting cloth and instructed him to clear and wipe down the coffee table. As Saff and I made tea in the kitchenette, I said, "Thanks for coming in for a while. And for talking to Dad. It means a lot to him."

She shrugged. "Disgusting as it is, I'm probably going to have to stay here tonight," she told me. "Sabina's arranged for us to go out in a big group of our mates, and after what happened today, I just can't face it."

"Oh, but Saff, you were really looking forward to seeing her," I said. "Why don't you just ring and see if you can have a quiet night in together instead?"

But Saff shook her head. "There's no way I'm telling her what happened. She'll just tell *everyone*. I don't want them all knowing I'm a loser."

"But Saff, you're not—" I began.

"Tell the TV people that," she said, giving me a tight smile and rummaging in her bag for her phone.

I took the tea through, and then came back for the sugar (Dad now took three, I found out). Saff was talking to Sabina, and I was surprised to hear her saying, "Well, I'm gutted I can't make it tonight, but I'm stuck here. The casting director wants me to stay on for callbacks…"

I hovered in the doorway until she'd finished speaking. Then, when she'd hung up with lots of air kissing and promising to let Sabina know the second there was any news about the part, I said, "Why did you say that?"

Saff turned around, startled. "I couldn't say I was laughed out of the first audition, could I? She'd tell everyone."

"Course you could," I said. "If they're real friends, they'll understand."

Saff sighed. "It's not about them, it's about me," she said. "I can't face being a failure, and I don't want them to see me as one. I'm going to be famous, Abs. I don't want to end up as just a beautician."

"Look, why don't you go out?" I said again. "It might cheer you up."

"No," said Saff firmly. "I'm feeling rubbish, and if I can't be the lively, bubbly Saff they expect, I'm not going at all."

"Suit yourself," I said, as we wandered back into the main room.

Saff asked about staying the night as well and Dad was really pleased. "You girls can have my bed and I'll take the sofa," he told us.

"Oh, *goodie*," said Saff, eyeing the saggy old bed with its shabby brown blankets.

I tried to get us all chatting then, but Saff and Dad just sat there, sipping their tea and looking as miserable as each other. After a few minutes of wittering on to myself, I did the goggly eyes look at Saff so she had to get the hint and make conversation. "This place is minging," she said.

"Saff!" I cried.

"What?" she protested. "You wanted me to say something, didn't you?"

"It's okay," said Dad. "I know it is. I am going to sort it out, I just—"

"When we first got to our flat it was gross too," said Saff, cutting him off. "I think it was worse than this – a close second anyway."

"Oh my gosh, and there was a rat!" I cried. "I can't believe I'd almost forgotten about that!" Me and Saff re-enacted how we'd seen it dashing across the floor and all screamed and clambered up on the table and chairs.

That made Dad smile, for the first time since I'd got there.

Then we told him how we'd cleaned our place from floor to ceiling, and done it up as best we could. Suddenly, Saff and I paused, and looked at each other. We'd both had the same idea. I got to my feet. "Right, come on, Dad," I said. "We're getting this place sorted, right now."

Dad couldn't believe it when we marched him into the kitchenette and raided the cupboard under the sink for cleaning products. He'd never seen either of us within a mile of a duster before. Some of the stuff we found looked a bit old, and definitely hadn't been bought by him, but it would have to do. Luckily we found some okay-looking rubber gloves shoved down the back of a drawer too. There was no way I was tackling any of it without them on.

We found a brush and I handed it to Dad. "Right, you do the floors – there's no dustpan, but you can use some of that old newspaper to sweep the bits into."

"Then when you've finished that, I'll get you a bucket of hot water to wash them down with," said Saff. "I found that mop behind the door but it's beyond revolting, so it's a hands-and-knees-with-a-cloth job. I'll blitz this dump and Abs is going to sort out the main room."

Dad just blinked at us. "Who are you and what have you done with my daughters?" he asked.

"Ha ha!" we chorused.

Well, Saff and I obviously had a lot of frustration to get out from how badly our days had gone, because we went totally Kim and Aggie, blasting the place for about two hours. Dad actually looked a bit *scared* at one point, but he got stuck in too.

When the kitchenette was spotless and sparkling, Dad came in to admire it. "It would be even better if we'd had some cream cleaner for the oven," Saff told him.

"I didn't even think you knew what that was!" he cried.

Saff swatted at him with a duster. "Oi! I'm not some little princess, you know!" she shrieked.

"Well, not any more," I said with a giggle, and then she tried to swat me as well.

When I'd cleared all the rubbish out of the main room and gathered up the washing into a black bag for the laundrette, Saff helped me get the revolting nets down and we put them straight in the big bin outside. There wasn't much we could do about the yellow curtains, but they didn't look so bad on their own, and we tied them right back with a bit of cord we found in a drawer.

As Dad made a start on washing the window, Saff sorted out all the old bottles and newspapers and stuff for recycling and I got busy cleaning the thick layer of dust off everything. It was a nice feeling, just getting on with things together. I'm not sure talking's *always* the best way to solve problems (I mean, just look at me and Marco – somehow we'd talked ourselves into splitting up). Having to pull some disgusting putrid hair out of a drain wasn't particularly lovely though, especially as it clearly wasn't Dad's. It made me feel completely sick and, before all this, there was no way I would have done it. But that was also before I scrubbed out The Most Revolting Toilet in the World at Rainbow Beauty. I felt like I could face anything now.

Saff found a pile of change down the back of the sofa while vacuuming behind the cushions. We were all hungry by then so she was going to put it towards some fish and chips, but I suggested making something instead. I thought cooking smells would be the finishing touch for the newly-sparkling flat, making it feel really homely.

Saff gave me her findings and Dad rummaged in his pocket and tried to hand me a crumpled tenner, but I told him to keep it. "Three pounds sixty-seven," I said, counting the change in my hand. "That'll be enough."

"You won't get dinner for that, surely?" Dad said.

"Yes, we will, and pudding too!" Saff told him.

Forty minutes later, we sat down round the little pull-out table we'd found buried under a stack of old newspapers. We'd made Mum's speciality economy tomato pasta, without the crème fraiche or mozzarella or basil. We'd been able to afford a courgette and a few mushrooms to go in it though, which Dad had been in charge of cutting up, and there were reduced-price strawberries for pudding. "Cooking as well as cleaning," he said to us, as we polished off the last few. "Honestly, I'm amazed."

Saff raised her eyebrows. "We haven't finished yet," she said. She looked him up and down and her lip curled. "You're next."

I grinned at her and said, "I like your thinking." Then I turned to Dad. "Now we can show you where our talents really lie," I told him.

He watched in amazement as we produced an array of colourful, delicious-smelling Rainbow Beauty products from our bags.

"So you're travelling light then?" he joked.

"Yeah, these are just the bare essentials," said Saff, taking him completely seriously. "I haven't even got my Mandarin Body Butter with me."

"I've got some," I told her. "That's an essential on *my* list."

So we ran Dad a bath in the now-squeaky-clean bathroom, filled it with Spicy Delight Bubble Bath, and sent him in there with one of my orange peel soaps, a pot of Lime & Ginger Sea Salt Body Scrub, an Almond Facial Exfoliator, the Mandarin Body Butter, and strict instructions to have a shave and wash his hair as well.

Saff put the TV on, but I couldn't concentrate on it. I kept wondering what Marco was doing, how the gig was going, if they'd gone on yet. I texted him a good luck message (I put a kiss on, then took it off again, then put it back), but he didn't reply. I guessed he was way too busy to worry about his phone. I hoped that was the reason anyway. I couldn't bear to think I'd lost him as a friend, as well as as a boyfriend.

When Dad reappeared about an hour later, he'd managed to find a clean pair of jeans and a shirt from somewhere too, and he looked like a new man. The Rainbow Beauty magic seemed to have worked.

Of course, I knew it wouldn't solve all his problems, but it had given him a kick-start, at least. And we knew it had affected him inside as well as out, because he had an announcement to make.

"I've been thinking, and I've decided to come down to Totnes," he said.

"What, tomorrow?" cried Saff.

"Yup."

My sister and I shared a glance. Mum would go mad, and as for Grace...

"I'll get the coach with you," he said. "I realize now I've been hiding up here like a coward. I need to face the music with your mum, and put things right with Grace too."

"Erm, you do realize she isn't talking to you, don't you?" said Saff. "And she won't want to see you."

Dad looked pained at that. "I know," he said. "But I'm the adult here. I need to see her and sort it out. Oh, thank goodness for you two. I'm so happy we're back together."

"It isn't as easy as that, Dad," I said. I didn't want him to think everything was better just because of one evening.

"No, it isn't," said Saff. "We're still *really* angry with you, you know."

Dad sighed. "I know. I guess I'll have to live with that, and just do everything I can to show you how…" His voice choked up and he couldn't speak for a moment. "…how much I love you and how sorry I am for everything that's happened. I'd do anything for you girls."

"Well, now you don't look and smell like a tramp, I think I could probably give you a hug," said Saff.

"I'm honoured," said Dad.

I smiled, watching them. When they broke apart, I said to Dad, "Do you really mean you'd do anything for us?"

"Yes, of course I would," he insisted.

Well, that gave me even more to think about. But I didn't say anything to him about my idea. I needed to talk to Mum, Saff and Grace first.

Chapter Nine

"Al! What the bloody hell are you doing here?" Mum shrieked.

"Look, Kim, I knew you wouldn't be pleased to see me—" Dad began.

Mum obviously remembered that her next client was waiting on the purple velvet sofa behind her then because, rather than killing him on the spot, she managed to smile and say, "I'm not entirely delighted, to put it mildly."

Then she marched him into the kitchenette, glaring at me and Saff on the way.

Of course, we knew we should have phoned to warn her, but when it came down to it neither of us had been brave enough to. I suppose we were hoping that Dad would change his mind overnight (BTW, we did actually get some sleep on the horrible saggy bed, amazingly). But when he handed us our tea in the morning, he was still set on going. Then at the station we were almost hoping he wouldn't get a seat on the coach, just thinking of how Mum would react, but it wasn't fully booked. Seeing the look on her face, he probably wished it had been now.

After Dad's makeover the night before, we'd sat around chatting, and we'd ended up telling him all about Rainbow Beauty, including the awful article and the problems we were having keeping it afloat. I didn't mention my Big Idea though. It was all just thoughts until Mum agreed. And given the reaction she'd just had, that didn't seem very likely.

Just as Mum and Dad reached the kitchenette, Grace came staggering out of one of the treatment rooms, carrying a huge pile of used towels in front of her face. "Hi, Saff," she called from behind them. "How did the audition go? And Abs, are you okay? Was it awful, seeing *that man*? I bet you wish you'd never—" She dropped the towels into the laundry basket and came face-to-face with *that man* himself. "Oh!" she gasped.

"Hi, Grace," said Dad nervously.

Grace just glared at him with her arms folded. "What are you doing here?" she demanded.

"Erm, well, I've come to see you," he stuttered. "I wanted to explain why I haven't been in touch. I didn't think you wanted me to be. And, well, things got a bit on top of me and I lost the plot for a while. Abbie and Saff can tell you. I was in a bad state."

"It's true," I said. "He was."

But Grace just stared at him. Then, "Excuse me," she said, as she picked up the laundry basket and walked out the door with it, to take it up to the flat.

"Oh," said Dad. "That went well."

"What do you expect, turning up out of the blue?" Mum snapped.

"I was hoping...I just wanted to talk to you and Grace," he mumbled. But he wasn't looking so sure about the whole thing now.

Mum glanced at the wall clock and sighed deeply. "Right, I'm going to treat my next client. I'll see *you* in the flat in one hour. You can say whatever you have to say and then clear off."

Dad just stood there, looking helpless. Mum gave me and then Saff a quick hug. "*Hello*," she said to us. "Saff, hon, I really am sorry about the audition. You can give me the full story later."

Saff shrugged. "It's okay. I'm over it," she said.

"That idiot producer wouldn't know talent if it bit him on the bum."

"Too right," said Mum, smiling at her. Then, "Go and check on Grace, would you, hon?" she said.

Saff nodded. "Sure."

Mum showed her client into one of the treatment rooms, and Saff hurried off upstairs. Dad wanted to go too, but I said I thought he should give Grace a bit of space. So I showed him around Rainbow Beauty. I talked him through all the products and then I made him a purple juice with beetroot for strength (he was going to need it once Mum got hold of him).

"I can't believe all this," he said, sipping his juice and gesturing round the reception area. "It's amazing how much you've achieved. I'm so proud of you all."

I couldn't help grinning. Whatever had happened between us, it still meant so much to me that Dad was proud of us. About ten minutes before Mum was due to finish, I took him up to the flat. Again, he was wowed by how nice we'd managed to make it.

It was so weird, him being in *our* kitchen. Saff put the kettle on and Grace pointedly ignored him (she was curled up on the sofa, reading a book, and she only said hello to *me* when we walked in).

About thirty seconds later Mum came up (and

demanded to know why Saff had given Dad some of *our* coffee).

"I see you've taken your rings off," Dad said, gesturing towards her left hand. "We're still married, you know."

"What do *you* care?" Mum snapped.

"Good point, Mum!" cried Saff.

As Mum and Dad started rowing about the details of their split, I turned on her. "That might be true, but this isn't helping, is it?"

Saff shrugged. "It is if it makes her feel better. Just because I'm talking to Dad again, it doesn't mean I think he should get off without facing the music!"

"Yeah, but——" I began.

Then a sickening cry pierced the air, like an animal caught in a trap. We all turned to see Grace standing bolt upright, frozen, with tears running down her face.

Saff gasped and Dad looked horrified.

My stomach flipped. "Grace——" I whispered.

Mum rushed over. "Hey, honey, it's okay," she gabbled. "We didn't mean to——"

But Grace just stared right through her. Then she came back to life.

And then she ran.

"I'll go," I said, dashing down the hall after her.

* * *

"Grace, wait! Where are you going?" I cried, jogging along the pavement behind her. But she didn't answer me, and she didn't slow down.

After a few more minutes I called out, "Grace, come on. I'd never have put these shoes on today if I'd known I'd be doing a marathon. You don't want me to break my ankle, do you?"

She still didn't say anything, but she slowed to a fast walk, so that was something, at least.

"Where are you going?" I gasped, when I finally caught her up.

"I don't know," she muttered. "Anywhere away from *him*."

After about fifteen minutes of very fast walking uphill in the strong sunshine and the wrong shoes, we ended up at the castle. At the ticket booth, Grace reached into her pocket and handed over a fiver to pay the two-pound-something entrance fee.

"I've got no money on me," I told her.

For a moment I thought she was going to go in and leave me standing there, but then she handed back some of her change to the man and gave me a ticket.

It was cool and shadowy inside the castle ruins. Grace pulled herself up to sit in one of the alcoves, and started to look more relaxed.

"Why here?" I asked, heaving myself up next to her. She shrugged. "I just like it."

I looked around me at the high, thick castle walls. There were only arrow slits for windows, a steep hill, a deep moat. *I* understood, even if Grace didn't. "You feel safe here," I said.

Grace laughed in surprise. "Yeah, I guess so," she said.

"This whole thing with Mum and Dad has affected you way more than you've let on, hasn't it?" I said then. When she didn't reply, I added, "I mean, you act all cold and hard about Dad, saying 'He's made his own bed' and all that, but inside you're really hurt about what's happened. Maybe the most hurt of all of us."

She still didn't say anything, but the tears had started to roll down her cheeks again.

"Oh, Grace, I'm so sorry," I said, pulling her into a hug. "I didn't mean to upset you."

"You haven't," she insisted, hugging me back. "You're just *right*, that's all. I only really feel okay here, or in my room studying."

"Is that why you haven't been going out with your friends?" I asked gently.

She nodded. "Yeah. It kept going round in my head — what if they don't really like me? Or what if

199

they do, but they change their minds when they get to know me better? I mean, I know I'm not the most bubbly person…"

"They like you the way you are, we all do," I insisted.

Grace burst into sobs then. "But I couldn't stand it if *they* rejected me too," she sniffled. "Not after Dad—"

"But Dad didn't reject you," I said firmly. "This is about him and Mum. I know it feels like he did though. I felt the same as you about that. I still do sometimes."

"I guess we all build walls around us to protect ourselves," said Grace, peering up at the thick stone.

"I guess so," I said. "Look, why don't you come back and hear what Dad has to say? It might make you feel better, you never know. It worked for me, anyway."

Grace just shrugged, but she did slither down from the alcove. I followed after her.

As we headed back past the ticket booth, the man on duty called out to us. "Hey, girls, you were only in there five minutes. Here, I can't take your money for that."

He handed Grace the entrance fee back and she smiled and thanked him. I beamed at him too – I doubt he realized how much that bit of change was to us.

"The least I can do is treat you to an ice cream," Grace said to me as we walked away, "after making you walk all the way up this hill."

"The very least!" I agreed. "I might actually *have* heatstroke this time!"

She laughed, then looked straight at me, suddenly serious. "Thanks, Abbie," she said. "I don't know what I'd do without you, I really don't."

I smiled at her. "No worries. Now, come on, my toffee fudge double cone with a flake isn't going to eat itself!"

When we got back to the flat, after our chat and everything, I hoped Grace might be ready to talk to Dad. But as we walked through the door, she suddenly looked really pale, like she was going to be sick.

"Too much mint choc chip?" I asked.

She shook her head. "Sorry, Abbie, I can't face him, I just can't," she muttered, and then slipped into her and Saff's room before I could stop her.

Mum and Dad came into the hallway then and soon we were all pleading with Grace.

"Please come out, love," called Mum. She looked really, really worried.

"No, not while *he's* still here," said Grace, through the door. She must have put a chair against it or something, because when we tried the handle, it wouldn't budge. Mum gave Dad a *Look what you've done* glare, but she didn't say anything out loud.

"There's no coach back until tomorrow, sweetheart," Dad called, leaning close to the door.

"Hon, we promise not to fight any more if you just come out and have dinner with us," Mum added. "You don't have to say anything, just come and eat."

Half an hour later, when we all sat down to our salad niçoise, Grace appeared by the door. She wouldn't catch anyone's eye, not even mine, and she ate her tea staring at the table, but at least she'd come out. No one else was talking either – I think Mum and Dad felt it was better not to say anything at all than risk starting another argument, and I could see Saff was exhausted.

I thought this might be the best chance I was going to get with us all there to reveal my new business-saving idea, and goodness knows, someone needed to kick-start the conversation. So I said,

"Going up to London gave me an idea for how we can get Rainbow Beauty back on track."

"Oh, yes, love?" Mum said.

"We create a product range, just four or five things to start with, and sell it in those posh skincare shops they have in the well-heeled areas," I explained. "I went into one with Em and Zo on Kensington High Street, and with what they're charging we could make a really decent profit."

"Wow, good thinking!" said Saff, perking up.

"Yeah, nice idea, Abs," said Dad.

Grace was about to say something, but then she stopped herself and went back to poking her food and staring at the table.

Mum sighed. "It is a really good idea, love, and I hate to be the bearer of bad news but I don't see why those shops would buy from us. They don't know anything about us or our products."

"That's why we have to show them, tell them… *persuade* them," I said. "We need to put together a nice leaflet, and let them sample the products."

"You mean, go up there?" Mum asked.

"Yeah," said Saff, getting on board. "We'd have to let them try the products out, so they can see how good they are."

"And we'd talk up how they're made from natural

ingredients, organic where possible," I added.

"You could offer a free gift to the person who places the order," Dad suggested. "That's what I do, I mean, what I used to do to encourage people to choose my company to run their event."

"I suppose we could, if they place orders over thirty pounds," said Mum.

"No, you should say for orders over a hundred quid, easily," Dad countered.

"You need to be realistic," Mum told him, looking irritated.

"I *am* being," he insisted. "You'll end up spending too much on the free gifts otherwise. You've always been too cautious, Kim."

"Well, you always took the high-risk strategies with your business, and look where that got you," Mum snapped.

Dad bristled at that. "Well, at least——" he began.

"Ahem!" said Saff loudly, and I did the goggly eyes warning look at both of them and then at Grace. Luckily they got the hint and stopped bickering.

Dad turned to me. "If you put together a range of, say, five products that are easily transportable and wouldn't need refrigeration then, even if you double the prices you've got downstairs, the shops would still get a good margin and you're only talking about…two or three of each product to get a hundred-pound order, aren't you?"

I turned to Grace, expecting her to chip in and tell me whether that was right or not, but she was refusing to look up from her plate, so I had to work it out myself.

"That's true," I said, eventually.

"I admit that does sound realistic," said Mum. "But anyway, it's irrelevant because we haven't got any money as it is, and we can't cover the costs involved."

"We could," I said, "if we're selective about the products we choose, and use mostly ingredients we already have."

"And we could design the leaflet ourselves," said Saff. "Summer could take photos of the range. She did a great job on my pictures."

"Grace," I said, addressing her directly. "Do you think we could afford to do this, if we're really careful?"

We all stared at her and eventually she looked up. She couldn't resist a bit of impromptu maths, Dad or no Dad. "I think we're looking at spending about two hundred, first off, in extra ingredients and packaging for the free gifts and samples, and on printing the leaflets – they'd have to be really good quality," she said. "So I suppose, if we waited for the red electricity bill rather than paying it now, and didn't order that new batch of things to make more body butters like we were planning... Yeah, we could probably just about afford it."

I thought Mum would be happy then, but she was frowning. "I've seen a problem, I'm afraid," she said gravely. "Someone will have to pitch to the shops initially, and then deliver the orders and, if it's successful, go back to show them other products. There's no point starting something if we can't keep it going. And couriers and sales reps are way out of our budget."

My heart started pounding then. I knew Mum would never let *me* go, there was no point even asking. "I can do it," Saff offered, "the initial sell-in at least."

"Not on your own, love," said Mum firmly. "And I can't go – we can't risk losing the remaining loyal clients we do have by me taking time out."

"Well, I was thinking..." I began. I looked at Mum, then at Dad. They both peered at me for a moment, confused. Then Mum just looked horrified, even more so than when she'd seen the rat on our first day here.

"Oh no!" she shrieked. "Not in a million years!

I'd rather starve in the street!"

"If we don't do this, you might have to," I pointed out.

"*Eh?*" Dad went, still looking confused. He turned to me, I raised my eyebrows at him and the penny dropped. "What, *me?* Become your sales rep?"

"Well, you did say you'd do anything for us girls," I reminded him.

"And I would, for *all* of you," he insisted. He tried again to catch Grace's eye but she pointedly looked the other way. Then he nodded towards Mum. "But there's no way *she'll* let me work with her."

"Excuse me, '*she*'?" Mum snapped. "I am *here*, you know. And you're right, by the way. You're not laying a finger on our business. You've already wrecked our lives once, there's no way I'm giving you the chance to do that again."

Dad went so pale, he looked like he was going to collapse. "I'm going to the shop," he croaked. He staggered across the kitchen, as if he'd just been punched in the stomach. Hard. "I mean it, Abs," he said, as he reached the doorway, "I'll do anything to help."

"Mum——" I began, when we'd heard the front door swing shut behind him.

"Mum what?" she cried. She was furious with

me. "I can't believe you even suggested that, Abbie! I know he's your father and of course you can see him if you want to, but I don't want *that man* anywhere near me, and certainly not anywhere near our business!"

It made my stomach flip over, hearing Mum be so horrible about Dad. I gave Saff a pleading look, but she just said, "I agree with Mum."

"Me too," said Grace, obviously deciding it was okay to talk now that Dad had gone.

I sighed. "Look, I know it's a shocking suggestion," I told them, "but it's the only choice we've got. It could save Rainbow Beauty. That's what this is about – it's not a way of letting Dad back into the family." I turned to Mum. "He'll be your courier, that's all. And he'll be working for free, of course."

Mum smiled grimly. "Well, he certainly owes us, that's for sure," she muttered. "I suppose he could deliver the products, just initially. But that doesn't solve the problem of how to get the orders in the first place."

"You wouldn't mind me pitching to the shops if Dad was there with me, would you?" I asked. Mum looked really horrified, so I quickly added, "I wouldn't let him say anything. He'd just be there as a responsible adult. Well, as an adult anyway."

"I suppose that would be acceptable," said Mum. "*If* he kept quiet."

"You should definitely do the pitches, you were great at the town fayre," said Grace. "The products were flying off our table once you'd shown everyone how good they were."

I smiled at her and she smiled back.

"Yeah, just bring out your passion for what we do and we'll sell tons," said Saff.

Well, as you can imagine I was totally blushing by then. "Thanks," I said.

"I think you should agree to Dad helping," Saff told Mum.

Mum looked at Grace. "Yep, so do I," Grace told her.

"But you—"

"We've got to think of the business," my sister said firmly.

"So will you?" I asked Mum.

"I'll think about it, that's all," she said. "I'm not promising anything. But I'm telling you, Abbie, if I do let him help, and he puts one toe out of line…"

Saff did an impression of Lord Sugar, pointing across the table and going, "Alastair Green, you're fired."

Even Grace giggled at that, but she fell silent again

as the doorbell rang. I went to answer it.

"I got you a Twirl," Dad told me, rummaging in a stripy carrier bag as he followed me up the stairs.

"Oh, thanks," I said.

Back in the kitchen, he handed a Ripple to Saff, and offered a bar of Fry's Peppermint Cream to Mum.

"Huh! I went off these years ago," she grumbled, but she took it anyway.

"And for my darling Grace, as always, since you were four anyway – Maltesers," he said, pulling one of those big-size bags out and trying to hand it to Grace.

She just let it slip through her fingers and drop to the floor. "You can't *buy* me," she said coldly, and walked off to her room.

"But Gracie, that's not what I—" Dad began. Then he sighed deeply and sank down onto the revolting brown sofa. "She really hates me, doesn't she?"

"Hate's a strong word," said Mum.

"It's more a combination of *loathe* and *detest*," Saff offered, unhelpfully.

"Girls, would you mind giving your mum and me some time alone?" asked Dad suddenly.

"Whatever. I'm going out with Emily now,

anyway," said Saff. And with that she stalked off to her and Grace's room to get ready.

"Okay," I said. I grabbed my book and my Twirl and went into my chill-out room.

I didn't mean to listen, exactly. It was just that the walls were really thin in the flat. Plus it was quite a hot evening, so I *had* to leave the door open a bit, or I would have baked.

Okay, fine, I admit it, I was totally eavesdropping.

"That sounds ominous, getting the girls to make themselves scarce," I heard Mum say. "What do you want to break to me now? There can't be any more bad news, surely?"

"I just...I thought we should talk about what's happened," Dad mumbled. "I'm sure you want to, you know, go over things." I could just imagine him sitting there, staring at the table, shoulders hunched, waiting for Mum to go crazy at him. I was waiting for it too, to be honest.

"I don't, actually," said Mum. "I don't see what good it would do to rake over the past. It won't change anything."

"Oh, okay," said Dad. He sounded surprised, and a bit suspicious too, as if this calm attitude was just a ruse of Mum's to give her time to go over to the toaster, unplug it, pick it up and throw it at his head.

"And it's a bit arrogant of you, don't you think?" she snapped. "Just deciding it's time to face the music and turning up out of the blue, *uninvited*. I have got my own life, you know."

He sighed. "I know. Could I just…can I just say one thing though, Kim?"

I could imagine Mum standing there, lips pursed and arms folded, possibly sidling closer to the toaster. "Go on," she said curtly.

"I know it's not nearly enough. I know no words can make up for everything I've put you through. But…I want to say I'm sorry."

"Al, don't," said Mum. Her voice had completely changed. She wasn't in toaster-throwing mode any more. Instead she sounded small, and shattered.

"I really am," said Dad. "I'm just so, so sorry about everything. Please let me help with your business. For the girls' sake, if nothing else. I've lost their home for them once. Let me help secure this one. I can't change the past, but I can help save the future."

My heart was pounding.

Neither of them spoke for what felt like ages. Then—

"Okay," said Mum.

"YES!" I cried. *Whoops!*

"Abbie, you might as well come in if you're listening anyway," Mum called.

So I did, and I gave her a big hug. "Thanks," I said, "thanks so much." And then I was so happy I gave Dad a hug too, even though Mum was watching.

"You won't regret it, honestly," Dad promised her.

"I'd better not," she said darkly. Then she added, "Let's get something straight, Al. I am your boss in this. What I say goes. No making suggestions, no changing plans. I tell you what to do, you do it and then you go away. Agreed?"

Dad shrugged. "Harsh, but fair. Agreed."

She gave him a steely glare. "Well, there's really no reason for you to stay any longer. I'll be in touch about the next step."

Dad glared back at her. "Oh, I'm not going anywhere," he said. "Not until Grace agrees to talk to me. I'll sit outside her door all night if necessary."

"No, you won't," Mum cried. "You're not staying here tonight, so don't think you are."

"Fine, I'll sit in the street then," said Dad defiantly.

"Fine."

"Fine."

Secretly I was quite impressed that he was refusing to give up.

He didn't sit in the street in the end though. Instead, I just happened to pop round to Liam's and just happened to mention what had happened and happened to say that if he happened to call round perhaps he could happen to offer Dad *his* sofa.

Half an hour later, he did.

Dad said, "Thanks, but no thanks, I'm waiting to talk to Grace."

Liam said, "Well, I'll leave you a key just in case."

So Dad sat outside Grace's door on the revolting hairy hallway carpet. But if he was stubborn, Grace was stubborner. He begged and pleaded with her, but she still wouldn't come out.

"Give her some space," Mum said, after about an hour. "Not everything works to your timetable, you know."

So Dad went back into the kitchen and Mum allowed him to have a cup of *her* coffee, and none of us heard anything from Grace and Saff's room for ages and ages. Saff had gone out long before, of course. After a while I went up to the door and called her name but there was no answer. Then Mum and Dad came up too, and called and called, but she still didn't reply.

Then we started panicking about whether she was okay, so Dad wrestled with the door until he got the chair out from under it on the other side and we all burst in. We found Grace fast asleep, her headphones in, curled round a pillow the way she did when she was little. There were tear marks streaked all down her cheeks. We fell silent and backed out of the room.

"Look, let her sleep on it," Mum said to Dad, more softly now, when we were back in the kitchen. "You just turning up like that today has been a real shock for her. Try again in the morning."

Dad sighed. "But I have to stay here. What if she wakes up and I've gone? I don't want her to think I've given up."

"If she wakes up in the night and wants to speak to you, I'll come and get you straight away," said Mum. "I promise."

Dad gave her an anxious look. "Will you really though?"

Mum pursed her lips and narrowed her eyes in a toaster-throwing way. "I keep *my* promises," she said curtly.

"Right. Well, I guess I'll be off then," Dad said. I hugged him again and said goodnight. Mum just folded her arms and gave him a death-stare.

Dad shrugged on his jacket. "Liam's just offered me his sofa because he's your mate, right?" he said to her. "You don't think he fancies me or anything?"

"Don't be so ridiculous," she hissed. "Anyway, he's way out of your league!" And with that, she bustled him out of the door and locked it behind him.

Chapter Ten

Dad came back round about 8 a.m. and as soon as Grace wandered into the kitchen, he started trying to talk to her. But she just stared straight ahead, made herself and Saff cups of tea and disappeared back into their room.

Me and Mum (and Saff, after a while) sat at the kitchen table, making awkward half-conversation with Dad for nearly an hour, in between taking turns to get ready.

"You're going to miss your coach if you don't go soon," said Mum, when it got to nine o'clock. After another twenty minutes, she made it very clear to him that he wasn't welcome to stay another day, and she and Saff went down to Rainbow Beauty to look at which manicure supplies needed to be ordered.

So Dad went and told Grace he had to go, but she didn't come out. "This doesn't mean I'm giving up though," he called through the door. "You'll see."

He gave me such a sad look, I reached up to hug him. "She'll come round," I said, even though I wasn't sure she ever would.

"Thanks, Abs," Dad muttered, but I didn't think he believed me.

"Come on, you'll miss your coach," I said. We hurried downstairs and he came into Rainbow Beauty with me to say a quick goodbye. We found Mum and Saff in the kitchenette, peering at the tap. There was a little bit of water spraying out from one side of it. Mum groaned. "Typical! It looks like we've got a leak, and there's no way we can afford a plumber."

"It's just the washer," said Dad, rolling up his sleeves. "If I just…"

He turned the tap and we all screamed as the whole top came off and water started spraying out in all directions, hitting the ceiling and soaking us all.

"Make it stop!" Mum screeched.

"I can't!" yelled Dad.

In seconds, Mum's silk blouse was wet through,

her hair was matted with water and her make-up was running all down her face. Me and Saff didn't look much better.

I grabbed a tea towel and Saff helped me to hold it over the tap, so at least then the water was just pouring down the sink.

"You idiot, Al!" Mum snapped. "I'm going to call Liam!" and with that she pushed past Dad and marched off to the reception desk.

"Well, I guess I'll be going," Dad mumbled. I felt even sorrier for him then.

"See you soon," I said. "In London." He hugged my and Saff's shoulders, but we couldn't hug him back – we had to keep pressing on the tap.

A minute later, Liam came bursting through the doorway, toolkit in hand. "I don't know why Kim called you," Dad grumbled. "I've had a look and it's a job for a plumber."

"GET OUT!" Mum screeched at him, from behind reception.

"Bye then!" called Dad and we heard the bell on the door tinkle as he made a quick exit.

Two minutes later, Liam had turned off the water at the mains, fitted a new washer to the tap and put the top tightly back on. Then he handed Mum the keys to his van. "You lot need a day out," he told her.

She looked down at them. "Oh, wow, that would be fantastic. Thanks, Liam. Won't you come though?"

"I'd love to, but I'm drowning in paperwork," he said. "Whereas you're just…drowning."

Mum looked down at her dripping clothes and then grinned at him. "Oh, Liam, what would I do without you?" she said.

"You'd be all lost and lonely," he sighed, pulling a sad face.

He was joking, but it was true. I was so pleased Mum had made a good friend. I knew *I'd* be lost without Summer and Ben (and Marco too – well, I *hoped* we were still friends, anyway, but he hadn't texted me back to say how the gig had gone). Saff and Emily were pretty much joined at the hip now, and maybe, after our chat, Grace would get up the courage to go out with Maisy and Aran too. No girl is an island and all that.

Once Saff and I had towelled ourselves off and Mum had completely changed and redone her hair and make-up (and we'd managed to persuade Grace that Dad really had gone, so that she would come out of her room) we all set off in Liam's van.

We went to the same beach he'd taken us to when we first arrived here. It was even busier now, being Sunday, and with the summer holidays in full swing, but we managed to find a place to put our towels down. We'd stopped in a lay-by on the way to buy some fresh local strawberries and now Saff was offering them round.

Grace took one and breathed in its heavenly scent. "Mmm, don't strawberries just *smell* of summer?" she said.

That got me thinking. "It would be lovely to put together a seasonal range for the London boutiques, and to sell at Rainbow Beauty too," I said. "You know, something very specific to us, to this place and time. That will make it stand out from the crowd more."

"What, like putting summer in a bottle?" asked Mum.

"Yeah," I said.

"Bringing Devon to London," Saff chipped in.

"Exactly. We've got to include the Strawberry Summer Moisturizer, of course," I said, picking another strawberry from the box. "That's the essence of summer."

"Yes, especially as we've still got lots of strawberry fruit extract powder and strawberry seed oil left from making the last batch," said Mum. "That way we can put in quality ingredients but keep our expenses fairly low."

"And we can make that the free gift for the person that places the order too," I said. "Apart from that, what's summery and Devony?"

"Picnics?" asked Saff.

"Yeah, but you could have those anywhere," I said.

"Devon cream teas?" suggested Mum.

I grimaced. "Nice idea, but I've had enough of cream," I said with a shudder, thinking back to the Strawberries & Cream Face Masks disaster.

"I just can't think," cried Saff dramatically. "What's Devony and summery? Cows?"

Grace sighed loudly and rolled her eyes. "You lot think you're really creative, but you're so busy with your heads in the clouds that you miss what's right in front of you...or in this case, right underneath your bums!"

Saff wrinkled her forehead. "What, my towel?"

"*The beach,* you dipstick!" I cried. "Good one, Grace!"

Suddenly, my mind went into overdrive. As Grace had said, it was right here, all around us. All the inspiration we needed.

First I came up with a shell and stone foot scrub, which uses mother-of-pearl (which I had to explain to Saff is shell) and pumice (which I had to explain to Grace is stone).

"We could use our Lime & Ginger Sea Salt Body Scrub too," Grace suggested. "We've got lots of the sea salt, so it won't cost us much to do. It's easy to make up and looks gorgeous in the chunky jars."

"Good thinking," I said. "And for the photos we could put it in a smoothie glass or something, with some cut pieces of lime on top, to get across how fresh and zesty it is."

"And let's include our Seaweed Body Mask, so then people can do a complete top-to-toe treatment at home," said Mum. "We've got plenty of seaweed powder, we'll just need more of the base ingredients."

"Good idea," said Grace approvingly.

"That won't be a problem," I said. "I can order from New Directions tomorrow and they'll be here on Tuesday." I was struck by a sudden thought. "Do you think the Strawberry Summer Moisturizer fits in with the theme now though?" I asked them.

"Well, it's great for after the beach," Mum reasoned.

"Yes, especially because strawberry seed oil is a powerful antioxidant, brilliant for repairing dry and damaged skin," Grace said.

"And strawberry fruit extract powder is great for reducing redness and improving the appearance of pores," Saff added.

I stared at them, and they looked at each other and giggled. "We do listen to you, you know," said Grace.

"We don't have any choice," said Saff, "you go *oooon* and *oooon* and *oooon*——"

"Oh my gosh, I'm in shock!" I shot back, and Grace pulled a face at me. It was nice to see her smiling again. "Okay, let's go for it then. And if anyone asks, I'll just say it's a Devon tradition to eat strawberries on the beach!"

Then we all agreed that we needed a body lotion to complete the range, but we couldn't think of any more of our current products that would fit the theme, so we decided to come up with something else completely new.

That was when we got a bit stuck though. "We've done shells and stones, and sea salt and seaweed," I said. "When you think of the beach, what else do you think of?"

"Fit lifeguards," said Saff dreamily.

"Typical! I don't think we can bottle those though," said Grace, with a grin.

"For me, it's the beautiful sunsets," Mum said. "When your dad and I were in Mustique…" And with that she launched off into a whole story about how they went on this barbecue boat and drank cocktails and ate giant prawns and watched the sun go down over the beach. It was the first time she'd talked about any memories with Dad in them since What Happened happened.

While Mum was speaking, my brain was whirring and suddenly an idea sparked. "How about a sunset-themed body lotion?" I suggested. "We could do it in a shallow, round tub with two different colours swirled together to make a sunset. We could have two scents too — how about cinnamon for red and orange for orange?"

"That sounds great," said Grace.

"Abbie, you're a genius!" cried Mum.

"I so bet you wish there was a GCSE in making up beauty products!" said Saff, making us all laugh.

"Definitely," I said, "especially if I could do it instead of Maths!"

So in the end we had five products in our range, and we'd worked out their full names. They were Strawberry Summer Face-Saving Moisturizer, Beach Feet Shell & Stone Foot Scrub, Lime & Ginger Sea Salt Body Scrub, Swept Away Seaweed Body Mask and Sunset Glow Body Butter.

"We'll need a name for the whole range too," Mum said, and of course they all looked straight at me as usual, expecting me to come up with something on the spot. And this time, amazingly, I did. "Simple," I said. "Beauty and the Beach."

"I LOVE that!" Saff squealed, and Mum and Grace agreed.

A bit later on we all went for a swim, even Saff, and our make-up ran (again!), and our hair got all salt-blown. But none of us cared one bit.

I did care a bit (okay, a lot) when we arrived back at Rainbow Beauty and found Marco there though. We stepped out of the van, all chatting about the whole London thing and our new mini-range (and looking like something left over from last Halloween), and I actually *tripped over him*.

You might not think that's possible, but if you're me, it turns out it is. I was walking backwards, talking to Saff about how we could photograph our Strawberry Summer Face-Saving Moisturizer with real strawberries in a basket of straw, the way they'd been displayed in the lay-by. Marco was sitting on the Rainbow Beauty steps with his long, gangly legs sticking out and I tripped and fell backwards right onto him.

CRINGE-ORAMA!

We both shot up really quickly and I started going

on about him being a health and safety hazard. Then finally I managed to ask, "What are you doing here?"

"Oh, nothing," he mumbled. "I was just passing so I looked to see if you were in there. Then I sat down for a minute because I was, you know, hot..." He trailed off, looking embarrassed.

"I—" I began, but then Saff stepped in and snapped, "She's got nothing to say to you, thank you very much."

Luckily Mum and Grace saw my desperate look and dragged her off up to the flat. Marco gave me an awkward smile and I tried to pat down my salt-encrusted scarecrow hairstyle, without him noticing that was what I was doing.

"So you're back," he said.

I looked down at myself, pretending to be surprised. "Yeah, wow, I guess so!" I said, trying to be funny. He just looked confused. Okay, make that trying and *failing* to be funny.

I sighed. "Yes, I got back yesterday. How was the gig? I was thinking of you the whole time. I'm so sorry I—"

"Yeah, fine," he said, cutting me off.

I waited. *Was that it?* Looked like it.

"Great. Good," I said.

He didn't seem to want to talk about it. Not with me, anyway.

"Well, erm, bye then," I said.

"Okay, bye then."

As I watched him mooch off down the road, Mum appeared in the doorway behind me. "What was all that about?" she asked.

"I don't really know," I said.

We didn't have any clients booked in until lunchtime on Monday, so we spent the morning in the kitchen, making up samples of our new foot scrub and body lotion and tweaking them to get the recipes perfect. We'd put a notice on the door of Rainbow Beauty, directing people to ring the bell for the flat if they wanted to come in or speak to someone about an appointment. I also popped down a couple of times to listen for new messages on the answerphone but, depressingly, there weren't any.

Still, at least the product development went well, and it was great to do something creative. With the Sunset Glow Body Butter, we had to fiddle about with the quantities of cocoa and shea butters and grapeseed oil so that the mixture was soft enough to make a nice swirl in the first place, but would set hard enough to *stay* in a swirl in the tubs even if you turned them upside down, and not just splidge into a splodge.

While we were experimenting, Saff suddenly opened up and started telling Mum and Grace how truly awful the audition had been (she'd just glossed over it before then). "So I've got no idea how I'm going to get famous when I don't have any amazing talents," she finished.

"You've got a talent for being a beautician," Mum pointed out.

"No, I mean a *proper* talent," Saff countered. "Something that will get me on TV."

Mum raised her eyebrows, but she managed to control herself and say, "Well, I guess that's something you're going to have to work out for yourself."

Saff looked at me and Grace. I think she was hoping we'd say, "Of course you'll be famous!" but neither of us did. She was a bit quiet after that, not her usual bubbly self at all.

"Are you going out with Maisy and Aran later?" I asked Grace, to change the subject. She'd called Maisy the night before, with encouragement from me, and Maisy had asked her to go and hang out on The Plains with them that afternoon, which is this street where everyone skateboards.

"Yeah, I might do," she said. "Let's see how this goes first."

When she went to get the packaging catalogue from downstairs, me, Mum and Saff did a kind of three-way "YAY" thing at each other. It looked like Grace was really starting to move forward and get over her fears.

When Grace came back with the catalogue, we looked at different coloured tubs for the Sunset Glow Body Butter, and eventually we settled on a red one, with a round orange sunsetty label on, which looked just right. We got the formula just right in the end too. The orange was the main scent, giving you a burst of citrus zest, with the warm spicy cinnamon coming through behind it.

For the Beach Feet scrub, we had to work out how much of the pumice and mother-of-pearl to use to give you a nice refreshing foot scrub without scrubbing your feet actually *off*. This involved all of us sitting on the side of the bath, nudging each other to move over and giggling and trying out the different blends, then washing them off with the shower hose. Luckily we decided on the perfect one (the one Mum tested) just before we got into a hysterical water fight.

I wanted them to help me sort out the leaflet design as well, so we headed downstairs to Rainbow

Beauty, because we all fancied a smoothie by then too. "Blueberry all round," said Mum, whizzing up a big batch. "It's good for your brain, and besides, we need to use them up before they go off."

We came up with a simple two-sided leaflet design, and looked in the mags on the coffee table to get ideas for style and typefaces, that kind of thing. I marked the pages of things I wanted to show Ben, who'd agreed to lay out the leaflet on his laptop.

Then we came up with some copy to introduce the Beauty and the Beach range. It read: *Sun-soaked sand, salty sea-spray, sumptuous strawberries and a magical glow at sunset. Your perfect summer beauty kit — handmade with love in Devon.*

Saff read it out in a husky M&S ad voice, and at the end she added, "*This isn't just beauty, this is Rainbow Beauty*," and I said, "Maybe that's your talent — voice-over artist!"

"No way," said Saff. "I want to be seen as well as heard!"

It was nearly time for Mum and Saff's client to arrive then. "You should get going," I told Grace. "Maisy said one o'clock, didn't she? Don't worry, I'll handle reception all afternoon, so there's no need to rush back."

Me and Saff and Mum all tried to look casual,

while psychically willing her to GO OUT! For a moment it looked like she was going to. But when she reached the doorway, she turned and said, "No, I'd better give it a miss today. I'm feeling a bit sniffly actually. I think I'll just get some more of my Maths project done, and maybe have a hot bath or something."

"A hot bath!" cried Saff. "Are you mad? It's about a gazillion degrees outside! Anyway, you don't look ill to me."

"Grace—" I began.

"Look, I just don't feel like it, okay?" she snapped. "Maybe another time." And with that she headed up to the flat.

Mum sighed. "I'd hoped she'd go for it after you talked to her," she said to me.

"I'm sure she wants to," I said. "She just needs that little extra bit of confidence."

"Hmm," said Saff. Mum and I both looked at her, but she wouldn't tell us what "Hmm" meant.

The next morning, a sunny Tuesday, we got things started at Rainbow Beauty, and then at about eleven I changed out of my pink uniform and went to meet up with Ben at the cafe. Mum gave me some money to treat him to a milkshake as a thank you for helping us out.

Soon we were tucked away in a booth, with Ben's laptop, the magazines, our layout ideas for the leaflet and a banana milkshake each in front of us. We were sitting opposite each other at first, and then I had to move round next to him because he was actually creating the leaflet on the laptop and I needed to be able to make suggestions and stuff as we went along.

"So, how was Marco's gig?" I asked as we worked.

"Great!" he said. "Really amazing! The crowd loved Headrush and hits on their website have gone up about a thousand per cent since. There's a video on YouTube and apparently the link to their demos is going round on Twitter as well."

"That's brilliant," I said. "I did ask him about it but he just said it was fine, so…"

"Yeah…" said Ben. "Summer told me about you guys splitting up, but I didn't know whether to say anything. Are you okay?"

I shrugged. "I suppose. I mean, maybe it's for the best… I guess that's what Marco must think…"

I waited. Of course, I wanted Ben to spill the beans on everything. To go, *No, he doesn't think that – we spent two hours discussing it, during which he got through three boxes of tissues and a giant Dairy Milk, and he's really gutted about it and he wants you back.*

Huh. Well, *that* just popped into my mind out of nowhere! Did I *want* him to want me back? Did I want *him* back?

But of course, what with Ben being a bloke, I didn't get any of that. Instead he just mumbled, "Yeah, bummer," and then started showing me some typefaces that were close to the ones I'd picked out from the mags.

When we'd finished, the leaflet looked A-Mazing. I couldn't help giving him a massive hug. Then he glanced at the time on his phone and said, "Oh, Marco'll be here in a minute."

I stiffened, going all red and flustered. "Oh! You didn't mention that."

"I forgot," he said. "But it's okay, isn't it? You're mates now, aren't you?"

"Yes, of course, it's cool," I stammered.

I agreed to stay for a milkshake with them but when Marco arrived he looked as awkward as I felt, so I found myself thanking Ben again and making an excuse to go.

When I got back, Saff was leaping about with happiness because her second client turned out to be

Sally, the tutor she's going to have when she starts beauty college in September (well, as long as her exam results are good enough). She'd booked under a different name as a surprise, so Saff had had no idea she was coming, and she'd been really impressed with her manicure. "I showed her my freehand nail art – you know, those little flowers I've been practising – and she loved it. She said I've got a real flair for beauty!" Saff cried, dancing round the purple sofas. "I gave her a load of our leaflets to give out."

I grinned. "Maybe that's your special talent," I told her. "You could be a famous beautician, you know, to the stars."

"Yeah, maybe!" Saff cried. "I could be flown around the world, visiting film sets and everything..."

"That's great," said Mum, popping out of a treatment room with an empty glass in her hand. "First things first, though. That loo needs a good clean, and then if you could put the towels on to wash..." She smiled sweetly at Saff and then went into the kitchenette to get her client some more water.

"It's not for ever, Cinders!" I called to Saff, and then the phone rang. "Good afternoon, Rainbow Beauty," I said in my best telephone voice. "How may I help you?"

235

"Abs? It's me," said Dad.

"Oh, hello!" I cried. "How's it going?" I spoke to him for a while, filling him in on how far we'd got with the products and leaflets. He told me he'd already got one appointment for us to pitch booked in for next Wednesday, which set my heart hammering.

"Oooh, it's really happening!" I squealed.

"Yes, love, it's really happening!" Dad repeated.

Then he spoke to Saff, because she wanted to tell him about Sally coming in. By the time she handed me the phone back, Grace had appeared, so I told her who it was and held it out to her, but she shook her head. I sighed and started to say goodbye to Dad.

"Did Grace get my letter today?" Dad asked, just as we were about to hang up.

A letter? Obviously Dad had meant it when he said he wasn't going to give up.

"Hang on," I said. "Grace, did you get Dad's letter?"

"Yes, I did," Grace snapped, "but I'm not going to read it."

I was just wondering how to tell Dad this when he said, "I heard." He sounded so downhearted, it was awful.

"Don't worry, I'm sure she'll read it soon," I told him.

But when Grace heard that, she just snorted and started folding the clean towels. Dad and I said goodbye and hung up, and I stood watching her, wondering if things were ever going to get any better between them.

Chapter Eleven

On Wednesday, Ben called in with the finished leaflet design, and we all gathered round to have a look. "All you have to do is drop the photos in when they're done," he told us.

"Oh, that's wonderful, love," said Mum. "Thank you."

"Yeah, it's fab!" cried Saff. "Thanks!" She launched herself at him and gave him a huge hug, which made him go completely red and forget what he was telling us about border widths.

"It's really good," I said, when he'd recovered a bit. "Thanks so much."

He smiled. "Glad you like it. If it's all approved

I'll get, say, twenty printed up at the print shop. You want heavyweight taupe recycled card with a matt finish, yeah?"

"Yes, please," said Grace, "and don't forget to ask for a discount."

As Ben was packing his stuff away (having promised Grace he'd get the price down if possible), he said to me, "Do you feel like hanging out?"

"I'd love to, but I'd better stay and get the product samples finished," I told him. "I rang Summer, and she's happy to do the pictures, and I need time before then to play about with packaging, see what looks nicest."

"Oh, cool, no worries," he said. "She's back tomorrow, isn't she? In time for the beach party?"

Ooooh! My ears pricked up at that! But I'd promised Summer I wouldn't say anything, so I managed to control myself and just go, "Yeah, she is."

"I suppose you two will want to hang out and catch up at the party," Ben said.

"Oh, yes!" I said. "We'll have loads to talk about." *YOU, for example!* I thought, and for a change I managed to stop myself from saying it out loud.

"So I'm guessing you won't want dates or anything," he said, and before I could reply, he

239

muttered, "Okay, well, I'll see you there then."

And with that, he left, getting a big chorus of "*Byeeeeeeeee!*" and lots of waving from his fan club, aka my mum and sisters.

Argh! He was obviously testing the water about whether to ask Summer to go to the party *as a date* and I'd totally messed it up. Whoops! I'd just have to make myself scarce on the night so they got to hang out on their own. I was sure of one thing after that conversation though: Ben liked Summer. As in, *liked* liked. Definitely.

I just knew that she had to go for it at the beach party.

And I couldn't wait to tell her so.

I got my chance the next morning when she came round to photograph the Beauty and the Beach range for our leaflets. She arrived looking even more beautiful than usual, in a pale yellow slip dress and flip-flops, which really set off her gorgeous tan. I noticed she also had a tiny slick of mascara on her top lashes, which made them even more impossibly long and lush. Once I'd got over the urge to run back upstairs to the flat immediately and put a paper bag over my head, we had a big squealy, girly hug. Mum,

Saff and Grace all said hello too and asked how her holiday was, which was nice of them and everything, but of course we really wanted them to leave us alone because we had to Talk, with a capital T.

But we didn't get a chance, not for ages anyway, because they were all helping us style the main shot of all five products together. We tried a few different things, and in the end we arranged them on some beach towels next to a punnet of real strawberries, Mum's designer sunglasses and a long, cool strawberry smoothie, dressed up with slices of lime and sprigs of mint. Summer sorted out the lighting, and Saff and I swapped the products round to see which looked best where. Once we were happy we had the best arrangement, Summer took the shots. Then Saff went off to sort out the treatment rooms, and Mum and Grace went to talk to someone who'd come in. I grabbed Summer's arm and grinned at her. "OMG, I have SO got something to tell you!" I hissed.

"You're back with Marco," she cried. "I knew it!"

"No, I'm not!" I gasped. "Why would you think that? Has he said something to you?"

Summer blinked at me. "Steady on! No, I haven't spoken to him."

"Oh. Right," I said. "No, it's something about you, and You Know Who."

She grinned. "What, me and Lord Voldemort? I always thought he was kind of fit!"

"Ha ha!" I cried, swatting at her. "Okay, so, I'm sure Ben likes you now – like, a hundred per cent sure."

Summer's eyes lit up. "Details!" she demanded.

"Yesterday when he was in here he mentioned the beach party," I told her, "and he asked whether you were going. He was saying he guessed we'd probably just want to hang out together, you know, with no dates or anything, and catch up after your holiday. Of course, being the total idiot I am, I went 'Yeah, probably', but then I realized – he was testing the water to see if he should ask you to go to the party with him! I'm SO sorry I blew it! But at least you know how he feels!"

Summer was just staring at me. "OM and double G," she gasped. "I thought he liked me, I mean, I *hoped* so, I was pretty sure, but from what you say… that's almost definite, isn't it?!"

"Definitely definite!" I cried. "And he's obviously as worried about getting turned down as you are, that's why he tried to sound me out about it first. Sorry I messed it up for you," I said again.

"Oh, don't worry about that," Summer insisted. "Just knowing how he feels is fantastic. Right, that's it – I'm asking him out at the party!"

Cue LOADS more girly squealing.

"What are you two so excited about?" asked Saff, wandering back over.

I looked at Summer but she gave a slight shake of her head. "Oh, just that these pictures are going to be great," I said.

Saff peered at me. "Are you back with Marco?" she asked.

"Why does everyone keep asking that?!" I cried.

When we were all gathered together, Summer showed us the shots of the whole range, and there were plenty of lovely ones to choose from. Then we took an individual picture of each product to put next to their descriptions. They all looked lovely, but the Sunset Glow Body Butter was best – the swirl of orange and red looked gorgeous.

Ben came along soon after (and when he said how nice Summer looked, we both had to stop ourselves from just screaming and leaping about, although Saff did give me a suspicious look – I reckon she suspected something was up). We chose the final shots and uploaded them onto the leaflet design, and just as the Beach Feet Shell & Stone Foot Scrub one was going into place, I happened to look in the direction of the door and saw a tall, black-clad figure skulking around outside it.

Marco.

As I slipped away from the group gathered round the laptop, I felt my heart pounding and my legs going all wobbly. I opened the door, making the bell jangle. He turned sharply and gave me an awkward smile. "Oh, hi."

"Hi."

I was trying to think of something, *anything*, to say, but I seemed to have forgotten the entire English language.

"I'm just waiting for Ben," he mumbled.

"Yeah, course! It's not like I thought you were here for me or anything!" I found myself shrieking, in a weird, hysterical way.

Marco gave me a funny look. I didn't blame him. "It's just that we're going for a kick-about when he's finished."

"Do you want to come in?" I asked, finding my normal voice again.

"I don't know," he said, peering through the glass. "Is Saff going to have another go at me? I mean, you *have* told her it was you who broke up with me, haven't you?"

I blinked at him. "Was it? I thought it more, you know, just sort of happened."

"Oh, right," he said. "Well, anyway, it doesn't matter now."

Cue more awkward silence. I thought about doing some kind of performance art thing, like we had to do at school, or perhaps singing a song, just to break the tension. *Control yourself, Abbie,* I warned myself. Being me, I couldn't *completely* manage that, of course – I found myself humming what I thought was a random tune and then going bright red with embarrassment when I realized it was that old song "Close To You". Yes, the one involving words about birds appearing when he's near and him being made by angels in heaven. Argh! "Are you going to the beach party?" I asked quickly, hoping he wouldn't realize what song it was. I partly hoped he wasn't – it was so cringe-makingly awful having one conversation with him, how on earth would we survive a whole party?

"Are *you*?" he countered. "Why are you asking? To avoid me? Are you going to not go if I go?" Wow, he was as edgy about me as I was about him. Did that *mean* something? Did I *want* it to mean something?

"No, it's not that, I was just making conversation,"

I insisted. "I'm going, and of course I hope you'll go too. We're mates, aren't we?"

"Yeah, mates," he mumbled, not sounding exactly happy about it. I wanted to ask him what that was supposed to mean. Didn't he even want to be mates? Or did he want to be *more* than mates? After a few more seconds of foot-shuffling silence, he said, "Look, tell Ben I'll meet him on the island. Usual place."

"But he'll only be a few minutes, why don't you come in—"

"No, you're alright," Marco insisted, walking away. Then he turned back. "See you tomorrow night, yeah?"

"Okay, sure," I said. I tried to sound casual but not cold. Just the right level of enthusiastic. I had been thinking that maybe at the beach party we could hang out together a bit, and talk, and maybe… But if he wasn't thinking that, I didn't want him to think *I* was. But if he was, I didn't want to put him *off* from thinking it. Oh God. Sometimes I wished I could just put my brain in a special tank and go on holiday without it for a week.

When I went back in, Ben was just packing up his laptop. I gave him Marco's message and we all said our goodbyes.

"See you at the party!" I said, and even though Summer and I were trying to act normal, we couldn't help bursting into girly giggles.

"What?" Ben asked.

"Oh, nothing," said Summer quickly. "I just have a feeling it's going to be a really good night, that's all."

"Especially for *you*," I told him, raising my eyebrows. Summer nudged me very hard in the ribs. Which was fair enough. But honestly, I couldn't help it, it just came out of my mouth on its own. Things do. Maybe it's a medical condition.

"Alrighty then…" said Ben, giving both of us a *Girls are mad* look. He was smiling to himself as he headed for the door though. I think maybe he'd guessed what was going on, i.e. that Summer was planning to Say Something at the party.

The postman dropped our letters in to us then, instead of putting them through the box for the flat, and there was another one from Dad to Grace. I found her in the kitchenette, washing up our mugs. I tried to give her the letter but she waved her wet hands at me. "Just put it on the side," she said. "Or in the bin. Whatever."

"Grace, remember our favourite book, from when we were little?" I asked her.

She rolled her eyes and gave me a *What are you on about?* look.

"You know, the one that Dad used to read to us? *We're Going On A Bear Hunt?*"

Grace shrugged. "Yeah, course. What about it?"

I sighed. "Well, this is the same, Grace. You have to deal with this Dad stuff. You can't go over it, you can't go under it, you've got to go through it. Like in the book."

Her whole body stiffened. "I don't want to talk about it," she said.

But I wasn't giving up. "Come up to London next Wednesday and present the products with me," I said. "I haven't booked my ticket yet. I need you, Grace. If they ask me about lead times and costings and testing certificates, I won't know what to say."

"Not if *he's* going to be there," she said firmly.

"But it's the perfect chance for you two to talk," I said.

"I don't *want* to talk to him. Ever."

I could almost *see* the castle walls go up around her. "Well, read this letter, at least," I said, putting the latest one down on the side. "That can't do any harm, can it?"

Grace just shrugged and stared at it with such a sad look on her face that I felt like my heart would burst. I wished I could wave a magic wand and make everything better for her, but I knew she had to do that for herself.

Summer gripped my hand as we rounded a bend in the cliff path and took in the scene on the beach below us. "It's beautiful!" she gasped.

She was right. I mean, wow. It was like being in a movie. A campfire blazed and fragrant smoke rose from a huge barbecue. Little tea lights in glass jars were scattered around on the low rocks and lined up along the drinks table, glowing warmly in the dusky light. Music, chatter and laughter weaved up to us and someone must have been handing out sparklers, because every few seconds a different face would leap into life under a spray of silver sparks.

"Keep walking, ladies, this is heavy," came a strained voice from behind us. That's when I remembered that Jim, one of Summer's older brothers, was carrying a huge cool box full of drinks. He'd been roped in to help, as had Jed, who I'd spotted manning the barbie with a couple of Totnes's trademark straggly-haired hippy dads.

Summer and I hurried down to the sand and I felt it cover my feet as my flip-flops sank in. For one mad moment while I'd been getting ready, I'd thought about wearing high heels. But in the end, Summer's simple look the other day had inspired me and I'd gone for a swishy knee-length turquoise dress and gemstone necklace, with the flip-flops. Saff had done my eye make-up using silver and turquoise, which looked lighter and more summery than my usual black and grey, and she'd also tousled up my hair in a free, wavy, this-didn't-take-ages-honestly style and painted little glitter stars on my nails. I don't have to tell you that Summer, of course, was Looking Amazing. This time, she was Looking Amazing in a swirly floor-length maxi-dress and loads of jangling bangles and beads.

We walked across the sand and had a chat with Jess, Bex and Rachel from our class at school. Then we got some drinks out of the cooler Jim had just put down, which turned out to be sparkling elderflower and apple (organic, of course). I spotted Declan, Tay and Chaz from Marco's band sitting near the fire on camping chairs. Tay was strumming a guitar and Chaz had swapped his drum kit for some bongos. Marco wasn't with them. Declan saw me and waved, so we went over to say hi. Someone handed us sparklers and we lit them in the fire and then danced around to the music with them, laughing.

Just as we were chatting, I felt someone come up behind me. I knew instantly it was Marco, but I pretended not to notice for ages. It was so nice, just being near him, without having to talk. Then, "Alright, mate!" said a familiar voice — Ben had arrived. So I had to turn and pretend to be surprised to find Marco standing there as well. He was wearing a striped blazer over his signature obscure band T-shirt and skinny jeans. I had to bite my lip hard, because for a moment I thought I was going to actually *say* what I was thinking. Which was *YUM*.

"Looking good, ladies," said Ben, doing his comedy smooth-guy thing.

"Not so bad yourself," said Summer, and I had to control my girly gigglyness. She was right, actually. He was wearing this really nice battered old leather jacket, which made him look older and cooler, and not so much like Mr. Nice Guy.

"I'll get us some drinks," Marco told Ben.

"I'll come with you," I said quickly, draining my bottle.

I was trying to leave Summer alone with Ben, of course. But as we wandered over to the drinks table, I realized it had looked like I wanted to be alone with Marco. My head started whirling again — did *he* think that? If so, would he be happy about it, or think I was some kind of crazy stalker, or worse, *just a mate*? I quickly told my brain to shut up and gave him a smile. "I hear there's been a lot of vibe about the band since the gig," I said.

"Yeah," he mumbled, as he rummaged in the various drinks coolers for something that wasn't made of fruit or vegetables. "The hits on our site have gone up massively, and loads of people have downloaded our demo. Oh thank God, a Coke. Do you want one?"

"Sure," I said, even though I don't usually drink sugary stuff cos it's bad for your skin.

He rummaged about and found me a can too, and then he told me all about how the gig went, and what had been happening since. Then we got talking about other stuff, like films and bands and whether raspberry cheesecake is the most delicious invention on earth (my opinion) or totally pointless when you can just have a Mars bar (honestly, *boys*!).

It was so nice just being together. It was probably only for about twenty minutes, but it felt like hours. When we got back to the group, the boys headed off to join in the volleyball and I pounced on Summer. "Well, did you Say Something, with capitals?"

She grimaced. "Not yet. I nearly did, but then… I didn't dare!"

"Summer——" I began.

"I know, I know!" she squealed. "I just want to be sure about how he feels first."

"I thought you *were* sure!" I cried.

"I was. I mean, I am. I just want to know *definitely* definitely…"

"Right, I've had enough of this," I told her sternly. "I'm taking charge here. Next time I'm alone with him I'm going to come straight out and ask him if he likes you."

"Don't you dare!" she shrieked. "Well, not unless he says something first, or it comes up naturally in the conversation, or if you're really subtle…"

"So not, 'Oi, my mate fancies you!' then," I teased.

"Oh, Abs, you'd SO better not!" she hissed.

"Leave it to me," I told her. Then we had to drop the subject because Amany and Iola from Art Club came over, and we all went to get some food and sat on a blanket on the sand, listening to Declan and Tay playing classics on their guitars while a rabble of voices joined in from all round the fire.

Soon it was too dark to play volleyball any more, so the boys came and joined us. They'd dodged the many salads and had plates loaded with ribs and home-made burgers. When they'd finished eating (i.e. about two minutes later) we all chatted for a bit, then Amany and Iola headed off, giggling, to find a rock to have a wee behind. Suddenly, Summer spotted some family friends who knew her and Marco from when they were little and dragged him off to chat to them, even though he claimed to have no idea who they were. It wasn't till she gave me a glance over her shoulder that I realized that was my cue to talk to Ben. I was just trying to work out what to say, when I realized I was shivering. It was getting too cold to just be in a slip dress and flip-flops, and all around me fleeces were appearing from nowhere and girls were pulling on jeans under their dresses. "Didn't you bring something warm?" Ben asked me.

I shook my head.

He smiled and tutted. "You city girls… Here, share with me," he said, shrugging one arm out of his jacket and putting half of it round me. I snuggled in, leaning against his shoulder, and found him still warm from the volleyball game.

"This jacket's cool, can I borrow it sometime?" I asked.

He smiled. "Sure."

"Listen, Ben, there's something I need to say," I told him. "It's about—"

I got the shock of my life then.

Because he kissed me. As in, on the lips.

Of course, I pulled back right away, and my side of the jacket flopped onto the sand. "Oh my God, what's going on?" I cried.

He stared at me in confusion. "I don't know! I just…I thought…"

"*What?*" I gasped. "You thought *what* exactly?"

He shrugged and mumbled, "Well, I don't know. I suppose just that we've been spending loads of time together, and getting on really well, and you ended it with Marco——"

"But *I* didn't…" I began, then shook my head in frustration. "Never mind, go on," I muttered.

Ben looked like he'd rather pull out his own fingernails than say anything more to me about it, but he forced the words out. "You were all giggly and cryptic with Summer when you were talking to me about the party, and just now she gave you a massive wink and dragged Marco off, and you're here with me and——" He trailed off, staring at the sand, probably wishing it would turn into the quick-sinking kind and swallow him up.

I clapped my hand over my mouth. Now I realized that when Ben had said about the beach party, he wasn't testing the water about asking Summer out – he'd been thinking of asking *me*. And when I'd said the party would be especially good for *him*, he must have thought...

"No, not *me*...I meant Summer," I said, then gasped and clapped my hand over my mouth again. Honestly, I should get it permanently taped shut.

"*Summer?*" he repeated, looking astonished. "Does Summer like me?"

"Yeah," I admitted. Well, it was too late to take it back by then. "She likes you and I thought – *we* thought – you liked her back." I dropped my head into my hands. "Oh God! What a disaster! What am I going to tell her?"

Thinking that made me automatically look round to see where she was. And then I didn't have to think about what to tell her, because I saw instantly from her face that she'd seen what had happened.

I leaped to my feet. "Oh no no no no no," I cried, leaping up and stumbling across the sand towards her.

Summer wrapped her purple fleece close to her. She wouldn't look at me.

"It wasn't what it looked like. I didn't... He kissed me, I didn't kiss him. I'd never do that to you," I gabbled. "Please say you know that."

"I know that," she mumbled.

"I'm so sorry," I said. "I didn't know he liked

256

me. Well, *of course* I didn't. I really thought he was into you." She just stared at her feet. "Summer, please, say something…" I begged. My stomach was churning and I felt like I was going to throw up all over her flip-flops.

"I think I'll head off now," she muttered. "I'm not feeling that great. I'll ask Jim to run me home."

And with that she walked off towards her brother, who was standing in the group gathered round the guitar players. "Summer, please stay…" I called, but she just kept walking. I stood there, feeling completely shocked, watching her talk to Jim, then seeing the two of them walk back up the cliff path, his arm round her, her dress swishing in the glow of the tea lights.

After a while, I turned to look for Ben, but he had gone too.

Then I searched for Marco, and I thought for a moment I'd spotted him walking away down the beach, with one of the glowing lanterns swinging from his hand. But…it couldn't be him. Because the boy I was looking at was hand in hand with a willowy girl in tight blue jeans. I recognized her as Lexi Brooks from our year. My heart started pounding and I felt dizzy and sick. It couldn't be Marco… It couldn't be…

But then the boy lifted the lantern and he and the girl hovered around it for a moment and then their faces blazed in the light of their sparklers and I saw.

The boy *was* Marco.

Watching him walk off down the beach with Lexi, turning and swirling so their sparklers danced in the air, I knew for sure that I wanted him back. And I also knew it was too late. I watched as the last little glow fizzled to nothing and I lost sight of him in the darkness.

Jim had come straight back after he'd dropped Summer home, and I had to wait for him and Jed to be ready before I could get a lift (which I'd absolutely *promised* Mum I'd do). I spent the next couple of hours wandering about, talking to different people, joining in with the singing, trying desperately to act normal but feeling in total shock inside. I wandered over to get a drink I didn't want, just for something to do, and while I was rummaging about in the cooler, someone came up beside me. I glanced up. It was Marco.

"Well, you moved on pretty quickly," I said flatly.

"I could say the same about you," he said, and gave me such a dark scowl I knew it could only mean one thing. He'd seen me and Ben kissing. Well, *thought* he'd seen that anyway. I sighed, suddenly feeling very tired, like I could just curl up on the sand and go to sleep. "*He* kissed *me*, it's not the same. I didn't kiss him back," I told him. "Anyway, even if I had, you and me aren't together so why do you even care?"

"Why do you care about me and Lexi?" he countered.

I didn't say, *Because I didn't really believe it was over. Not for good. Because I thought you still liked me. Because I thought, hoped, we'd get back together. Because I thought we had something special.* Instead, all I said was, "I *don't* care." Then I handed him my Coke. "Here, I don't want this any more," I told him. "It's no good for me."

And then I turned and walked away.

Chapter Twelve

I was completely distracted all the next day at Rainbow Beauty. It was much quieter than it should have been for a Saturday, but whenever Mum *was* busy with a client, I tried calling Summer from the phone on reception. I left messages the first couple of times, saying how I hoped she was okay and to please, *please* just ring me. And I sent four texts from the mobile, but I didn't get a reply to those either. Summer had a pedicure booked in at four with Saff and I wasn't sure whether she'd even turn up or not. We were completely empty just after three o'clock, so I spent half an hour anxiously arranging and rearranging the pedicure stuff, lining up colours I thought Summer would like and hoping, *hoping* she'd come.

It was a relief when she walked in a few minutes early, looking stunning in a pale blue tea-dress with tiny flowers on. There were only the faintest signs of tiredness and tears on her face; but they were there, if you knew to look for them, like I did. I was so nervous about seeing her, my stomach was doing flips – I didn't know if she'd be angry with me for what had happened. I wouldn't have blamed her – I felt terrible for being too dim to notice Ben liked me. But instead she just gave me a wobbly smile, and when I rushed over and swept her up in a hug, she didn't push me away.

"You do know I didn't, I mean, I would never—" I started gabbling again, as soon as we broke apart.

"Course I do," she insisted. "And I know it's not Ben's fault either. I'm the one who misread the signals. Thank goodness he doesn't know how I feel," she added, with a shudder. "At least we can just forget about it now and he'll never need to—"

I gave a small, strangled groan and she stopped talking. "Abbie?" she said. "You didn't, did you? Oh, please tell me you didn't!"

I buried my head in my hands and nodded. "I'm sorry!" I cried. "I was in shock, and it just came out."

"OMG, I can *never* face him again!" she gasped, looking like she wanted to dive behind the smoothie counter and live there permanently. To be honest, when *I* thought about seeing Ben again, I felt like joining her.

"Do you still like him?" I asked, when she'd recovered a bit from the whole HORROR of the situation.

She shrugged. "Well, I can't just switch off how I feel. But if he's not into me, I'll have to get over it."

"That's the same situation as I'm in," I told her. "With Marco, I've been feeling like, well, I hoped that maybe he might still like me and…"

She gasped. "Abs! Why didn't you tell me?!"

"I only knew for sure at the beach party," I said.

"Oooh, I knew it wasn't over between you two!" she squealed. "I'm amazed it took you this long to realize it!"

"It *is* over," I said flatly. "It's pointless even talking about it now because he's into someone else."

"Oh my gosh, who?" Summer gasped, her eyes goggling out at me.

I told her about seeing him going up the beach with Lexi, after she'd left the party.

She frowned. "Did he see you and Ben, you know…?"

"Yes," I said, cringing again just from thinking about it.

"Well, maybe he only went off with her because he thought you'd gone off with *him*," she reasoned.

"Maybe," I conceded. "But if that's why he did it, then he's even more jealous and immature and egotistical than I thought!"

"Oh, come on, Abs," Summer cried. "I'm not saying he *isn't* all those things. But he's also obviously still crazy about you, to go and do something so stupid."

A little silver fizz of happiness sparked inside me then, like one of last night's sparklers trying to light. But the sensible part of me snuffed it out. "The fact is, he thought I would do that, right in front of him, with his best mate!" I cried. "If that's what he really thinks of me, he can do one!"

Summer sighed. "Oh, come on, be reasonable — he saw it with his own eyes. At least, he thought he did."

I folded my arms. "No, I'm taking this as a warning not to get involved with him again. It is absolutely, *definitely* over between us," I declared...

...just as Ben and Marco walked in.

There was so much awkward embarrassment in the room I thought the windows might blow out, like in action movies, and we'd all go flying backwards onto the pavement. After a few seconds of agonizing silence, I started to wish that *would* happen.

Ben couldn't look at me or Summer, Summer couldn't look at Ben, Marco couldn't look at me, and I couldn't look at him or Ben. So basically there was a lot of shuffling about and pretending to be very interested in the walls and ceiling.

It was a huge relief when Mum appeared from one of the treatment rooms and came over to us. Ben pulled the printed leaflets for the London shops out of his bag and we all admired them. Then Mum's client emerged and she had to go and prepare her bill, and Saff called Summer over to talk about nail polish colours. Marco had to go and urgently fiddle with his mobile outside the door, so I was left with Ben.

"Sorry about last night," we both said at once… then grimaced. "So you——" we both began again.

"You go first," said Ben.

"Oh, I was just going to say, so you haven't fallen out with Marco over this? I mean, not that it's any of his business, not any more, but——"

"Yeah, we're solid, man," Ben said, doing his joke rude-boy voice. "I just told him the truth – that it was a stupid spur-of-the-moment thing and that it didn't mean anything. He was cool with that – after a while, anyway."

I sighed. "Ben, I'm sorry I don't feel—"

"It's fine," he cut in. "I'll get over it." He grinned and nudged me. "You're not *that* special, you know."

"Oh, thanks!" I cried. Then I said, "Anyway, what were you going to say?" because I could see how much he wanted the floor to open up and swallow him.

"Oh, just, are you and Summer okay?"

"Yeah, course. She knows I wouldn't do that to her, thank God. But, look, she's really embarrassed about you knowing she likes you, so play it down, yeah?"

"Of course," he said. "I'm a proper gent, you know. And a true mate."

I smiled at him and he smiled back. "I know," I told him. "I really do know that."

Marco knocked on the window then, and pointed to his stomach.

"Gotta head off," said Ben. "We're going for burgers. We thought we'd skip the hitting each other and go straight to the male-bonding-type thing."

"Have fun," I told him. I could see that Marco was already walking off up the road.

Ben turned just as he reached the door. "He told me nothing happened with Lexi," he said. "He didn't kiss her or anything."

"And why would I care *what* he does?" I asked, raising my eyebrows.

Ben raised his right back at me. "I'm just saying, that's all." And then he was gone.

"Come and chat while I have my nails done?" said Summer, as I wandered over to her and Saff. "What do you think of this?" she asked, waving a bottle of electric blue nail polish in my face. "Is it too jazzy for me?"

"Nah, nothing's too jazzy for you," I said. I linked arms with her and we headed into the treatment room I'd prepared.

"You know, after that disaster I think we should swear off boys altogether," she said.

"Too right," I agreed. But inside, the little silver sparkler had fizzed into life again, and written *Marco* in the air. And this time, I couldn't snuff it out.

Okay, so you know when I said that Grace just needed an extra bit of confidence to take the plunge and go out with her friends? And you know Saff went "Hmm"? She wouldn't tell us what she meant at the time, but on Monday morning, we found out.

Mum, Grace and I were sitting round the kitchen table, eating cereal, when Saff staggered in, holding up a hanger in each hand. She'd put together a complete outfit on each – a checked shirt and leggings on one side, with a cool belt and Converse, and a ruffly orange dress on the other, with gold sandals and loads of bangles hung over one of the straps.

"Grace, which one?" she asked.

Grace looked them up and down. "That dress is really short – you'll be flashing your knickers all day, but then that shirt will barely cover your bum, so you might want to swap the leggings for jeans."

Saff grinned. "Not for me, for you, you dipstick!"

"What?" cried Grace.

"You're getting a makeover," Saff announced.

"Oh no I'm not," Grace said.

"Oh yes you are," said Saff, as if they were in a pantomime. "And Abbie's helping."

"Am I?" I asked.

"Yep," she said, then turned back to Grace. "We're doing hair, clothes, make-up, nails, the works. We all think you need a confidence boost, don't we?"

Grace glared at Mum and me.

"Well, we just want you to be happy, love," Mum said sheepishly.

"And how is this supposed to help?" Grace

snapped. "A bit of mascara isn't going to magically make me feel better, is it?"

"It's working on the principle of *look good, feel good*," said Saff. "It's going to be tasteful, and reflect the real you, so don't worry."

Grace grimaced. "Well, it better do. I don't want to end up looking like a WAG."

"Don't worry, you won't, you haven't got the boobs for that," said Saff.

"Oh, thanks, I can just feel the confidence building up already," said Grace sarcastically.

"Great," said Saff. "See? Told you this was a good idea."

So, an hour later, we'd finished working our magic and Saff finally agreed to let Grace go down to Rainbow Beauty and look in the full-length mirror. She'd wanted to blindfold her before the big reveal, but Mum said that would be dangerous, what with the narrow stairs and everything, so we settled for walking her through the door backwards and then me putting my hands over her eyes.

"Ta-da!" cried Saff as I pulled them away.

For a moment Grace just stared at herself, as if she didn't even know who was looking back. We hardly recognized her ourselves. Saff had put some loose curls into her straight brown hair and clipped up the front so that it tumbled casually onto her shoulders. Grace had gone for the shirt, leggings and baseball boots combo and it really showed off the shape of her legs, which we never usually saw because she just wore baggy old jeans all the time.

I hadn't gone too mad with the make-up, because I knew it really wasn't her thing, but I'd outlined her eyes in a soft brown pencil and blended it in well for a smudgy, smoky look. Then I'd added a couple of layers of brown/black mascara which really brought out her eye colour, and a slick of tinted lip gloss. Amazingly, by the end, Grace was completely in our power and had agreed to Saff putting purple nail varnish on her as well.

"You look great!" Mum declared.

"Amazing!" I said.

"I actually look okay," Grace marvelled.

"Just okay?" cried Saff. "Come on, you look seriously cool!"

But I was pleased with "okay". For Grace to think she looked okay was a major big deal. I knew Mum thought so too, because we shared a knowing smile.

"Right then, off we go," said Saff.

"What? Where to?" cried Grace.

"You know yesterday we were talking about how we need a local publicity drive for this place, as well as doing the London stuff?" said Saff.

"So? What about it?" said Grace, looking uneasy.

"So, we're giving out Rainbow Beauty leaflets in town and telling people all about what we offer, to try and get ourselves more bookings through the week, and ideally to get fully booked for next Saturday."

Grace was horrified. "No way, I'm not doing that!" she shrieked. "You know I don't do chatting. Especially not with strangers."

"It's part of my Confidence Training Programme," said Saff. "The more you get out there and talk to people, the easier you'll find it."

Grace didn't look convinced, so I said, "It's for the business." Of course, I knew she'd do anything to try and help Rainbow Beauty survive.

"Okay, fine, but if it's hideous I'm coming back," Grace mumbled.

Mum promised her that she could manage on her own for a couple of hours and that making sure we didn't have *another* horribly quiet week was a priority. Saff and I hustled Grace out of the door before she could change her mind.

* * *

Soon, we were standing in the high street with big smiles on our faces, talking to people and handing out leaflets. Well, Saff and I were anyway. Grace was skulking about behind us, looking flustered and stressed out.

"Come on," said Saff, "you haven't even spoken to one single person yet. The next lady who walks by, you have to tell her about Rainbow Beauty."

Hearing that, Grace looked like she was going to make a run for it down the street, so I quickly said, "You *don't* have to say anything. Look, that girl in the blue coat's coming this way. Just smile and hand her a leaflet, that's all."

"And if it goes wrong, you never have to see her again, so it doesn't matter," Saff pointed out.

We didn't think Grace was going to do it. But just as the girl had almost walked right by us, she leaned forward and gave her a leaflet.

"Oh, thank you," the girl said, looking at it.

"We're a new beauty parlour," Grace gabbled. "Come and try us out sometime."

Saff and I looked at each other in surprise.

"I might do that," said the girl, then walked on.

"I did it!" cried Grace. "*And* I said something! I didn't think I would but then I just thought, *Go for it!*"

We pulled her into a huge hug. "Well done, Gracie!" I cried.

"Right, you've got to do two more now," said Saff, "to really get used to it."

I thought Grace would say *No, one is enough, thank you,* but she rose to the challenge and talked to two ladies, one straight after the other.

And then I spotted the boy looking our way, talking to his mate.

Saff noticed too. "Hey, look, he's SO checking me out," she said, automatically flicking her hair and pouting. "Abs, don't stare!" she hissed, so I turned away and then glanced back at him as casually as I could.

"Actually, he's looking at Grace," I told her.

"Me?!" Grace cried.

"Yeah, you!" I said, grinning at her.

She gave him a quick glance. "But I don't even know him. He's not from our school, I don't think."

"Go and talk to him!" squealed Saff. "Go on! This can be your next challenge."

Grace looked like she was thinking of bolting again. "But what would I say?" she cried. "He's hardly going to be interested in a massage and leg wax, is he?"

"No, but his mum might be," I said, "or ask if he has a sister."

"Or a girlfriend," Saff added, "and if he says no, get in there!" And before Grace could argue, she virtually shoved her across the pavement.

Grace kept glancing back at Saff, looking like she wanted to kill her, but she did go up to the boy and chat for a moment. Then she handed him a leaflet and hurried away. The boy walked off down the hill with his mate, but he kept looking back at Grace and smiling.

Saff and I just about managed to control ourselves until they'd gone into the gaming shop, and then we exploded into girly screams. "I can't believe you did that!" I shrieked. "Major respect!"

Grace was blushing and grinning, her face all lit up. I don't think she could believe it either.

"You should have got his number," said Saff.

"Nah," said Grace. "It was just a bit of fun." She sighed and shook her head. "I still can't believe I did that!"

Then the smile suddenly dropped off her face and Saff and I followed her gaze to a group of girls coming down the street.

"Oh no, it's Richanne and her lot from school," Grace hissed, looking panicked. "I don't want them to see me."

That got Saff's back up. "What, is she bullying

you?" she said. "Because if she is, I'll have a word—"

"Oh no, nothing like that," Grace said quickly. "It's just, the way they look at me, I know they think I'm such a geek. And when I go by them at school I'm sure they're whispering about me. I just don't want them to notice me, that's all." She glanced behind us, sizing up whether the New Age shop or the veggie cafe would be the best place to hide in.

"But that's exactly why you have to give them leaflets," said Saff.

"What?!" gasped Grace. "No way!"

"Yes way," Saff insisted. "Go and do it. You've done brilliantly this morning. This is the ultimate challenge. They make you really nervous, yeah? So face your fears – talk to them."

"And we're here for you," I added. "If they *are* bitchy, we'll step right in, won't we, Saff?"

My sister nodded. "Course."

Richanne and her two mates were about to walk right past us. Grace steeled herself. "Hi!" she said brightly. "We've just opened a new beauty parlour down on The Parade." She handed them each a leaflet. "We do loads of great treatments, facials, massages—"

"Do you do nails?" one of the girls asked.

"Yes," said Grace. "Luxury manicures with hand treatment, file and polish."

"I might come. Look at the state of mine," the girl said, holding her nails up for Grace to see.

"You could all come in together," Grace suggested. "You get a free smoothie or fresh juice each and there are gorgeous beauty products to buy, all handmade too."

"Do you do acrylics?" asked Richanne, looking up from the leaflet.

Grace looked at Saff. "Yes, and gel nails, nail tattoos and nail art," Saff said.

"Cool," said Richanne. She was peering at Grace. "You're in our year, aren't you? You're that new girl."

"Yeah," said Grace.

"I thought I'd seen you around," said one of Richanne's mates.

"Alright?" said the other.

"Alright," said Grace, looking a bit bewildered.

"Thanks for this," said Richanne. "We might be in soon, then."

We all said bye and they went off down the street.

"Wow, well done!" I told Grace.

"I don't think she's got it in for you," said Saff. "She hardly even knew who you were!"

"I know," said Grace in surprise.

"If you'd just given them a smile or chatted a bit at school, I bet they'd have been friendly," I said.

"Knowing you, you probably just blanked them out of nerves, and so they didn't bother with you either," Saff pointed out.

"Hmm," said Grace. I could almost see the cogs turning in her head.

"Grace Green, you have officially passed my Confidence Training Programme, Level One, anyway," Saff announced then, with a flourish.

Grace smiled wryly. "Thanks," she said. "Do I get a medal or something?"

"No, but you do get a reward," said Saff, looking all smug and mysterious again. She glanced at her watch. "You're meeting Maisy and Aran on The Plains to hang out and then you're off to the cinema." She held out a crumpled tenner. "This is from Mum. She said to get yourself a sandwich too."

Grace just gaped at her. "How did you get in touch with Maisy and Aran?"

"Facebook," said Saff, looking very pleased with herself. "Aran's quite fit, isn't he? If you're into Geek Chic. Tell Maisy I'm here anytime she wants a makeover, though. That fringe doesn't do anything for her. Now, come on, you don't want to be late!"

"You're a nightmare!" Grace cried. "Thanks, though. And you, Abs."

I smiled at her and Saff said, "No worries." Then she linked arms with me on one side and Grace on the other. We set off down the hill and Grace did a little skip to get her steps in time with ours, like we always used to. Left, right, left, right, left, right.

We left Grace at The Plains with her mates and when we got back to Rainbow Beauty, I found another letter from Dad amongst the post. Clearly he wasn't giving up on Grace. As I put it on the kitchen table, I just hoped that Grace hadn't completely given up on *him*.

When Saff and I got down to Rainbow Beauty the next morning, Grace was already there, setting up for Mum's first client, who'd booked a massage and body treatment package. Dad's letter had gone from the table, but I didn't say anything to her about it. I didn't want to risk upsetting her just when she was starting to open up.

"Hiya. Did you have a good time yesterday?" Saff asked her. She'd been out with Emily when Grace had got back the evening before. Grace admitted that she had, and told her about the film and how funny

Aran was on The Plains, trying to show her and Maisy how to skateboard when he hardly had any idea himself. "Thanks for making me come out of my shell," she said then. "I just needed someone to, you know, push me a bit."

Then she turned to me. "And, Abs, I've been thinking about what you said, about London. I've decided to come with you tomorrow."

"Wow! That's brilliant!" I said. "I'll book our tickets then. I've been holding off, hoping you'd change your mind."

"And can you show me how to do that eye make-up you put on me yesterday?" Grace asked then. "I don't want to wear it all the time, but it would be good to know how to do it, so I've got the choice."

"Sure," I told her. When she went to talk to Mum in the kitchenette, I said, "Well done, Saff, you really helped her."

Saff beamed at me. "I'm glad you think so," she said, "because you're next on my fix-it list."

"Erm, what?!" I cried.

Saff just did her smug mysterious look, and said, "It's nearly ten, he'll be here any minute."

"He?!" I shrieked. "You mean Marco?"

Saff raised her eyebrows. "*Oh* yes."

"Oh *no!*" I screeched. "Saff, what have you done?"

Grace sprang back over, looking gleeful. "You're getting Saffed too, are you?" she cried. "Fab!"

"No, you don't understand, Marco doesn't even *like* me any more," I gabbled. "He went down the beach with someone else at the party… Saff, if you've forced him into coming here today… Oh my God, I'm going to look like some kind of crazy stalker!"

Saff just did The Look again and said, "Wait and see."

I was completely torn – wishing and hoping Marco wouldn't come, because it would obviously be *hideously* embarrassing, while also hoping he would. "You could have warned me," I cried. "I've only got a tiny bit of make-up on and my hair's all over the place."

The bell above the door jangled as Marco walked in. Luckily the urge to run up and hug him was cancelled out by the desire to throw myself behind the smoothie counter and hide, so I managed to stay still. "Saff—" I began.

"Shut up and smile," she hissed at me, then swished over to greet Marco. "Thank you for coming, it's so kind of you!" she gushed. "I was just explaining to Abbie that I'm developing a new unisex luxury hand and nail package and you've agreed to be my guinea pig. Please do follow me to the treatment room, everything's ready." She grabbed Marco's arm and dragged him across the reception area, winking at me unsubtly on the way. "And while you're here you could buy something nice for your new girlfriend," she added loudly.

"I don't have a new girlfriend," said Marco, looking completely bewildered.

Saff turned round to me, raised her eyebrows and gave me a big double thumbs up. OMG, CRINGE! My face went so burning hot I had to drop down behind the reception desk and pretend to be looking for something. "Oh, here's my pen!" I exclaimed. *And here's my dignity, crumpled up on the floor next to it,* I thought.

"Oh, Abbie, I forgot fresh towels, could you bring some in for me, please?" Saff said in her serene therapist voice. Then she virtually shoved Marco into the treatment room and closed the door.

"What on earth is she playing at?" I hissed at Grace.

Grace grinned at me, her eyes gleaming. "I don't know. But I can't wait to find out!"

I muttered something about wishing I was an only child and marched off to get the towels. I took them to the treatment room and Saff came out to meet me, closing the door behind her.

I tried to hand her the towels but she wouldn't take them. "I've just remembered, I've got to go out," she said. "You'll have to do the treatment. All the stuff is set out for you. It's a hand spa, exfoliate and massage, cuticle nourish and moisturizer, and nail tidy, of course. No need to thank me!"

She beamed at me and swished off towards the door. *Thank her?* I felt like strangling her. "But I can't go in there, with him!" I hissed. "We're barely talking! And anyway, I don't know how to do all that stuff you just said!"

"Course you do, you'll be fine. Enjoy," said Saff, and with a jangling of the bell above the door, she was gone.

Grace snorted with laughter from behind the reception desk and I glared at her.

Of course, I'd planned to go into the room and tell Marco Saff had set us up. But when I walked in and our eyes met, I found myself just saying "Hi".

"Hi," he said.

Unusually for a nail treatment, Saff had lit all the candles, the scent of bergamot from the oil burner filled the air and soft music played. Marco was sitting on a chair, still looking bewildered, with the little manicure table set up in front of him. "Erm, Saff's had to go off somewhere and she wants me to do your hands instead," I said then. "Sorry about this, it's completely embarrassing."

I expected him to make some excuse to leave, but instead he said, "That's okay."

"Oh! Is it?" I asked.

He shrugged. "Sure."

"Oh, right." I hadn't imagined actually having to *do* the treatment. I'd just thought he'd leave, and then I'd wait till Saff got back, and then I'd kill her dead. But, hey, maybe I *could* pull this off. Surely I'd had enough luxury hand treatments to know what to do? I started the little spa thing bubbling and put the special mineral salts in. "Here, put your hands in, like this," I said, taking his hands and placing them into the bubbly water. I felt that familiar spark jump between us as I touched him, and I had to actually force myself to let go.

"Oh, weird!" he said, wiggling his fingers in the water.

We didn't talk much after that, apart from about the treatment. For a start, I had to concentrate so I didn't muck it up and somehow disable him from playing the guitar ever again. And anyway, it was nice, just being together without any pressure or arguments. I looked up in the middle of doing the exfoliating bit and found him gazing at me. He just smiled and I smiled back, and then I told him off about the state of his cuticles.

Best of all was the hand massage. It was supposed to only take ten minutes, but I'm sure I spent way longer than that. His nails were quite tidy for a boy – short and neat on his left hand and longer on his right, for picking guitar strings, so I hardly had to do anything with the file. At the end, I blew away a few bits of nail dust and said, "There you go, all finished."

"Is it?" he said. "What a shame." He gave me an intense look, like he wasn't just talking about the treatment. I hoped he wasn't, anyway. But I didn't say anything back. I didn't want to spoil the moment with my stupid big mouth, in case he *did* only mean his nails.

Then I took him out to reception and got him to write down what he thought of the different bits of the treatment, to try and make it look like a completely professional thing (luckily Grace wasn't around, so she couldn't go all giggly and embarrass me even more). Then I said "Thanks for coming" and he said "No worries" and that was it.

The second he left, Grace and Saff came springing out of the kitchenette.

"So, how did it go?" Grace asked.

"Are you going to kiss me or kill me?" asked Saff, with a wicked grin.

I narrowed my eyes at her and said, "I haven't decided yet."

Chapter
Thirteen

On Wednesday, Grace and I got into Victoria Coach Station at about five o'clock and fought our way through the evening rush hour on the boiling hot, packed-out Tube to get to Dad's. He'd offered to meet us at the station but I'd said we'd be okay because I knew my way to his place now. As well as my backpack with my overnight stuff slung over my shoulder, I was carrying a nice smart leather bag of Mum's with the things for our pitch in.

Dad had told me on the phone that he'd fixed up six appointments for us, so I'd brought ten of the free gift Strawberry Summer Face-Saving Moisturizers in their lovely rosebud packaging with me. I hoped that we'd get an order from every single shop, and that we might even find some other ones to just pop into as well. The bag also contained samples of all five products in our Beauty and the Beach range, as well as the gorgeous leaflets we'd created, and an information file containing the cosmetic testing certificates and ingredients lists, in case anyone asked to see it. I'd checked and double-checked that I had everything, and then got Grace to check too. Then finally, Mum and Saff had given us the biggest hugs and wished us luck, and we'd headed off to get the coach.

Grace and I went through the ticket barriers at the Tube station and spilled out into the fresh air. Looking at it now, Dad's new area didn't seem as dodgy as I'd remembered. The lovely, leafy trees lining the road really stood out against the clear blue sky and I didn't notice the graffiti so much. There was a lively, just-finished-work atmosphere and we passed a pub with every outside table taken and people standing on the pavement. A woman with a cute toddler in a buggy passed us and smiled, and I smiled back. Grace wasn't smiling though. She was shuffling along as slowly as possible, like she was on the way to the dentist or something.

"It'll be okay, you know," I told her, as we turned into Dad's road.

"I hope so," said Grace.

When we got there, Dad welcomed us in with smiles and hugs (I hugged him back, Grace just stood there) but I could tell he was nervous.

"The place still looks nice," I said, as we stepped into the main room. Sunlight streamed through the huge sash window onto the sitting area, which now had a cleared, polished coffee table and clean throws and cushions hiding the old sofas.

"Yes, I've been keeping it tidy after all your and Saff's hard work," Dad told me.

Grace hadn't said anything yet. Not even hello. She was just staring around her, taking everything in. I guess, even though the place looked the best it could now, it was still tiny, with scrappy mismatched furniture and grotty yellow curtains. And I'm sure it was a shock to see Dad's bed in the corner too — to realize that this was *it*.

"I'll put the kettle on," I said, heading for the kitchenette. "And call Mum, tell her we got here okay."

I knew Grace was giving me *Don't go*-type looks, but I went anyway. I felt like they'd never get anywhere unless I gave them a bit of space.

"Did you get my letters?" I heard Dad ask.

"Yes," Grace mumbled.

"Did you read them?"

Pause. "Yes," Grace admitted.

I couldn't hear any more because the kettle was making too much noise, and then because I was ringing Mum. We only spoke for a minute or two, to save credit – I just said we were there safely and she said good luck to us again. Then I purposefully took ages making the tea. When I walked back into the main room, clutching two mugs in one hand, the third in the other, and with a packet of biscuits I'd found in the cupboard under my arm, I found Dad and Grace sitting at the little table. Dad had turned that corner of the room into a little office, and the table was covered in neat stacks of paper.

"I'm going to brief Dad on the products, prices and ingredients, and go through the testing certificates," Grace said. "We all need to know the information ready for tomorrow. It won't look very professional if we're umming and ahhing."

"Good idea," I said. I put their mugs down on the table and went over to flop on the sofa. "I'll listen in," I said. "I could do with a recap on that stuff too."

"No, you're first up," Grace told me. "You're going to be presenting the products, so let's pretend Dad's the customer and you do your pitch and then we can give you some feedback."

"Grace, you really have to stop watching *The Apprentice*," I grumbled. "Can't I even have my tea first?"

"Nope," said Grace.

Usually I would have just curled up on the sofa anyway, but I knew that the real reason she was insisting I got involved was because she wasn't ready to just talk to Dad on his own. So I stood up, got the products out and arranged them nicely on the coffee table. Then I shook hands with Dad. "Thank you very much for taking the time to see us," I said. "I'm Abbie Green and this is Grace, my sister, and Alastair, my father..." I went through the whole pitch, showing each product, talking about the ingredients and their properties, and emphasizing how they were all natural, handmade, and organic where possible. I made sure Dad smelled the gorgeous zing of the lime and ginger in the sea salt body scrub and felt how smooth and silky the seaweed body mask was. I demonstrated a little of the foot scrub on his hand, lathering it up with a bit of bottled water and wiping it off with a baby wipe (also from the bag). And I encouraged him to sample the moisturizer and body butter. All the time, Grace was watching like a hawk, and scribbling down notes.

"So, how did I do?" I asked her.

"Very impressive," she said. "But, Dad, you did just go 'Oh lovely, oh wonderful' all the time. We do need to be prepared for some tough questions. Here, *I'll* be the customer now. Abbie, demonstrate the range again."

"Grace!" I cried. "My tea's half cold as it is! Can't I at least just—"

"No, you can't," she said sternly. "We have to be completely prepared for tomorrow. Everything hangs on this – the future of our business, our home, our *life*. Everything."

Dad looked very awkward when he heard that. "Girls, I just wish I could make everything alright," he gabbled, before Grace could cut in with any more business-speak and stop him. "I'm so sorry about everything that's happened. I really am."

Grace looked rocked to the core for a moment, and I was worried she'd bolt for the door. But instead she said, "There's no point dwelling on the past."

"I just wish there was more I could do to help..." Dad muttered.

"Be as prepared as possible for tomorrow," said Grace. "That's all you *can* do. Now, Abbie..." She flipped to a new page in her notebook. "Why should I order your moisturizer for my shop when I already stock a natural, completely organic one?"

Before I launched into my answer about how ours is packed with all the skin-saving properties of our strawberry ingredients, I caught Dad's eye and gave him a quick smile. He'd tried to talk, to *really* talk to Grace and she hadn't run away. That was something at least. I wanted him to know that just because they hadn't hugged and cried and all that, he'd still got somewhere. He gave me a small smile back and I knew he understood.

Grace interrogated me about the quality of ingredients and the products' shelf lives and order turnaround. She even dropped the Sunset Glow Body Butter on the floor to test the strength of the packaging (luckily, it passed). It was like playing some kind of crazy verbal tennis game, as she fired question after question at me, and I shot answers back, making sure to stay detailed and to the point, while keeping a smile on my face the whole time.

I really put my foot down after that though, about the tea, I mean. I went to make a new cup and then sank into the sofa. Grace sat at the table and went through the information file with Dad and then fired loads of questions at him too, which he batted back expertly.

"You *are* quite good at this," she said, grudgingly impressed.

"Well, I did used to *be* in sales and marketing," Dad pointed out, with a cheeky grin.

"You ran events," said Grace flatly.

"I ran my own events company," Dad corrected. "I marketed my business, I pitched to clients, I secured orders and I delivered the event, i.e. the product. That's what we're doing now."

I froze for a moment. I really thought Grace would say something like, *No, it's what me, Mum, Saff and Abbie are doing now. You're just helping.* But to my surprise, she didn't. Instead she just said, "Let's look at the figures next."

Leaning over their notes at the table, making calculations and agreeing on final trade and recommended retail prices, Grace completely forgot to be distant and cold with Dad. "No, hang on," she was saying, frowning at the calculator, "I said we were looking at a 45% margin on the Strawberry Summer Moisturizer, not 34%, so long as the strawberry seed oil is kept to 0.5%."

They could have been sitting at our kitchen table in the Ealing house before any of this happened, going over his latest event or her homework. They were like two peas in a pod – and I guessed that was why what Dad did hurt Grace so much.

"Oh yeah," said Dad, tapping in the figures again.

"So that gives us £20.25 profit on each order of five units. That's not enough, Grace, I think we need to charge £11 per unit instead of £9 — that gives us £30.25 profit per five-unit order. That's more like it."

Grace frowned. "That means setting the recommended retail price at £15.99, or the shops won't make enough profit. I'm not sure people will pay that for a 100ml cream," she said. "Abbie, what do you think?"

I wasn't sure either, so I phoned Mum.

"She's sure they will," I told Dad and Grace when I'd rung off. "Only she says to round up to £16 because 99ps look common on this sort of thing."

Dad snorted with laughter. "All credit to her, she's right," he said. "£16 it is."

After another hour they'd finalized the price lists and Grace and I had written out ten nice copies in the hand lettering we used for the product labels (Dad's scrawl wouldn't have done at all). By the time we'd finished, it was nearly eight o'clock. My head was spinning and my stomach was rumbling.

"Come on, girls, I'm taking you out on the town," said Dad. Grace and I glanced at each other and luckily, she smiled. That was the phrase he always used when we were about to go out somewhere. It used to mean smart restaurants, but that night it was fish and chips, eaten at one of the little tables in the chippy.

"Well, it's not exactly the Savoy," mumbled Grace, banging the bottom of a ketchup bottle.

"What do you mean?" Dad teased. "You've got actual plates, haven't you? That's posh!"

Grace pulled a face at him.

"Er, a gherkin! Why do they *do* that?" I cried with a shudder, picking it up off my plate with my fingertips.

"I'll have it," Grace and Dad said together. Then they smiled at each other, and suddenly sitting in that chippy together was better than any posh restaurant.

"Oh, I really hope it goes well tomorrow," I said. I'd been feeling more and more nervous the closer we got to the pitches, and now the butterflies in my stomach were putting me off my chips.

"Don't worry," said Grace, "we're completely prepared. It'll be fine."

"Yeah, and with your enthusiasm and passion, you're our secret weapon," Dad told me.

But later, sharing Dad's bed with Grace as he snored away on the sofa, I found I couldn't sleep. I kept checking my phone and seeing the time get later and later, while thinking of all the ways that our pitches could go wrong the next day. I finally fell asleep about three o'clock in the morning, with the fear whizzing round my head that, rather than our secret weapon, I might be our secret disaster waiting to happen.

When Grace and I woke early on Thursday morning, Dad was already up. He'd put on his one smart suit – he said the bailiffs had taken the rest but he'd been wearing this one and they hadn't quite been horrible enough to leave him in his underpants. As he reached across me for milk in the kitchenette, I was taken by surprise by the smell of his shaving foam, and the clink of his cufflinks. It took me right back – that was how it used to be every morning, as he reached across for the juice or the toast rack. It made me so sad suddenly, for everything we'd lost. Combined with how nervous I was about the day ahead, I thought I might explode. I couldn't eat anything at all, and I noticed Grace didn't either, until Dad persuaded us to force down a bowl of cereal each, saying that Mum would kill him if he let us go out without some kind of breakfast.

Luckily I had the Beauty and the Beach range to help me pull myself together (I wanted the samples to look a bit used anyway, so the first shop didn't realize they *were* the first). I used the body and foot scrubs in the shower to really wake up my skin and then put on the Sunset Glow Body Butter and Strawberry Moisturizer when I'd dried off. Luckily, the Rainbow Beauty magic worked once again and I felt like I'd just been on the beach, refreshed by the sea and filled with sunshine.

I'd put on a nice blue top, with smart white trousers and sandals, and Grace looked great in a blazer and pencil skirt. As I checked and double-checked everything was in the bag, Dad gave his shoes a final shine, then wiped off a bit of shaving foam that Grace had spotted behind his ear. Saff's GCSE results were due that day, so we all texted her good luck. Then, "Ready to bring Rainbow Beauty to the masses?" Dad asked.

"Ready!" Grace and I said together, and we all strode out of the flat, buzzing with nerves and excitement.

But the excitement part didn't last long, unfortunately. The first pitch was awful, and the second was worse. At the first shop, the one I'd been into with Em and Zo on Kensington High Street, the girl didn't even know we'd made an appointment. Worse, she said the buying was down to her boss and that he'd been called away suddenly and wouldn't be back until the next day. We all kept smiling, and showed her the products anyway, but it was so disappointing, knowing that she wouldn't order anything.

At the second one, the manager welcomed us in, but then when I started the pitch she just seemed really distracted, and she kept going off to talk to her staff or deal with customers. It really threw me and I ended up rushing it, and forgetting half the things I was supposed to say. When I'd finished, she said that while she thought the products were very nice, they already had a couple of natural, organic ranges and she didn't have room for another. Luckily Dad and I managed to say "Thank you for your time" politely and hustle Grace out of the shop before she could shout "Well, why did you invite us to pitch then?!" (which is what she did as soon as we were back out on the street).

As we set off for the next appointment, which was a few streets' walk away, it felt as if all our confidence had evaporated. Grace was still angry and brooding over the rudeness of the last woman we'd seen, and Dad was going over and over what had happened at the first place, saying how keen the manager had been on the phone, and if only he hadn't been called away...

"Right," I told them sternly. "We need to pick ourselves up and focus on the next appointment."

"Well, if they're all like that—" Grace began.

"You can't just quit after a couple of knock-backs!" I cried. "What would Lord Sugar say?"

Grace didn't reply, but she perked up at the mention of her idol.

"We are going back with a full order book," I told them sternly. "We've worked too hard not to, and besides, what will we say to Mum if we don't?"

Dad actually looked *scared* then and he seemed much more determined after that.

I don't know if it was my little pep talk, or if we were just lucky with the next appointment (probably both), but things started to look up. We were right on time to meet Caroline, the owner/manager of Tiger Eyes, a beautiful shop on Kensington Church Street. She had lots of gorgeous natural brands already and I found myself worrying that she'd say the same as the last lady. But I pushed those thoughts aside and got on with my pitch, making it as lively and interesting as I could.

Caroline asked a lot of questions and made loads of positive comments while she was trying the range. "I love your ideas, and the quality of the products is excellent," she said when I'd finished. I couldn't help grinning at Dad and Grace — I was sure we had an order in the bag. "But that's not enough," she added, to my surprise. "I have a business to run, so convince me."

So then it was down to Dad and Grace to show her that she could make a good profit for not too much of an outlay. They did an amazing job, explaining the figures and reassuring her that although we were a small business, there wouldn't be any delay if she needed to order more stock. "In fact, if you order now, we can guarantee you delivery of the products on Monday," said Dad.

My eyebrows shot right up then. *Monday?* What would Mum say to that? But I kept smiling. We had to get the order, we just had to.

"I'll take five of everything," said Caroline. "That qualifies me for the free gift, doesn't it?"

"It certainly does," said Dad.

Grace and I managed to stop ourselves from jumping up and down and going "YES!" but we couldn't get the huge grins off our faces. Grace wrote the order in our book, along with Caroline's details. We all said goodbye really professionally, shaking her hand and everything, but then, when we got round the corner, we did do the jumping-up-and-down-going-*YES!* Not just me and Grace — Dad as well.

We were on a roll after that. At the next shop, the girl said sorry but she was too busy to look at the products after all, but then Dad mentioned the order from Caroline at Tiger Eyes and that got her interested. She tried them out, and loved them, and then got her manager to come downstairs and have a look. She was impressed too and we got another order!

We came out and didn't even make it round the corner this time before we started high-fiving and whooping and cheering.

When we'd calmed down a bit, Dad said, "I really hope this is the start of something." He was looking right at Grace and I knew he wasn't talking about the London orders.

"Me too," said Grace.

"Oh, I'm so glad you two are working things out!" I exclaimed. I was so happy and buzzed-up I couldn't help myself. Dad gave me a smile, but of course Grace freaked out. "Right, come on then," she said, "let's stop off in that cafe before you two go completely Emo on me." She turned to Dad. "You can buy me a coffee and a panini."

"I'd be honoured," he said. I could see how pleased he was, after the Maltesers incident and everything.

We got our coffees and our number and when we found a table, Grace popped to the loo.

"Thanks for getting her here," said Dad, taking a sip of his cappuccino.

"That's okay," I said. "Thanks for not giving up on her."

Dad looked horrified. "I would never have done that! However long it took. Even if Grace never spoke to me again, I'd still have kept trying. I left your mum, not you three."

"I know," I told him. "I know that now." I paused. "Dad, can I ask you something?"

"Sure, go ahead," he said.

"Why are boys such idiots?"

Dad almost spat out his coffee. "What's brought this on?" he asked.

I explained about what had happened with Ben at the party (skating over the kissing bit, obviously – it was my *dad*, after all!). Then I said about how Marco had seen us (and obviously thought I'd just *do* that to him, with his best mate) and about how he instantly went off with some other girl. "He's such an immature idiot!" I finished.

Dad sighed. "Welcome to male bravado," he said.

"What?" I asked, feeling bewildered.

"He was feeling hurt and rejected by you, so he

went off with someone else to try and make it look like he didn't care," Dad said. "It's called *male bravado*. All of us have it. And it stuffs things up for us every time."

"Oh," I said. "Dad, if you know all this, then how did you still manage to mess up so badly with Mum?"

"Perhaps it's only now that I'm getting wise to what an idiot I've been," he said.

"About time," said Grace, sliding into the booth next to him. But she was smiling. And then our paninis arrived, hot and yummy and oozing with cheese.

We had three more appointments left after our break. We checked each other for strings of mozzarella or panini crumbs, Dad and I popped to the loos, and then we all went to get on the bus to Chelsea. As we were getting off, there was a gabbled call from Saff saying she'd got good enough GCSE results to get on her beauty course at college – just. I went mad jumping up and down screaming, and when she heard, Grace joined in. Dad took the phone and told Saff how proud he was. When he hung up he had to wipe away a couple of tears and pull himself together before we went into the next shop.

The manager in that place was very nice, but after a quick look, she said the products weren't right for them. As we strode down the pavement to the next appointment, I realized that, this time, getting the brush-off hadn't fazed us at all. If anything, it had just made us more determined to get the next order.

So at Pure Beauty we smiled and talked and sold our hearts out and, excitingly, the manager ordered ten of each unit! We couldn't believe it and we were so happy we ended up giving both her and her assistant free gift moisturizers. When we got outside, I thought Grace might say it was giving too much away, but in fact she agreed with Dad that it was good PR, and they had ordered a huge amount, after all. As with the other two orders, Dad promised the products for Monday, which I could tell had impressed them even more.

Our last stop was a lovely little vintage-looking shop off the King's Road. I thought it looked perfect for our products and I was right, because the manager, Lissa, ordered eight of the body butter and sea salt scrub, and five each of the other products. As Grace wrote up the order, I didn't think things could get any better – and then they did! Lissa said she'd call her other store and arrange for them to see us too, if we had time.

Well, it was a massive rush because we had to get back to Victoria for the coach, but of course we said yes! We really did feel like we were in *The Apprentice* then, leaping onto a bus and then running down the road to get to the other shop as quickly as we could. The second shop was bigger, and because we'd been recommended, we got a warm welcome and our first offer of a cup of tea all day. The manager, Massimo, was really keen on the products, and he said he'd try the two scrubs in the men's section too, as well as the women's. We couldn't believe it when he said he'd take twelve of each of those, and ten of everything else. I really had to stop myself from hugging him!

I'd known we were running late for the coach, but it was only when we were back on the pavement that we realized exactly *how* late. There was no time to get our overnight stuff from Dad's, or wait for a bus – instead he just leaped into the road and flagged down a taxi, gave the driver what was probably his last tenner in the world and bundled us in.

I pulled down the window. "Bye, Dad! See you soon!" I called.

Grace squished up next to me, leaned out and waved.

"Bye, girls! I love you!" Dad called, running alongside the taxi.

"I love you too!" I cried.

Then, just as we were pulling off into the stream of traffic, Grace called out, "I love you too, too!"

We waved and waved, and Dad waved back. He looked like a different man to the one I'd discovered in the grimy bedsit. Now he seemed so determined, standing tall, suited and booted and shaved and cufflinked. He looked like Dad again, except maybe a little bit older. And definitely a little bit wiser. And, as he blew us kisses, he looked so proud of us too.

Grace and I didn't talk much on the way back — we were too tired and there was so much going on in our heads. On the coach with Saff I'd had six hours of fashion and beauty tips, celebrity gossip, and being read quizzes and star signs out of magazines, which is great, most of the time. But that's the nice thing about Grace, you can be quiet with her. So we shared my iPod, which I'd put in the smart pitch bag along with the cheap phone, luckily (and my make-up bag, of course!). Grace leaned on the window and I leaned on Grace. I closed my eyes, listened to Adele and thought back to the pitches, and the orders we'd got and, most of all, to what Dad had said about Marco.

Chapter Fourteen

Grace and I had got back to Totnes at half ten and found Mum and Saff waiting for us at the coach stop. I'd called them from the coach and told them we'd got 135 orders, so we all had a big squealy hug about that, and about Saff's results too. When we got into Liam's van, which Mum had borrowed, she turned the radio up and we all bobbed about and joined in with the song that was on.

She nearly crashed when I mentioned that Dad had promised the orders by Monday though. "But we'll be busy at Rainbow Beauty all day Saturday," she cried. "I was about to tell you – your leaflet drive really paid off, and Saff's tutor's been spreading the word. We've been busier over the last couple of days and we're almost fully booked for Saturday. *And* we'll have to get the stuff up there on Sunday somehow. That only gives us tomorrow to make the whole lot…"

"And packaging and labelling, that always takes ages," added Saff unhelpfully.

So that explained why, first thing on Friday morning, we were all in the kitchen (including Summer and Emily) in our aprons and hairnets, ready to start. Mum had taken the van keys back to Liam on Thursday night and had a minor panic attack on his doorstep about how much there was to do. He'd rung around and found a mate of his who was working in London on Saturday anyway, and he agreed to drop the products off at Dad's. She was so lucky to have Liam as a friend – we all were.

So, anyway, we got started on the body and foot scrubs, but even though they were the quickest to put together, they were taking much longer than we'd thought because we were making such big quantities. Soon it was getting near to ten o'clock and one of us would have to go and get Rainbow Beauty opened up and ready for Mum's first client, who was due at half past.

"We're never going to get all this done in time,"

Mum groaned. "Abbie, you'll have to call in the boys too."

Well, hearing that, Summer and I looked at each other in absolute horror. "But I can't," I protested. "For a start, we've got these gross hairnets on, and anyway, it's really awkward with Ben, and as for Marco——"

"I don't care what's going on between you all," Mum cried, "everyone has to muck in. Grace, you can ring Maisy and Aran too."

"No problem," said Grace, reaching for the mobile. When she'd spoken to Maisy, she handed the phone to me. I was about to start arguing again, but Mum gave me such a stressed-out look that I just called Ben, explained the situation, and asked him to crowbar Marco out of bed on his way over and bring him too.

So, an hour later, when Mum was downstairs doing her treatment and Grace was looking after reception, Marco and Ben walked in the door. Maisy and Aran were sitting on the revolting brown sofa, leaning on books and writing out labels. Summer and I were starting on the Strawberry Summer Face-Saving Moisturizer and Emily and Saff had got into a rhythm and were streaking through the rest of the foot scrub orders.

"Hi!" we all called out as they walked in (I guessed Grace must have sent them up). I tried to hold a funnel over my face to hide the hairnet (or at least to hide my red-cheeked embarrassment about wearing it). "Saff, it's awful that he's seeing me like this!" I hissed. "I can't believe I'm saying this, but – *help!*"

"Don't worry, I've got a plan," she whispered back, then sashayed over to the boys. "Hi, guys, thanks for coming," she said. "Marco, you come and stand next to Abbie and start filling these bottles with moisturizer. That way she can get on with the seaweed body masks."

She handed him a pink striped apron and hairnet and physically walked him across the room and put him next to me. Hmm, so her genius plan was to make him look as silly as I did, whilst also pushing us together again. Honestly, I thought I might melt into a huge puddle of embarrassment and drip through the ceiling onto Mum's client downstairs. But instead I smiled and showed him how he had to scrub his hands at the sink.

Ben was on packaging duty, so he didn't have to wear anything ridiculous. Saff showed him how to tie little bits of ribbon and paper rosebuds round the bottlenecks, along with the cute handwritten labels that Maisy and Aran were making. She said his first effort wasn't up to scratch, but his second try passed the test. "I didn't think you'd be that good at this, you know, being a bloke and everything, but you've got a very delicate touch," she told him. "Just a bit more curling on the ribbon and we're there."

"Oooh, you and your *delicate touch*!" Marco teased, but Ben just grinned at him and said, "Nice hairnet, mate." Funnily enough, he shut up after that.

By the time Mum came up from her appointment, it was almost twelve, and we'd finished bottling up all the moisturizers and were starting on the second batch of seaweed body masks. The sea salt body scrubs were all in their jars, with green and orange ribbons to tie the labels on (curled perfectly by Ben), and Maisy and Aran had almost finished the labels for the moisturizers.

I thought Saff had finished meddling once she'd put Marco and me next to each other, but she obviously didn't think she'd done enough, because after about an hour she sent us two downstairs to make drinks for everyone. "And tell Grace to come up, could you?" she added. "We need her to check the ingredients list for the Shell & Stone Foot Scrubs before we start on the labels." She glanced at Mum and they grinned at each other. All I could do was slope off downstairs, with Marco trailing behind me, and try not to look like I knew what they were up to.

As soon as Grace saw the two of us come in, she just gave me a huge, knowing grin and hurried upstairs, without me even giving her Saff's message.

I put Marco on apple-chopping duty for the energizing yellow juice Maisy and Emily had asked for, and we chatted normally, about music and TV and his band and stuff. Then, just as I was blitzing up some strawberry smoothies for Mum and Aran, he said, "Abbie, can I talk to you?"

Seeing as we already *were* talking, I knew he meant *talk* talking. Ooh-er, I didn't like the sound of that.

"Sure," I said, because what else *could* I say?

"Well, you know we've been getting on so well? Like, when you did the nail thing on me, and this morning..."

I braced myself – this was where he'd say how great it was that we were mates again. (Urgh!) And probably how he liked someone else. (Double Urgh!) Or worse, how he was already *with* someone else. (Humongous, planet-sized URGH!)

"So—" he said, and, oh God, don't ask me what I was thinking, but I found myself whizzing the blender over his words and doing a big bad-acting thing of mouthing, "I can't hear you!"

He said it again, whatever it was, but I still wasn't

ready for the blow, so I went onto a higher speed, and the blender screeched like a washing machine on spin. I shook my head. "I still can't—" I mouthed.

"I wish we hadn't split up!" he shouted.

I was so surprised I got all mixed up and took the lid off the blender before I'd let go of the whizzing button. Smoothie splattered everywhere, covering me, him, the counter and the wall behind us.

"Turn it off!" he screeched.

"I'm trying!" I screamed. My hands were so slippery it took ages to get the button to press down.

"What are you saying?" I asked, when I'd finally managed to turn the stupid thing off and wiped the strawberry smoothie out of my eye.

He looked down at his strawberry-splattered jeans. "Yuck! I'm saying...do you want to get back together?"

Well, I felt like my brain had turned into a blender then, as so many thoughts were whizzing round it at high speed.

First of all I just thought *YEEEEEEEEEEEEES!!!!!* obviously. Then I thought, *Thank goodness he still likes me and there's no one else*. Then I thought about why it went wrong between us – because there was so much going on for both of us – and how there still is. I didn't want to *not* be with him, but I wasn't sure whether to risk getting back together again. We'd only just got our friendship back – what if it went wrong again and we weren't so lucky next time? I couldn't bear to lose him completely.

"So, how about it?" he asked again.

I reached out and took his hand, feeling that familiar spark ignite between us. "I don't know," I said.

Marco looked a bit taken aback. But that was honestly what I felt, so that's what I said. I guess it wasn't what he'd hoped for. He didn't let go of my hand though.

"Your mum says you might want this," said Aran, walking in, swinging a tray in front of him. "Woah, what happened here?" he added, seeing the state of us.

"It's all a bit of a mess," I told him, "but we'll get it sorted, don't worry."

"I hope we will anyway," said Marco. Then he gave my hand a squeeze.

And then he let go.

Liam had got back from work about five and brought fish and chips for everyone, which gave us all the boost we needed to get everything finished. Then he mucked in to help with the final bits and pieces and towards the end we all got really silly and hysterical, especially when Saff pointed out to Marco that he could have taken his hairnet off two hours earlier, when he'd gone on to label-sticking duty.

By about nine o'clock, the products were all set out on the kitchen table, beautifully packaged and looking absolutely gorgeous, ready to go to London. We'd even done a few extra of each to sell at Rainbow Beauty. When everyone had gone (after we'd thanked them about a million times for coming to the rescue), Mum, Saff, Grace and I just stood for ages, leaning against the kitchen counter in a daze, staring at the colourful, beautiful spread in front of us.

"Oh, girls! I can't believe we've done all this!" Mum exclaimed, pulling us into a hug. "I think you're all...' Her voice choked up with tears and she looked at Saff. "Can I go on, or is this going to give you a mascara crisis?" she asked, with a sniffly giggle.

"It's fine, I'm taking it off in a minute and having an early night," said Saff, grinning.

"Well, in that case," Mum continued, "I just want to say that I couldn't be prouder of you girls. You are the most wonderful, resourceful, brave and spiritful—"

"Is that even a word?" I teased.

"It is now," said Mum. "...*spiritful* daughters I

could ever have hoped for. And, although your dad and I have our differences, it's only fair to say that I know he feels exactly the same way. And *you* know he does, don't you?"

"Yeees," Saff and I chorused.

"Yes," Grace said softly, and I gave her an extra squeeze.

Then Saff let go and stepped over to the table. "Right, brace yourselves, I'm about to go all Devon on you," she said. Then she leaned over the jewel-like beauty products in their gorgeous bottles and jars and wiggled her fingers as if she was weaving a magic spell. "I hereby send the Rainbow Beauty magic out into the world, to spread happiness and joy wherever it goes!" she chanted. Then, "All join in," she said solemnly.

Smiling, we reached for each other's hands and stood beside the table.

"One, two, three…" she counted.

"We hereby send the Rainbow Beauty magic out into the world, to spread happiness and joy wherever it goes!" we cried. Then Saff made a big whooshing magic-sending noise and Mum and Grace clapped. I just smiled, and sank into the delicious cosy glow I felt inside, like sinking into a big hot bath full of thick, creamy, spicy, fruity bubbles.

* * *

On Saturday morning when my alarm went off at seven, I was still so tired from all our hard work that I felt like ignoring it and going back to sleep, but Mum had already leaped up and was springing around the room being disgustingly cheerful. "Come on, Abs, rise and shine," she cried. "I took a couple more calls late yesterday afternoon and we're fully booked now. This is our chance to get Rainbow Beauty back on track and prove just how fabulous it is!"

"If you want *me* to be fabulous, I'll need a cup of tea first," I grumbled. But despite my fuzzy head, I was feeling excited too. We were about to hit the London market with our products – now this was our chance to turn things round closer to home as well!

When I got downstairs in my pink uniform and carefully-done hair and make-up, I found Saff standing outside by the blackboard, with the chalks in her hand and a cheeky grin on her face. She'd written: *...heavenly, with beautiful handmade products and an indulgent ambiance..."* Review by Geneva Grant, *The Totnes Echo.*

"You can't put that!" I gasped. "That's not what she said!"

"Yes, it is!" Saff insisted, shoving the offending article into my hand.

I scanned it and saw the phrase that Saff had lifted (completely out of context). "Well, okay, she did *say* it," I conceded, "but she didn't mean—"

Saff just grinned even more and propped the board up on the pavement, and I decided not to argue.

Mum and Saff both had five bookings, including a couple of ladies that Trish, one of our regulars, had sent our way. After we'd been open a while, a steady stream of people started coming in just to have a juice or smoothie and buy some products too. Grace and I recognized one of them as the girl with the blue coat she'd spoken to in town. Grace was really pleased she'd come and welcomed her like an old friend. About three o'clock, Richanne and her friends all tumbled in too, giggling, hoping to get their nails done. "We haven't made appointments because we had to be sure we had the money first," Richanne told Saff, who'd just finished with a client.

"That's okay," said Saff, "I'm sure I can fit you in. You can all come in together."

"Alright?" said Grace cheerfully, striding confidently up to them.

"Alright," they replied.

"Put your jackets on the pegs if you like," Grace told them, "and here's our juice and smoothie menu, for you to choose your complimentary drink."

They all smiled and said thanks, and I felt *so* proud of her. She was really finding her way now – with Dad, and Maisy and Aran, and the girls from school, but most importantly, with herself.

The day went really well. Grace smiled. Saff listened. I glided around serenely, NOT looking like a sweaty mess. The Beauty and the Beach range sold like hot cakes, which we all agreed boded well for sales in the London shops. I'd left the display of the Beauty and the Beach samples up after our photography session, and stacked the newly-made products on the shelf underneath it. Even ladies who didn't know each other gathered round the display together, testing the products out, chatting about them and, most importantly, buying loads. Some were planning to give them as gifts, so I offered to make sets up of the five products in a nice wrapping, nestled in yellow shredded paper and done up with extra ribbon and rosebuds. That turned out to be so popular I made a sample gift set up like that too, and added it to the display table, so people could see how nice they looked as a present.

We sold even *more* after I'd done that!

Summer and Emily came in about four o'clock, to give us a hand tidying up. Emily helped with catching up too, as Saff was a bit behind with her nail clients, but apart from that, we ran pretty much to time all day (leaving that little bit of space between the appointments made a huge difference).

When we'd waved our last client off and turned the sign on the door to *Closed*, we all burst into a big round of clapping and cheering.

"We've done it! We've done it!" cried Mum. Then, "Grace, *have* we done it?" she asked, when the noise died down.

Grace frowned over her pages of figures and tapped at the calculator. "Well, if every Saturday's like this, and we can increase our bookings during the week by twenty per cent – no, hang on…" She tapped away a bit more and scribbled down a few numbers. "Make that twenty-five per cent, and the London orders keep coming, and we keep having new ideas…" She looked up and smiled. "We're going to be fine."

"Thank goodness," said Mum.

"Yippeeee!" cried Saff.

I just beamed, feeling like I might burst with happiness.

"I can't believe I'm about to say this," Mum said then, "but I've decided to offer your father the job of handling the London side – getting new orders and things. Commission only, of course. I must be mad but—"

"Oh, Mum, that's brilliant!" I cried, pulling her into a hug. And Grace and Saff obviously thought so too, because they launched themselves on her as well.

"Talking of new ideas, I've decided to put gift sets together for a few more of the products, like I was doing today with the Beauty and the Beach range," I told them. "And I'm going to make the themed table a permanent thing, with samples of a set of products displayed in a really attractive way, with props. That was a real talking point today, and it led to loads of sales too."

They all cracked up laughing then, for some reason. "What?" I cried. "I am!"

"I know you are, love," said Mum, "it's just—"

"You can't stop thinking about this place for a second, can you?" said Grace.

"Well, I wasn't talking about starting right *now*," I grumbled. "So I'm dedicated to our business, so what?"

"That's great, love," said Mum. "We're just

saying, don't let it take over your whole life, that's all."

"Yeah, we've done so well today, let's just kick back and celebrate for a while before we start on the next thing!" said Saff. She winked at me. "Why don't you call Marco, invite him over?"

"I'm not sure he'd want to come," I mumbled. "Not after I knocked him back yesterday."

"You knocked him back?" Saff repeated. "When? *Why?*"

Well, they were all doing the goggly eyes thing at me then, including Summer, who also demanded to know why I hadn't told her what had happened during the smoothie-making IMMEDIATELY afterwards.

"He was still around till nine and then you all went home," I told her lamely. I turned to Saff. "And then I was so tired, we all were..."

"Rubbish excuse," my sister declared. "Well, better late than never. Come on, then – spill los beanios."

So I had to tell them about what he'd said when we made the strawberry smoothies (and got them all over the wall), about wanting to get back together.

"Aw!" they all swooned, even Summer, and Saff told me I was crazy for turning him down.

"I'm just so busy," I protested. "With the

business, and you lot, and getting used to how things are now..."

Mum and Summer were looking nonplussed. Saff was actually shaking her head and *tutting*.

I gave Grace a pleading look, begging her to come to my rescue, but she just said, "I agree. You need some fun in your life. Marco makes you laugh. You couldn't stop beaming after those dates you had."

"Oh my God," I cried dramatically. "*Grace* is telling me to loosen up. *Grace.* Things must be really bad."

"The cheek!" snorted Grace, but she was smiling.

I sighed. "Maybe you're right," I admitted. "But I've turned him down. He's not going to come back for more rejection, is he?"

"Oh, love, but surely, if you just explain..." Mum began.

I looked at Summer. "No," she said, "knowing Marco I'd say he probably won't."

Mum and my sisters left it then, and I tried to forget about it too and enjoy the evening – like Saff said, kick back and chill out for once. We put some music on, ordered pizzas and made juices for everyone to use up all the bits of leftover fruit. Ben turned up soon after Maisy and Aran – Summer must have texted him (those two were almost back to normal after spending the whole of the day before together) and Liam came in (clutching a bottle of champagne) just as his fave ham-and-pineapple double crust arrived.

But Marco didn't show up, even though Summer got Ben to text him. Standing with all my friends and family, chatting and laughing and dancing around, I realized how much I wanted him there. It was like a bottle of Spicy Delight Bubble Bath with the sandalwood missing...

It just wasn't quite right without him.

When Mum said we needed some more strawberries, I offered to pop to the corner shop. Everyone else seemed to be having such a good time, I didn't want them to have to go, and I felt like getting some air anyway.

Outside the shop, there was a little table of fruit and veg. I picked up four big punnets of strawberries and balanced them on top of one another, then walked carefully towards the shop doorway – and straight into someone.

Marco.

"Oh no, I'm so sorry!" I cried. "I was getting these to make drinks for Mum and—"

Cringe-makingly, the strawberry punnets had lurched forward and were now leaning on *him*, and I had to wriggle my hand up between them and his shirt to balance them back onto myself. As I nearly slipped over, I realized that some had fallen out and squished under my sandals too.

He grinned at me. "What's that, some kind of old-fashioned smoothie-making method, like those people who tread grapes with their feet? Why do they *do* that?"

"Because the fungus on feet really gets the grapes fermenting," I found myself saying. *What?!* What on earth was I going on about *foot fungus* for?

"Here, let me take those while you—" he began.

"Thanks," I said, handing him the stack of punnets. Then I bobbed down and picked up the rest of the stray strawberries, the unsquished ones, anyway. When I came back up, the smell of strawberries was all around us, and the air between us was electric. Marco looked at me and I put the strawberries I'd picked up back into the top punnet and...suddenly I found myself saying, "Ask me again."

"What, about the foot fungus?" Marco said.

"No, I..." I began, but the smile on his lips showed me he was only messing around.

"Do you want to get back together?"

"Yes," I said.

He smiled his slow, lazy smile and took my hand. I felt that rush of electricity between us, and I know he did too, because he squeezed my hand a little. Then our eyes locked and you can guess what happened next.

Yep. I kissed him.

And, well…WOW!

It was wonderful, magical, and amazing. So amazing, in fact, that afterwards, I was completely on another planet and I forgot to go and pay for the strawberries, so Mr. Trewis had to come out of the shop and call after us.

When we reached Rainbow Beauty, Marco hesitated at the doorway. "Come on in, everyone's here," I told him.

He shrugged. "Sure, okay."

So we walked in and loaded Grace up with the strawberries. Then I looked at Marco and smiled the biggest (probably gormless-est) smile and he smiled back at me in his gorgeous, stomach-flipping way. I took his hand and led him over to Summer and Ben, ignoring all the winking and whispering that was going on (well, *pretending* to ignore it anyway!). When I said we were back together, Summer gave me the most massive hug and whispered in my ear that she'd always known we'd work it out, and Ben did that complicated cool handshake thing with Marco, and then added a big uncool thumbs up and said, "Nice one, mate."

Mum and Liam whizzed up some strawberry cocktails, with fizzy elderflower for us and champagne for them, and Saff handed them round, giving me a big smile with mine (*and* she only hummed a few notes of the wedding march, *and* she did it pretty quietly, so not too bad, I suppose, for Saff). I caught Grace's eye to tut about Saff and she beamed at me.

"A toast!" cried Mum, tinging her glass with a teaspoon. "I'd like to thank every single one of you for your part in getting Rainbow Beauty off the ground. We couldn't have done it without you and we appreciate it so, so much!"

"Hear, hear!" called Grace, raising her glass towards our crowd of friends, and Saff and I echoed it. Then I went over to Grace, pulling Saff with me, and put my arms round both their waists. Mum joined on next to Saff and I thought she was going to start crying again for a moment, but there was only a beaming smile on her face.

Then Liam said, "I'd just like to say to Kim, Saff, Grace and Abbie that starting up a new business, especially after all they've been though, takes courage, strength and, perhaps, a little bit of madness.

But they've done it, and it's wonderful, and so are they!"

Everyone clapped and cheered at that, and Saff went into full actress-taking-a-bow mode, while the other three of us blushed about a million degrees and grinned our faces off.

I beamed at Liam. "I'd like to say something," I announced. I took a deep breath and reached for the words to sum up everything I felt inside. "When we got here, we were broke and hurt and, let's face it, terrified of what the future might hold. We didn't know we were this brave. We didn't know we were this strong. Okay, so we knew we were a little bit mad..." Everyone laughed at that. "Being here, starting again, with you guys to support us, is what's *made* us all those things," I said then. "And, as well as a little bit of madness, I'd say we've got a little bit of *magic* too, helping us on our way. The magic of friendship and hope and inspiration and...fun!"

"You said it, sis!" cried Saff, as everyone clapped and cheered.

"Well said, Abbie," said Mum, raising her glass again. "So – here's to our Strawberry Summer!"

"To our Strawberry Summer!" we all cried, clinking our glasses together. Then Saff put on "Girls

Just Want To Have Fun", and the Rainbow Beauty
magic weaved around us, and we laughed and chatted
and danced all night.

 The End

There's an autumn chill in the air,
but nothing can dampen Abbie's spirits at

Rainbow Beauty

Well...almost nothing

Turn the page for a sneak preview of
the next fun and fabulous book

Blueberry
Wishes

I'd just re-done the display table, with spicy, warming things now that it was officially autumn. I love how the air changes and summer suddenly stops, and you start to think about the leaves falling and getting all cosy and snuggly indoors. I wanted to bring some of that into Rainbow Beauty, so I'd put our Spicy Delight Bubble Bath and Warming Cinnamon and Sandalwood Massage Oil on a rich red gold-embroidered Indian throw borrowed from my friend Summer's house. A pile of Bath Bombs, some Rose and Geranium ones with little rose petals in, and some with lavender flowers, sat in a bronze bowl, like delicious sweets. I couldn't help smiling as three women gathered around, smelling the products and chatting about them.

Just then, a treatment room door opened and Trish, one of our regular customers, emerged, followed by Mum. "Hello, girls!" Trish said, beaming. "Oh, I'm walking on air, I am! Your mother's a marvel!"

"Hi, Trish," we all chorused.

"Abbie, you are always looking so happy!" Trish cried. "You're like a little ray of sunshine! And so talented, making up all these lovely products. You're beautiful, too!"

By this point I was obviously blushing about a zillion degrees. And that last bit made me splutter. "Oh, I'm not!" I cried. "My skin and hair are so pale that if I don't wear loads of eye make-up——"

"...it looks like I haven't got a head," finished my loud-mouth sister Saff, doing an impression of me.

Trish just smiled at that. "Have you got a boyfriend, love?" she asked me then, making me splutter even more. "My son——"

"Yes, she has," Saff informed her. She did a little wiggly dance and sang, "His name is Mar-co. And she lurves him!"...

Things are finally going right for Abbie and her family...until a swanky new spa opens nearby, threatening everything they've worked for.
Could this spell the end of Rainbow Beauty?
Find out in...

ISBN: 9781409546238
eBook also available

The Future Game

What will your life be like in the future? Take some
inspiration from Summer and Abbie, cosy up with
your BFFs and answer these questions together.
In five, ten, twenty or even fifty years...

> Where do you live? Town, country or by
> the sea? New York? Paris? Mexico City?

> What is your home like? Castle,
> cottage or city apartment?

> What dream job do you do?

> Do you have any cute or quirky
> pets? What are they called?

> Who's the lurrrve of
> your life?

> What new skills have you learned? Can you
> drive? Speak Mandarin? Cook a soufflé?
> Scuba-dive? Play the guitar? Tap dance?

> Imagine a typical day in the future!
> What are you up to?

Strawberry Summer Smoothie

Whizzing up a *Rainbow Beauty* fruit smoothie is a delicious way to help ensure you're eating plenty of fresh fruit – perfect for feeding your skin and hair with yummy goodness to give you a gorgeous glow.

Remember the Rainbow Beauty motto:

Beauty from the inside out!

You will need:
1 banana
6 large strawberries
150g (5oz) natural low-fat yoghurt

If you don't have a jug-style blender or smoothie-maker, you can use a handheld blender instead.

1. Peel the banana and cut it into thick slices. Rinse the strawberries and dry them on a paper towel. Cut out the stalks and chop the strawberries in half.

2. Put the fruit in a jug-style blender with the yoghurt and whizz together until smooth. Then kick back, relax, and enjoy!

Catching up with
Rainbow Beauty
author
Kelly McKain

How do you come up with all your ideas for the Rainbow Beauty products?

I really don't know! I just pretend I'm running a beauty parlour and think about what people might like to buy. It helps to do lots of research too — what a hard job I have, trying out beauty products, experimenting with fragrances and getting pampered!

What is your favourite Rainbow Beauty product from this book?

The Sunset Glow Body Butter — I'd buy loads of that! I love the idea of the colours swirled together, and the delicious orange and cinnamon smell. Yum...

What's your perfect beach party outfit?

I'd go for a loose bias-cut sky-blue slip dress and flip-flops, maybe with loads of bangles, like Summer.

And I wouldn't forget my fleece and jeans to pull on later – *brrrr!*

If you ran a quirky London boutique, what would you name it, and why?

I loved making up the boutique names in Strawberry Summer and I think I'd go with Lily Loves for my own place. I have no idea who Lily is – it just popped into my head!

The Green girls always bounce back from disappointments and problems. How do you stay strong when things get tough?

I tell myself it won't last for ever and that things will get better. I ask myself what I can do to help fix or improve the problem – it always feels better to take action rather than worry or stew over something. And if all else fails, I curl up with a good book, eat loads of choc and sleep on it. Things often seem better in the morning when you've had time to rest and recover – and a solution may come to you in your dreams too!

For all the latest news on Kelly, go to www.kellymckain.co.uk

Calling all Abbie fans!

For exclusive Rainbow Beauty material
log on to

www.kellymckain.co.uk/rainbowbeauty

Join in with all the latest
Rainbow Beauty chat online

Be the first to know about
Rainbow Beauty competitions and giveaways

Download gorgeous Rainbow Beauty
screensavers and friendship vouchers

Learn how to do your own DIY manicure
– perfect for that Saturday sleepover

Discover Kelly's fave pampering treats

And lots, lots more!